I0591968

Author: Beth Prentice

Website: www.bethprentice.com

Copyright 2021 Beth Prentice

The moral rights of the author have been assured.

BOOKS BY BETH PRENTICE

The Westport Mysteries

Lizzie

A Sinister Sign ~ The Prequel

Dangerous Deeds

Give Murder A Hand

Deathly Desire

The Christmas Gift – A Mini Lizzie Mystery

Molly

Wicked Little Lies

Chloe

Killer Unleashed

Deadly Tails

Alexandra

Invitation to Murder

Gracie

The Ivory Veil – a novella

The Aloha Lagoon Samantha Reynolds Mysteries

Deadly Wipeout

Lethal Tide

Fatal Break

Tidal Wave

The Dandelion Ponds Mysteries

In High Spirits

The Hollyday Spirit - novella

That's the Spirit

The Dun Roamin' Romantic Mysteries
Tilly ~ Before Dun Roamin'
Matilda's Wish
Matilda's Secret - Coming Soon

MATILDA'S WISH

A DUN ROAMIN' ROMANTIC MYSTERY

BETH PRENTICE

PROLOGUE

Fate. It's a fickle master. One minute I was riding the wave of happiness and success. Everything in my life was just the way my ten-year-old self had imagined it would be. I had a successful bakery specializing in cupcakes, my days were filled with sugar filled creations and customers lined the streets to buy my wares. I had a gorgeous kind-of boyfriend, and my parents were on a trek to Machu Picchu, their phones out of signal, leaving me alone.

But was Fate happy? No. It was not. Fate was only happy once it set me up and then ripped the carpet out from under my feet so that I fell flat on my face.

I'm Tilly Lockhart, and this is my story.

*B*ack *on my feet.*

Those words played on a loop in my head, like a mantra. It was the only way I could keep moving forward.

I stood on the pavement and took a deep shuddery breath, adjusting the container I was holding. Looking up at the foreboding building at the top of the steps, I gulped. Two stories of dark brick, and soulless windows glared back at me, daring me to enter. The busy streets of Westport buzzed behind me with vehicles and pedestrians bustling about their day as the threat of rain loomed dark overhead. A bus pulled to a stop at the traffic light, horns blared, and in the distance a siren screamed someone's pain. But it all fell into the background as the brass sign on the high gloss black door in front of me alerted me to the fact that I had reached my destination.

Blackburn & Associates
Attorneys at Law

I'd received a call two days ago from the secretary of Gregory Blackburn the Third, requesting an appointment with me. I did tell her when she called that I thought she had the wrong person, but she confirmed she was after Matilda Mary Lockhart of 76 Ivy Road, Westport. I was only Matilda on my birth certificate, and it was technically my parents who lived at 76 Ivy Road. I was just staying there while I got back on my feet, but there was no doubt that she had the right person and so the appointment was set up.

My stomach contracted with anxiety as the events of the recent past played through my mind. One month ago, today, I had closed the door on my beloved cupcake shop. The shop that had held all my hopes and dreams, where I belonged and where I could help people.

Sure, my cupcakes didn't cure the world of disease, or end wars but they definitely made people happy. I loved seeing the smiles of my regular customers light up when I kept a stash of their favorites aside, just for them. I loved seeing the mums call in after school to buy their children a treat for getting a good report card, and I loved those special occasions like Christmas and Valentine's Day which gave me the opportunity to create the most amazing, sugar filled delights. To see it all fall in a heap because I sucked at business had broken my heart.

Baking cupcakes was what I was good at, and I wasn't good at much. I had a list of failed careers behind me as a testament to that, but hey, no one could say that I hadn't tried.

"Look out!"

I spun on my heel at the sound of a bicycle bell. A Lycra clad cyclist with a beer belly, cursed loudly as he swerved around me, causing me to squeal. My heart missed a beat and the plastic container I was holding slipped from my grasp, my hands fumbling to catch it before it hit the ground.

"Bugger, that was close!" My entire body shook as I clutched the container tight. Like I wasn't anxious enough. I did not need to destroy the one thing that may put me on Mr. Blackburn's good side.

I'd spent hours last night baking this batch of cupcakes to give to him in the hope that he would go easy on me. I hadn't been told what this meeting was about, but I was certain that it was to do with my looming bankruptcy which was why I'd decided to sweeten him up with sugar. My plan may not have been perfect, but it was the only one I had.

I stood in front of the floor to ceiling windows inside Gregory Blackburn the Third's high spec office, watching the rain pelt the glass. Smoothing a few stray locks, I looked around. The glass topped desk glistened under the overhead lights; a high-backed leather chair pushed neatly under it. Dark oak shelving holding many intimidating looking books lined the wall, and the plush white carpet felt luxurious under my feet.

I slipped off my high heeled pumps and dug my toes into the soft carpet using it like a stress ball. My stomach rumbled. I'd missed lunch, and low sugar levels didn't help my anxious mood. I loved sugar in all its forms. To be low on it was a terrible, terrible thing.

My gaze fell to the container of cupcakes that sat on the chair. Moving to it, I pulled back the lid and peeked inside to double check they were all safe. Gratitude swept over me as I eyed the rows of deluxe Butterfinger cupcakes with the ganache filling, their red icing balancing the fondant legal scrolls I'd spent hours making.

The scent of chocolate and sugar filled my senses and a calm enveloped me. My creations were safe.

Smiling, I adjusted one of the cakes slightly to the left in order for the rows to line up perfectly, just as the door behind me abruptly opened.

I jumped and the container slipped from my hands. It fell through the air as I fumbled after it. But alas the Gods of coordination had already favored me once today, so instead of an

Olympic worthy save, my fingers slipped against the smooth plastic, flipping it upside down. It landed perfectly with a thump. Urgh.

Mr. Blackburn walked toward me, his made to measure expensive suit molding to his body perfectly, his hand extended for me to shake. "I'm so sorry to keep you waiting." His eyes dropped to the mess on the floor.

"I'm so, so sorry," I stammered, dropping to my knees. The red icing and dark rich ganache were oozing their way into the fibers of the white carpet, and the world spun as the blood drained from my face.

"What on earth...?" His voice faded.

"They were cupcakes," I mumbled, hurriedly attempting to scoop the mess back into the container. "I made them for you, but..."

I looked up and our eyes connected.

His jaw clenched and his shoulders tensed. I could see how as a lawyer he could intimidate his opposition.

"That was very thoughtful of you," he said, tersely.

I flicked a dollop of icing from my fingers, ready to scoop some more.

"Leave it! You're just making it worse."

I wasn't sure it could be worse.

I sat back on my heels and gulped.

"I'm sorry. So sorry," I mumbled.

"Don't worry about it. I'll get my secretary to clean it up after our meeting."

"Please send me the bill for the cleaning." Or add it to the cumulative total, more like.

"Really, don't worry about it. It's not a big drama." He waved his hand dismissively, yet his eyes belied the truth. "Why don't you take a seat and I can fill you in on why you're here."

My stomach did a little flip with apprehension.

He unbuttoned his navy jacket and moved fluidly around the desk, sidestepping my shoes that I'd left near the window.

Mr. Blackburn wasn't at all what I was expecting. To be honest I'd been imagining a man who was about to retire and had lots of nose hair. This guy was definitely not old and from what I could see, his nasal hairs were perfectly well-groomed. Just like the rest of him.

Sitting back on my chair, I licked my fingers to remove the mix of cake and icing, regret momentarily displacing my anxiety. These cakes tasted as good as they looked. Not that Mr. Blackburn would ever know.

He sat behind the desk, his nose scrunched and his eyes narrowed studying me, before he opened a drawer and offered me a box of tissues.

"Thank you."

He stared at me for a bit before his finger moved to the edge of his lip. "You have ummm, you have some there."

Oh geez.

I swiped at my lip. "You're younger than I expected," I blurted out before my brain could stop my mouth.

He smiled, flashing a perfect set of dimples. "You were probably expecting my grandfather. He retired a few months ago and passed the business to me."

I tried to remember to think before speaking next time. But nerves did that to me.

"I've just finished the remodel. Brought it into the twenty first century so to speak."

"So, the carpet was new?" Heat flushed my cheeks as I cringed.

"Ah, yes. Laid just last week."

"Did I mention that I'm sorry?" I whispered.

"Yes, but don't worry about it. Now, let's get on to business, shall we? Do you mind if I call you Matilda?"

"It's Tilly, actually. But really, I'm not fussy. Just don't call me late for dinner." I nervously laughed.

Gregory Blackburn the Third didn't seem to get my joke. Oh well, I tried.

He opened a folder on his desk. "Now you're probably wondering why I've asked you here today?"

That was an understatement. "Am I in trouble?" My stomach tightened as I prepared myself for what was to come.

"No."

Huh?

"Quite the opposite, in fact." He shuffled the papers in front of him and cleared his throat. "You're here for me to read you the last will and testament of your great aunt, Matilda Mary Lockhart."

"You can just call me Tilly."

"Pardon?"

"You can just call me Tilly. You don't need to keep saying Matilda Mary Lockhart."

"I was referring to your great aunt."

"Huh?"

"Your great aunt," he repeated on a sigh. "She passed away a few months ago." His brows furrowed. "You didn't know?"

"Sorry, but I honestly have no idea what you're talking about."

"Okay, let me start at the beginning, then. Your great aunt passed away and we're here today to read her last will and testament."

"How am I related to this great aunt exactly?"

"Well, it appears that she and your great grandfather on your father's side were siblings."

"And she kept the Lockhart name?"

"She never married."

"Oh. How old was she?"

"Ninety-five."

"Geez," I chewed my thumb nail. "You said she passed away a few months ago?"

"Yes, she passed on October 8th, about ten weeks ago. Probate holds these things up."

"How did she die?"

"Please be assured she passed peacefully in her sleep." Sincerity shone from his eyes. "She'd had good health and it was old age catching up with her in the end."

"Okay. Well, that's good at least. But why am I the one who's been called here? Why didn't you tell my dad or his cousin, Tony?" I pushed my back into the chair and crossed my legs, my foot jiggling.

"I was instructed to call you as the sole beneficiary of her estate."

I sat up straight. Did he just say *estate?* And *sole beneficiary?* Now he *really* had my attention.

*M*y heartbeats were fast in my chest as my car idled at the entrance to the property. It was pretty unimpressive, just two rusty iron gates held back by bricks, allowing visitors to pass through. A worn sign advising me this was *'Dun Roamin'* swung from a white timber mail box. It leaned precariously, the tall grass swaying gently as the breeze moved across the flat plain and I expected a tumbleweed to stop by any second. I looked ahead of me, down the gravel driveway. There, in the distance, was a group of trees. I guessed that was where I'd find my new home.

Swallowing the anxiety that sat like a heavy lump in my throat, I depressed the accelerator and moved my powder blue Fiat 500 forwards onto the gravel, leaving the safety of the single lane road behind me. The roadside grass disappeared, and crops rose high from the ground obscuring the life I knew from view.

A cloud of dust billowed behind my car. I shivered. What was I doing? I wasn't this person. I actually couldn't remember the last time I'd driven on gravel. And my little car was not appreciating the rough drive.

Ignoring my racing pulse and the tightness in my chest, I took some deep calming breaths and concentrated on driving, only stopping when my path was blocked by a large cow. Thankfully I wasn't driving fast, but a trailing cloud of dust surrounded me when I hit the brakes, and the car came skidding to a halt only meters from the cow's white belted black coat. Once the dust had settled, the cow looked me in the eye, casually chewing a blade of grass hanging from its mouth.

I swallowed hard against my dry mouth. I'd never been this close to an animal heavier than my car before and if I was completely honest, it scared the beejeezus out of me. Plus, I had no idea what I should do next. The cow didn't seem fazed by my presence and definitely didn't appear to be moving any time soon.

Assessing my options, I wondered what I knew about cows. Hmmm, I knew they were large, gave us milk, that they had the biggest, most beautiful eyes, and according to the nursery rhyme they could jump over the moon. None of which was going to help me now, though.

Okay, what would David Attenborough do? He'd probably send his camera crew to shoo it away, is what he would do. Without a camera crew to do the job for me, I wondered if I should drive around it. But that would put me in the crop. I could move closer to the cow to see if it took the hint and got out of the way, or I could get out of the car and shoo it. I gave my horn a little toot to see if it would move along. When it didn't work, I opted for option A and drove around it.

"Eeeek," I squealed, flattening the crop. The cow looked me in the eye as I maneuvered past it.

Only once the cow was clearly visible in my rear vision mirror, I released the breath I was holding, and continued along the gravel path until I reached a T-section. Wondering which way to go, I took a guess, turned left, and followed the path through the tall, pretty flowering oleanders.

My thoughts raced over the events of the last week. I still

couldn't quite believe how Fate had changed its mind so quickly again. One minute there I was on the verge of bankruptcy and then the next I was an inheritee. I'd never inherited anything before, let alone a farm. Even though Mr. Blackburn had informed me that it was technically half a farm as Matilda had sold the other part off a few years before.

I had to live here for a year before the deed was transferred into my name, and if I left before the time was up, the inheritance would go to the local Arts society. As much as I liked the arts, I couldn't bear to lose this opportunity. So, I could do this, right? I mean, how hard could it be?

I pulled to a stop in front of an old timber house and some of the happiness the inheritance had given me evaporated.

Concerned I may have lost complete blood supply to my white knuckles, I loosened my grip on the steering wheel and leaned my body weight forward, giving myself a better view of the traditional Queenslander with the wide verandas. Its high-pitched roof was more rusty than not. I could see that once upon a time the house had been painted white, but it had peeled away, revealing aged timber beneath it. The five steps leading to the front door were old and rickety, the grass surrounding the building was brown, and the one-eyed dog looking in my direction from the top of the steps looked plain sad.

This was Dun Roamin? My shoulders sank along with my hopes as a weight settled heavily in my stomach. I'd imagined a sprawling farmhouse, lush gardens, and a dog contentedly sleeping on the airy verandah enjoying the afternoon breeze. I mean it was worth three point six million dollars! For that kind of money in my home town of Westport, you could get a mansion overlooking the ocean.

I indulged my anxieties for a moment by hyperventilating, before dropping my forehead to the steering wheel and attempting to control my breathing as any confidence I'd had disappeared into thin air. I was a city girl through and through. I loved buildings, and shops, and...and...bitumen roads.

I lifted my head once again, and the dog made its way down the steps toward my car. I pressed my nose to the inside of the glass window and looked down as it lifted its back leg and peed all over my front wheel. Argh!

I sat back, rested my head against the car seat, and closed my eyes. A three point six-million-dollar property, plus nearly a hundred thousand in cash. With that kind of money, I'd be able to pay back all my debts, return to Westport and reopen my cupcake shop. I'd loved that shop with all my heart, and I'd cried for weeks when Mum, Dad and the bank had all asked for their investment money back.

This inheritance had come at a fantastic time. I mean, obviously it wasn't a fantastic time for Great Aunt Matilda. No, I was sure she would have much rather been here enjoying the money herself.

The questions I still had about the inheritance zipped through my mind. Why did my great aunt have the exact same name as me—Matilda Mary Lockhart? Why was it that when I spoke to Dad about it, he professed to not knowing anything about her, yet Mum insisted that it was his idea I be given my name? Why did the will state I had to live here for a year before the transfer? And why was it left to me instead of my dad or his cousin, Tony? After all, Matilda was their aunt before she was mine.

I opened my eyes and looked back at the house. I needed to do this. Not just for the money. I needed not to fail at something. Especially before I'd even tried. And yes, I didn't know my Great Aunt Matilda, but she obviously wanted me to have this farm for a reason, didn't she? Who the hell knew what the reason was, but I guessed in time I would figure it out. So, I just needed to stay positive. Sure, the house looked old and dirty from the outside, but it could all be fixed, right?

I killed the car motor. With a determined enthusiasm, I

grabbed my handbag off the seat, plucked up all my courage and opened the car door, stepping my (albeit fake) Louboutin clad foot out into the hot afternoon air, and almost breaking my ankle as my heel twisted on the gravel.

Immediately a thousand flies swarmed at me, some landing on my shirt, some trying to get into my mouth. I learned pretty quickly that I needed to keep my mouth shut. That wouldn't be easy for me, but looking around at the farm, I figured nothing about my new life was going to be easy.

The sound of the wind whistling through the trees brought with it the scent of fresh country air, and I filled my lungs before the dog sniffed at my feet. I had a moment of fear it would cock its leg once again, but instead it wagged its tail and jumped up against me.

"Good doggy," I said, tentatively patting its head as it placed its snout on my hip.

Its short brown hair and skinny body reminded me of a Dingo, while its black snout and deep brown eyes were more like those of a German Shepherd. Its scent was like musk mixed with dirt.

"What's your name?" I asked

He gave a friendly woof and sauntered off toward the shade.

I was considering following him when a white and brown goat sprang through the nearby garden bed, a green shirt clamped in its jaws. It quickly disappeared along the side of the house. The dog turned a disinterested eye after it, before making three anticlockwise turns and settling into a divot in the dirt.

I let out a loud sigh. Was it normal farm behavior for a goat to eat clothing?

An elderly gentleman came walking hurriedly across the dead grass, swearing loudly, "Get back here, ya mangy bugger!" He stopped abruptly once he saw me. "Oh! G'day!" he said in a wheezy voice, placing his hands on his waist and sucking in some much-needed oxygen.

"Hello. Um...are you okay?" I squinted at him, my eyes stinging from the hot dry air hitting my contact lenses.

He straightened up and raised his palm to me. "Yep, yep. I'm fine. You must be Matilda. We were expecting you a bit earlier today."

"Yes. That's me." I wiped the dog slobber on my tailored shorts and extended my hand toward him, smiling. "Sorry, I didn't mean to be late. I got caught up with packing my car." I didn't add that I'd spent hours deliberating over my outfit because I wanted to impress these people.

He took my hand in a large, almost bear like grip and gave it a hearty shake. "Well, I'm pleased to meet you, Matilda. I'm Wallace. Wallace McKenzie, but you can call me Wally."

Mr. Blackburn had explained to me that it was the McKenzie family—Wallace, his son Randall, and his grandson Noah, that had purchased the other half of Dun Roamin' a few years before. The configuration of the break-up of the land was a strange one, but I was relieved that I wasn't solely responsible for keeping a farm running.

"Lovely to meet you, Wally. And please call me Tilly."

Wally McKenzie was quite possibly the cutest man I had ever met. Now, I didn't mean cute as in a *I have a thing for old men* kind of way. No, I mean he was cute in an adorable kind of way. His false teeth looked slightly too big for his mouth, his ears were long with large, flappy lobes, his skin was wrinkled, and his head was bald. But when he smiled, sunshine and mischief shone from his eyes giving me a glimpse of the man beneath. I liked him already.

"Sorry about that." He jabbed his thumb in the direction the goat had disappeared. "Goatie got into the washing again."

"Oh! Does that happen often?" The last thing I wanted was for my underwear to be eaten by a goat. Or worse still, left lying around the farm for the McKenzie men to find.

"More often than I care to think about," he muttered

narrowing his eyes in the direction the goat had ran. He then nodded toward the house. "You found it okay, then?"

I followed his gaze toward my new home. "Yes. I found it."

"She doesn't look much, but she's got heart."

"It's not what I was expecting," I replied quietly, biting my lip with my understatement.

Both Wally and I stood looking at the house, simultaneously waving our hands in front of our faces, shooing the flies away.

"Matilda was a stubborn one," he broke the silence. "Never would accept help keeping up the place. But I'm sure it's not as bad as it looks."

I liked his optimism, but seriously doubted his assumptions. "You really think so?"

"Nope, but you got to have hope, right?" he laughed, happily slapping me on the shoulder. "Did Matilda ever explain the layout of the land to you?"

"I'm sorry but I didn't know her. The solicitor explained it though."

"Gregory Blackburn the Third?" Wally's nose scrunched as if he was saying a dirty word.

I nodded. "He told me I own two thousand acres of agricultural farm land, the house, some outbuildings, and an assortment of animals."

"Good, good. But did he explain how it's all broken up?"

"Yes, he even drew me a map." I opened my handbag and retrieved a piece of paper Greg had used to draw a rough outline of the property. He'd given me the official plans as well, but his hand drawn map was the one I truly understood. I spread it open and showed it to Wally. "He said the farm's been divided into four one thousand acre lots, with three houses occupying the area in the middle." I ran my finger around the circle which was drawn around the houses. "You own the two plots on the opposite diagonal, which amounts to two thousand acres exactly," I pointed to two different areas of land. "This is your house here, and these two are mine." I looked at Wally to make sure I'd understood everything correctly.

"That's right." He rubbed his stubbly chin. "Matilda never did explain to us why she broke the land up the way she did, but we've been renting these two thousand acres ever since we've been here, and it hasn't caused us any problems. We were hoping you'd be happy to continue the rent arrangement."

"You have *no idea* how happy I am to continue with it." I beamed.

I turned to look at the house. "I should probably go inside for a look. The solicitor didn't have any keys, but he mentioned they may be here." I looked at Wally expectantly.

He shrugged. "You don't need to worry about keys. This is the country. We don't lock things out here."

"You don't lock your house?" My mouth hung open and I choked on a fly that flew straight in.

Wally laughed, a deep wheezy sound coming straight from his chest. "Got to remember to keep your mouth closed."

"Yes, well…" I couldn't finish what I wanted to say. I was struggling to control the gagging. The fly was stuck in my throat and tears stung my eyes.

Was the year up yet?

"I'll leave you to have a look around," Wally said, once I'd gotten control of myself. "Let you get acquainted with the place. Don't worry about unpacking your car though. As soon as Noah gets home, I'll send him over to help with the lifting."

"No, it's okay. I can manage," I croaked.

"Alright, well I'll be off then."

As he turned to walk away, I looked at the house, and a chill ran over my skin. "Wally?" I called, swiping at the moisture escaping my lashes. "Um…what's it like in there?"

"I don't know. I've never been past the refrigerator in the kitchen."

"Really?"

"Yep. Matilda wasn't one for visitors."

"But she hasn't been here for months. Didn't you have a look around?" I knew I would have done.

"Nope. It's not my place."

"Well…would you like to have a look now?"

Wally studied me for a moment. "That'd be great. And how about I chase away that ghost you're afraid of?" He indicated with an outstretched hand that I walk ahead of him.

The hinges squeaked as I held back the flyscreen door and pushed the solid entry door open. It creaked backward and the smell of moth balls drifted up the hallway toward me, making me sneeze. I blinked, adjusting my eyes to the darkened interior.

My heels clicked on the timber boards and echoed down the hallway as Wally walked in behind me. Moving slowly and taking everything in, I felt as if I were here to visit a long lost relative. In a way, I guess I was.

The floor plan was pretty simple. The hallway was central with bedrooms to the left and right, their entrances close to the front door. Walking deeper into the house I came across a room containing a baby grand piano covered with framed photos, and there was a bathroom across the hall. The kitchen and living area were toward the back. The walls were vertical tongue and groove boards painted in a dirty cream color, and the windows were covered with closed floral curtains. I stopped in the kitchen, my breath catching in my throat.

The will had stated I had to be living here within the seven days of it being read out to me. I'd used the seven days well, using the online search engines until the wee hours of the morning. I'd learned a lot about the surrounding area of Littlebrook. I didn't read every one of the five hundred and seventy-one million results the search engines had given me on how to run a farm, but I felt as if I now had a basic understanding at least of the nine rules of farming. But mostly I used those hours imagining the large farmhouse kitchen I'd inherited and the time I was going to enjoy baking over the hob.

In my daydreams, the cabinets were white and made in the shaker style, the oven was large and stainless-steel, and the bench tops were stone. To think I was delusional was an understatement. The only thing in here remotely like I had imagined was the timber floor. Only in reality, it was scarred and worn.

A row of cupboards ran under the window, holding a dull porcelain sink. The cupboards had no doors, only floral fabric bunched on a wire concealing the contents from me. Above them was a battered wooden shelf holding a radio, several white and blue tins, and a smattering of cobwebs. A small table was pushed against a wall, a lone chair tucked under it. I scanned for the oven only to find it was an old fire heated stove where the floor seemed wonky. I stifled my disappointment and opened the back door to look at the verandah.

Wally silently followed me.

"What's in that building?" I pointed to a small hut only meters from the rear steps.

"The dunny. A thunderbox to be more precise."

My head snapped around to him so fast I kinked my neck. "But…but I saw a bathroom. Back down the hallway," I stammered.

"Yep. It was a bathroom alright. Just not a toilet. I know for a fact it's over there. Noah always tried to convince Matilda to get one put inside, but she wouldn't. Told him it had been like that all her life, so why change it?" Wally shrugged.

"So…there's no inside toilet?" I asked quietly.

"Nope. Sorry love."

I nodded and blinked back the tears. It was all going to be okay. *It was all going to be okay.* I would call a plumber and have him install an inside toilet pronto. In fact, was now too late in the day to call him? I looked at my watch. Four thirty-five. Hmmm.

"Wally, can you recommend a local plumber who can install a toilet before it gets dark tonight?"

Wally laughed his deep wheezy laugh. "Oh my," he said, holding onto his side. "It's going to be fun having you around. You've got a good sense of humor. I like that in a girl."

"So…a plumber won't be able to get here today?" I closed my eyes hoping I'd misheard him.

"The closest plumber who can do a job like this is in Westport."

And Westport was a good hour's drive away.

A small squeak escaped my lips but I covered it with a cough.

"I'll leave you to get acquainted with the place," Wally said. "Noah will feed the animals tonight, just like he's been doing. You get yourself settled and tomorrow I'll introduce you to the clan."

"The clan? How many are there?" I asked, the weight in my stomach growing substantially.

"Well, let's see. You already saw Goatie. That's Clifford the dog over there. There's Izzy the cat. You've got a chook pen with three chickens in it. There used to be more, but some have died of old age. You've got an ex-race horse, a miniature pony, and four cows. Oh, and I nearly forgot the cockatoo."

I'm not sure how he nearly forgot the cockatoo who was squawking so loud I almost had to cover my ears.

I sighed. The chooks, the cows and the dog I expected to find on a farm. Even the cat. But the rest of them were definitely off my radar.

"Like I said," Wally continued, "I'll introduce you to them tomorrow. It's nearly time for Family Feud so I better get going." With that he saluted me and made his way through the house and out into the hot afternoon air.

It was only as he was leaving that I remembered the cupcakes I'd made for the McKenzie's were on the front seat of my car.

"Oh, before you go, I have something for you!" I scurried after him, down the front steps which creaked and groaned under my weight. I tiptoed to my car to stop my heels getting stuck in the gravel. I beeped my Fiat unlocked and grimaced as heat rushed out of the open door, hitting me. I said a quick prayer that my cupcakes had survived.

"I baked these this morning. I hope you like them." I opened the lid on the container and let out a contented sigh as I looked at my beautifully decorated creations. I'd spent ages on them, making little farm animals and machinery out of royal icing, and I was grateful the heat hadn't destroyed them.

Wally accepted the open container and inhaled deeply, his nostrils flared as he peeked inside.

My stomach flipped. I really wanted him to like me. And my cupcakes of course.

"Are these red velvet?" he asked.

I nodded.

"Keep this up, girl, and I may just ask you to marry me." He beamed.

I giggled. I just wasn't sure if it was from happiness that he liked me, or hysteria at my lack of plumbing and menagerie of animals that I was about to become responsible for. Whatever it was I made a mental note to bake another batch as soon as I figured out how to use the stove. Or bought a new one—whichever came first. Oh, as if I was even going to try to work that stove out. Nope, tomorrow I'd call the electrical goods store right after I called the plumber. Thank goodness Aunt Matilda had left me some cash.

As Wally walked away whistling, I grabbed my black polka dot suitcase from the car and tiptoed back to the house. I stood inside the front door and placed the case on the floor, wondering which bedroom to put it in.

I glanced left to right. Two doors stared back at me, but

neither called my name. Making a decision I opened the door to my right.

Unlike the front door, these hinges didn't creak. Instead the door slid silently open revealing a room I guessed to be about three meters square. The double sized iron bed with the floral bedspread told me this probably used to be Great Aunt Matilda's room. I stood on the threshold unsure about whether I wanted to enter or not.

It was strange. It looked as if she had gotten up that morning and left. From where I stood, I could see her slippers neatly under the bed, her dressing gown was hanging on a hook near the door, and a slight layer of dust covered the floor.

I screamed as something ran past my legs, into the room and up on to the bed. Clifford. He turned anti clockwise three times and then settled down with a sigh. My heart ached with the thought of him missing Matilda.

I patted his dusty back while I looked around, trying to get a sense of who Matilda really was when a photo sitting on the mirrored dresser caught my eye.

I'd seen the photo before. It was of a married couple on their wedding day - my great grandparents, Milton and Emily Lockhart.

I didn't know a lot about my family history. My dad had completed the family tree when I was a kid, but other than the saga of how my great grandfather Milton had been thrown out of the family once he had married my great grandmother Emily, I didn't know much more. I don't think anyone really knew why my great grandmother Emily was hated so much, only from that moment on, our side of the Lockhart family never spoke another word about the family before them. Now, I wondered about the series of events that would have taken place at the time.

The frame was cool against my fingers as I brushed away the thin layer of dust and looked closely at my heritage. Had my great grandfather left the farm willingly? How long had he lived here before that day? And did he ever regret his decision?

I returned the photo to its place on the dresser and picked up another which sat behind it. This one was an artificially colored black and white photo of a beautiful young woman with porcelain skin, sitting demurely with her feet crossed at the ankle. Her long dark curls tumbled over the shoulders of her vibrant blue dress which matched the color of her piercing eyes. A gold key hanging on a chain rested low on her chest, and she held a bouquet of peonies in her hand. It had to be Matilda.

My stomach gave a flip as I looked at her eyes sparkling with youthfulness and vitality and recognized them as my own.

I ran my finger over the glass and a cool breeze danced across my shoulders, making me break out in goose bumps. I quickly replaced the photo and hurriedly left the room, knowing there was no way in hell I was sleeping in there tonight.

a sudden wave of emotion hit me, and I fought back tears as I pushed open the door to the other bedroom. When I'd found out about the inheritance, I'd given a whoop of joy thinking I'd happily live anywhere for that amount of money. But I'd forgotten to think about the reality of it. Now that truth was crashing down around me.

I'd given up my life in Westport for this. Sure, my shop had failed and I had no job, but I had friends, family and Warwick, the particularly gorgeous policeman who was my kind-of boyfriend. We'd only been dating a few short months, but it was the longest relationship I'd had for a long time.

The hinges complained as the room opened up, revealing that it was identical to Matilda's in size and shape, only this one had a single bed in the center of the room with a similar floral bedspread covering it. A dark timber wardrobe stood against the wall and a matching dresser sat under the room's only window.

I sighed and placed my suitcase on the bed, my thoughts jumping to the adorable little room in the apartment I'd had above my cupcake shop in Price Lane, Westport. This room was as far from that as I could imagine. Emotion clogged my throat and the smell of moth balls clogged my sinuses.

I liked familiarity. I liked the feeling of my own sheets, and the scent of my candles. "It'll be better when I've filled this room with my own belongings. Surrounded by familiarity I won't feel so overwhelmed." Saying it aloud didn't help. It just made me sound even more depressed.

I pulled out my phone from the back pocket of my shorts and dialed Warwick. I knew he'd be too busy to chat for long, but I also knew he'd have the right words to settle the uneasiness swirling in my stomach. Unfortunately, the call failed to connect.

"Bugger." It appeared Dun Roamin' had no mobile coverage.

I dropped the phone onto the quilt and placed my face in my hands. I let the tears flow for a few minutes but then I flicked them from my lashes and straightened my shoulders, swallowing hard.

"Stop Tilly," I scolded myself. "You can do this. Don't let fear stop you." I stood and paced the room giving myself the pep talk that I needed. "Fear may slow me down occasionally, but I'm determined to make this work. It has to work. It just has to."

A second later, I got startled at the sound of the splintering timber on the front steps.

"Hello," a deep male voice called out.

Well, *that* definitely wasn't Wally.

I hurriedly spun on my heel, catching my reflection in the mirror over the dresser. On the upside to farm life—there was no humidity which meant my hair was still silky smooth. My make-up had faded considerably as the strain of the day had taken effect, my shorts sat low on my narrow hips, and my silky singlet hung loose from my lack of cleavage. I figured I didn't look great, but it was as good as it was going to get in the next thirty seconds.

Stepping into the hall, I politely smiled at the good looking stranger waiting at the door, all while trying to slow my sudden erratic heartbeat.

He beamed at me and any semblance of control I had over my heart flew straight out the proverbial window. But a lesson my dad had taught me when I was younger was 'act in control, even when you're not'.

"Oh hi." My tone was somewhere in the Minnie Mouse range.

"Tilly?" His dark blonde hair fell forward over his forehead and his blue eyes shone so brightly it was impossible not to notice. "I'm Noah."

I nodded—the only thing I was capable of.

"Gramps told me to come over and introduce myself. Hope you don't mind I called you Tilly and not Matilda? Gramps said you preferred it."

"Oh no, I don't mind what you call me," I trilled. "Gramps?"

When the solicitor had explained the McKenzie men to me, I'd assumed Noah to be a kid. Boy, was I wrong.

"Yeah. Wally is my grandad."

"Yes, of course he is. You can tell. The ummm, resemblance is uncanny."

Noah's grin flashed. "I get that a lot. I just hope I'm not as wrinkly as he is."

"No. You're definitely not." I was about to say 'you're perfect' but thankfully caught myself just in time.

"I hear you have a full car and need help unloading it?"

"Oh well, yes. It is full. But I can manage, thanks."

"It's no problem." He headed back down the groaning stairs. His biceps pulling tight against the sleeves of his T-shirt.

"What *is* this?" He stopped in front of my little Fiat and placed his hands on his hips.

"Ah…it's my car." Well, he may have been good looking but obviously he wasn't so smart.

"Wow, I don't think I've ever seen a car this small before. Did you have any problems getting here?"

"A few. It appears that country roads aren't made for Fiat 500's."

I unlocked the doors and opened the back hatch as he let out a long, low whistle.

"I'm impressed with how much you got in there."

To be honest I'd surprised myself with exactly how much I could fit into the hatchback. "I just brought the important things."

The rest of my possessions were being delivered, but with me I had fifteen pairs of shoes of varying heel heights, two suitcases filled with clothes, underwear and toiletries, my pillow, and one box of my favorite things—mostly items I needed to make and decorate cupcakes.

When life got tough, I baked. Lately I'd been baking a lot, hence the waist band of my shorts was quite a bit tighter than normal.

Noah grabbed at the box of kitchen items and I picked up the box with my shoes. I did notice the smile tilt the corner of his mouth as he glanced my way, but what would he know? He was a man, and a man would never understand the importance of a good heel and how they made your legs look longer and your butt look better. Plus, whenever I wore them, I felt more confident, and I needed as much of that as I could get.

As the heel of my knock-off Louboutin dug into the gravel as I turned, I wondered if I should reassess my choices.

"Can you put that one in the kitchen please?" I called over my shoulder, stepping onto the bottom stair tread.

The entire staircase wobbled under my weight.

Maybe it was time to stop eating my own cupcakes.

I looked at Noah. He was staring at my butt.

An entire butterfly family erupted in my belly as I confidently strutted up the next two steps.

Maybe Great Aunt Matilda was watching and didn't approve of my behavior because at that moment the sound of splintering wood cracked the air as the plank under my feet plummeted to the ground, taking me with it, screaming all the way.

Thank goodness the fall was less than a meter drop. Still, I was mortified as I landed in the dirt with a dozen pairs of shoes scattered around me.

"Shit!" Noah raced to my aid. "Are you okay?"

Sure, but I was worried the heat from my face would cause the old timber to catch fire and the house would burn down.

Would I still need to do the twelve months stay then?

"Umm...yes. I'm fine." I wasn't about to tell him I thought I'd broken my coccyx, and I was going to be getting splinters out of my ass for weeks. Plus, it seemed I had broken the heel of my favorite shoe.

I released a deep sigh which came all the way from my soul.

Noah reached for my hand. Grasping tightly, he easily pulled me to my feet, the force lifting me over the bottom two stair treads and into him.

Surprise flashed in his eyes when the momentum got the better of me and I smashed into his body nearly knocking him over. He stumbled backward but managed to stay on his feet.

"Thanks," I muttered, my face flaming as my hands slapped against his toned chest.

"Sorry." He shrugged, releasing his hold.

"It's no problem." I definitely wasn't complaining. Warwick hadn't been around for a while and this was the most action my body parts had felt in quite some time.

I wiped my hands across my backside, flicked off the dirt and dead grass, turned and looked at the front steps. They were a disaster.

"We should probably go in through the back door." Noah's gaze followed mine. "I'll come over and fix those later."

He obviously got his optimistic nature from Wally. What I was looking at appeared beyond repair. But then, going by how hard his body had felt under my hands, I figured he had a lot of skills I didn't know about.

With Noah's help I refilled the box with shoes and then limped my way to the back of the house. Part of the limping was from the broken shoe, and the other part was from the searing pain coming from my tail bone.

"That box stays in here," I told Noah as he came into the kitchen behind me. "I'll just put this one in the bedroom." With that, I kicked off my shoes, then headed down the hallway.

By the time I returned, Noah had made himself comfortable on the lone chair, his elbows resting on his knees, looking lost in a memory. "I haven't been in here since Matilda left us." His gorgeous blue eyes clouded.

"Oh really? Wally said Matilda didn't like visitors."

"She didn't, but she did like me to come in and have a drink with her once in a while."

I smiled, leaning against the door jamb. I didn't know her, but already I liked her style.

"Your cupcakes are better than hers." He smiled, eyes downcast.

"You tried my cupcakes?"

"Sure did."

His stunning eyes came up and locked on mine.

"Um…would you like a cup of tea?" I needed a distraction to make him stop looking at me quite so intently. "I have another batch of cupcakes in that box too."

"You talked me in to it."

"Well that wasn't hard." I laughed.

"Hey," he said, lifting his hands into the surrender position. "Red velvet cupcakes are my favorite. And it's not every day I get to eat a Massey Ferguson 186."

"A what?"

"A 186."

My mind was blank.

"It's a tractor," he explained. "The cupcake I ate at home had a little red tractor on the top of it. It looked like the Massey Ferguson we have."

"Oh of course, yes a tractor! Totally knew that."

He laughed and a little dance started deep in my belly. Oh boy.

I busied myself looking around the kitchen, trying to find cups and a kettle, and tea for that matter.

"If you're wondering where the tea is, it's on the top shelf over there." He pointed toward the shelf above the counter next to the window. "I never did understand why Matilda kept it in a place she had trouble reaching." He moved past me, lifting the tin down. His old worn jeans sat low on his hips, and I caught a glimpse of flesh when he lifted his arms.

Hmmm. I obviously had a lot to learn about Matilda, but one thing I knew already was she wasn't stupid.

"Thank you," I said, accepting the tin he held out to me. "Now, can you tell me where the kettle is?"

"Why don't I just make it?"

"Because it would be rude. You helped me so the least I can do is offer you a beverage."

"Any beverage?"

I nodded, wondering what other beverages we had.

"Well in that case, I'd rather have one of the beers in the fridge." Noah grinned.

"There's beer in the fridge?"

"Yep. I put them there the last time I was here."

"When was that?"

He gulped as the spark in his eyes once again dulled. "The day I found Matilda."

I wanted to ask him about her and how he found her, but it felt too soon.

Noah pulled two bottles of beer out of the fridge. He twisted the bottle top off one, and passed it to me, before repeating the process for his own. I watched him place his lips around the glass bottle and his Adam's apple bobbed up and down as he swallowed. His eyes momentarily closed, and his long lashes shadowed his cheeks. The heat of the day had left a sheen on his olive skin, and an unusual mix of strength and vulnerability oozed from him.

Suddenly this year of living on a farm had taken a turn for the better.

I made a mental note to learn from Matilda and leave things in places I couldn't reach. And I really needed to quickly replace the stove so I could make more cupcakes. That way he might visit every day.

"You look just like your photo," Noah said.

"Which photo?"

"The one Matilda kept on the piano. She talked about you all the time. You look surprised."

I was stunned. "Um…well…um…can I see the photo you're talking about?"

"Come on, I'll show you." He led the way to the room with the piano.

Earlier when I'd wandered around with Wally, I'd noticed the baby grand piano was covered with framed photos, but I hadn't yet looked at the photos themselves. This time I moved toward them shocked as the faces of my family looked back at me.

How? How did Matilda have all these photos?

Noah picked up a picture of me on my graduation day from Westport's School of Culinary Arts. Holding it out to me, he said, "She was really proud of you."

I swiped at the dust and looked at the photo closely. It had been a hot sunny day in December when it had been taken. I remembered how uncomfortable I'd been in the cap and gown.

I put the photo back on the piano and looked at the others of Mum and Dad, of Grandpop John and Grandma Audrey, his brother, Malcolm, with his wife, Vera, of Dad's cousin, Tony, and his wife, Christine, with their son, Ethan. There were probably about forty photos all up, a lot of which were of me.

I picked up a framed newspaper clipping of me standing outside my cupcake shop on the day it had opened.

"She raved about that shop when you opened it. I went there, you know?" Noah's voice was low and intimate.

My head whipped around to him. "You went to my shop? To *All Things Nice?*"

"Yeah. Matilda asked me to. We Googled your menu before I left and she picked one out for me to bring her home."

"Which one?" I gasped.

"I can't remember what it was called, but it was a raspberry one. Chocolate cake with a raspberry filling and a big pink flower on top. She loved it. Every time I went to Westport after that she asked me to bring her one home."

I didn't know what to say. Or think. How was it that she had all of this, yet I'd never heard of her?

And why didn't I remember seeing Noah before today?

"Are you okay?" The concern showed on his brow.

"It was called raspberry truffle," I said, barely above a whisper. "It was my favorite too." I placed the frame back on the piano and gulped. "I think I need to get back to that beer now."

———————

"That's a really pretty sunset." I followed Noah onto the back verandah, and sat next to him on the two-seater iron couch.

He looked at the sky. "It looks like a storm's brewing. We haven't had rain in a very long time, so let's hope those clouds dump right on top of us."

Over the plains and to the west, the storm clouds partially covered the horizon. Mother nature was showing off with the awesome color she was bouncing off the clouds and throwing about the sky.

"Red sky at night, farmer's delight. Red sky in the morning, farmer's warning," Noah said. "My mum used to love that saying. Red skies always remind me of her." He gave a small smile and took a swig from his beer bottle. "She passed away a couple of years ago. At the time I was getting ready to go and start my own farm. But once she got sick, I couldn't leave Dad to cope alone. Since she passed, he just hasn't been the same."

"I'm sorry," I said quietly.

He looked down at the bottle in his hands. "Thanks. We're getting there. Well…Gramps and I are. Dad—he's not doing so well."

"Is there anything I can do?"

"Like what?" Noah's voice was soft, just above a whisper.

I shrugged. "I could bake some more cupcakes for your dad. They make everyone happy, don't they?"

He let out a small laugh. "Well, they certainly make me happy."

Good to know.

I paused for a moment before asking, "How much of that land out there is ours?"

"Between us we have four thousand acres."

I smiled. "Yes, but I have no idea how big that actually is."

"Oh. Well we go all the way down to the creek which separates us from the Barrett's property. I'll take you for a drive tomorrow and show you."

"That would be awesome."

Just at that moment a wolf whistle came from the garden.

I jumped.

"Polly! What have I told you about that?" Noah called, laughing. "You know it embarrasses me."

"Who are you talking to?"

"Polly. Haven't you met yet?"

I shook my head slowly.

Noah stood. "Come on. I'll introduce you."

He led the way between the large oleanders, stopping when

31

we reached a bird aviary. So, this was who had been making all the squawking noises earlier.

"Polly, say hello to Tilly." Noah put his fingers through the wire.

"Nut-uh!" squawked the Sulfur Crested cockatoo, running down the branch toward him.

Noah frowned down at the bird as she sidled up to the wire, rubbing herself as close to him as she could get. "Polly, don't be rude. Say hello."

Polly turned her backside toward me and dropped her head to her feet. It didn't take a genius to figure out what she meant. Then she turned back to Noah and whistled once again. "Polly loves Noah!"

He looked at me, a blush starting around his ears. "She has a bit of a crush on me."

Polly had good taste.

4

*M*other nature sure was irritated. If the storm raging against the house was anything to judge by, someone, somewhere had really upset her. I let out a sigh and rolled onto my side, clicking the magic button on my phone. There was no reception out here but the screen did tell me the time. 2.55 a.m. Ugh!

To say I wasn't overly happy about being woken up was an understatement. It had taken me ages to get to sleep. Firstly, because Great Aunt Matilda's guest bed was damned uncomfortable. Springs seemed to have appeared out of nowhere, digging into my spine with every movement. Secondly, the numerous amount of clocks in the house chimed every bloody hour. I had no idea why anyone needed to be reminded it was the early hours of the morning, and why they needed cuckoo's screaming it out to them (actually I didn't understand why they needed that at any time of the day!). And thirdly, Clifford took up more than his fair share of the bed.

I'd never owned a dog before, let alone slept with one, but when I'd turned off the light and put my head on the pillow, I heard his whimpers at the door and couldn't ignore him. The instant it was opened he ran in, claimed his spot on the doona, and made himself comfortable. And that's where he stayed, no matter how much I tried to reclaim my share of the bed. Eventually I'd managed to curl in a small ball and fit into the top left-hand corner of the mattress, where I eventually fell asleep. That was until thunder shook the walls and lightning had lit up the room.

I was grateful for the lightning. The one thing about sleeping on a farm an hour outside of Westport was that once the sun had set, it got dark. Like, really, *really* dark. I'd never in my life been anywhere like this. In town we had the glow of the streetlights streaming through the cracks in the blinds to light up a darkened room. Out here there were stars. They were pretty, but they didn't illuminate too much, especially after the storm clouds rolled completely in.

I wasn't scared of storms, but I was a little scared of how well this old house would hold up against one. I sat up and flicked the switch on the bedside lamp. The light cast an eerie glow around the room, and I broke out in goose bumps as the house creaked and groaned.

I pulled the sheets closer and watched Clifford. He was happily snoring, the storm completely off his radar. Either he was used to them, or he sucked at being a guard dog. I guessed the noises were normal and I had nothing to worry about. Sensing he was being stared at, he opened his one eye and studied me. Obviously, he didn't find me all that interesting because he then rolled onto his back, stretched his legs as far as they would go, and sighed as he relaxed once again into the doona.

The sudden sound of a radio blaring from the kitchen made me jump. Clifford sat up, his ears pointed and alert. Stillness surrounded us both as I held my breath, my heart pounding, wondering who had switched it on.

My eyes flicked to the lock on the bedroom door. I had

pushed it across, but I didn't think it would be much of a deterrent for anyone wanting to enter. Pulling back the covers, I quietly padded toward my box of shoes. They may not be practical for life in the country, but a three-inch spiked heel definitely served as a weapon. With the shoe in my hand, I stepped up behind Clifford who was already waiting at the door, his tail wagging.

My hand trembled as I turned the doorknob, barely breathing, straining for any unfamiliar sounds over the melody of John Williamson's *True Blue*. As I pulled the door toward me, the hinges creaked loudly and I cursed at the noise.

Flipping the hallway light switch, I quietly made my way to the back of the house, my guard dog at the ready.

The guard dog was encouraging until I remembered he only had one eye and two teeth, and was already running ahead of me, his tail wagging profusely.

Thunder rumbled, lightning lit the windows, and the wind howled through the many cracks in the walls as I kept my eyes wide. By the time I looked into the kitchen, Clifford had stopped near the stove, his tail beating a tune against the curtain under the bench, and was gazing up happily.

My heart skipped another beat as I flipped the light switch and saw nobody there. "Clifford, what are you wagging your tail at?"

I turned the radio off and the sound of the rain hitting the tin roof replaced the song.

"Woof!" Clifford looked at me and wagged his tail even harder. "Woof!"

"Clifford! Stop it!" I snapped, rubbing the goose bumps on my arms.

I really wished he would stop looking at thin air as if someone was standing there.

Attempting to ignore him I looked around for who or what

had switched the radio on, but nothing looked any different to how it looked before I went to bed.

A bright flash of lightning lit up the night sky, silhouetting the figure of a man outside the window. I screamed, Clifford barked, and the lights flashed off.

My grip on the high heeled shoe tightened. I wasn't the bravest girl on the planet, and I would have felt a whole lot better with more than one choice of weapon. But as footsteps fought with the sound of the rain, I knew I had to make do with what I had.

The lights came back on, and I pushed my back against the wall, held my breath, and watched the door handle turn.

"Wh...who...who's there?" I called.

"Tilly!" A deep voice boomed urgently back at me. "It's Noah! Are you alright?"

"Noah? What are you doing here?" My eyes jumped to the old clock on the wall above the refrigerator as the first of the clocks struck 3a.m. What would Noah be doing at my back door at witching hour?

"Tilly!" The door rattled, shaking me out of my confusion. Crossing the kitchen, I turned the old metal key in the lock, and opened it to a very wet Noah. As he scanned me from head to toe, I pulled my T-shirt down to meet the band of my night shorts, suddenly feeling self-conscious.

"Are you okay?" He flipped the hood of his oilskin rain jacket down. Water dripped onto the floor as he moved. "I heard you scream."

"Well...yes. I did scream but I didn't expect to see you standing at the window at three in the morning." I replied, willing my heart rate to slow down.

As I noted the small water droplets on the end of his long eye lashes, I didn't think I had any chance of it happening in the near future.

"I came over to check on Polly. She hates storms, and I knew she'd be freaking out." Yeah, well, she wasn't the only one.

"And then I saw a ladder had been left near your window, so I came to move it before the wind knocked it over and smashed the glass."

"Oh." I let go of the breath I'd been holding. "Well, that was really nice of you," I replied, as lightning once again flashed, causing the dim overhead bulb to momentarily die.

When the light came back on, Noah was standing close, looking down at me. "Are you really okay?" The concern was etched on his brow.

"Yes. I'm really okay." Clifford had returned to the sink, once again wagging his tail and looking into thin air. "Apart from Clifford doing that and creeping me out."

"Don't worry about him." Noah's deep voice had an instant soothing effect on my nerves.

He moved to Clifford, kneeling to rub him behind the ears.

Unlike a few minutes before, when the kitchen felt cold and scary, the room now felt warm and inviting, and I knew it was all due to Noah's presence.

"Whatcha doing boy?" he asked Clifford. "Can you see Matilda? Is she here with us now?"

Clifford responded with a short sharp yap as if to say yes, and gave Noah a big sloppy kiss on the chin.

"Matilda is not with us," I said, more to reassure myself than anything else.

"Dogs are pretty in tune to these kinds of things." Noah gave Clifford one last pat, and then pulled himself up to his full height. He looked at me and laughed.

"What's so funny?" I asked, trying to ignore the sexy crinkles around his eyes when he smiled.

"You look upset that Matilda may still be here."

"I'm not upset. I don't believe in this kind of thing," I said, dismissively. Maybe I did believe in it, but admitting it meant it could be true, and I liked the idea I could convince myself otherwise.

"Okay. Your prerogative." Noah turned to the door as thunder rumbled. "I should get going."

"Will you be okay?"

"Yeah. It's only a quick run and I'll be home."

"But there's still lightning out there."

"It's on its way out now. I'll be fine."

"How was Polly?" I asked, wanting to delay his departure.

"She's okay. I'll take her with me as I go. She has a stand outside my room where she'll happily sit until daybreak."

I wondered if he'd mind me sitting on a stand outside his room. I chose not to ask, and instead said, "Thank you. And thanks for checking on the ladder situation."

"No problem. I noticed you locked the door," he added, flipping his hood back up.

"Of course, I locked the door."

"Huh, I'm surprised it actually worked. I'm sure it hasn't been locked since 1897 when the house was built."

That was something I'd never get used to.

"Good morning Tilly," he said, his eyes locking onto mine as his smile warmed my insides.

"Good morning Noah," I called, as he took the back steps in one stride.

As he disappeared into the night, I locked the door and looked at Clifford. "Are you coming back to bed?"

He stood, wagged his tail, and trotted up the hallway.

As I was turning off the kitchen light, I noticed a woman's hat on the little table. A hat which was definitely not there when I'd gone to bed.

I woke bleary eyed. After Noah had left I'd attempted to sleep. It was difficult as my mind seemed to want to use the time to go over every little detail of my life and how I had found myself so far from the home I had always known. I didn't know why my mind wanted to do that, it's not like it came up with any answers. I mean, it would have been far better to use the time to think about Noah and how damned sexy he was. Alright, I'll admit that maybe some of the time was used for this purpose, but then I remembered my kind-of boyfriend Warwick and figured I should find a way to give him a call and check to see how things were between us.

I hadn't seen much of Warwick in the last few months. Westport police officers were kept very busy and I knew how important his work was to him. That didn't leave him a whole lot of time for a girlfriend. But he had paid me a visit the day before I moved my life to Dun Roamin' when he'd dropped off a bottle of champagne and some delicious chocolates, so that meant something, right?

With no phone signal, I opened the notes on my phone and typed: *Call Warwick*. I then added *Call plumber, buy stove, get a phone plan that got coverage or have the landline reconnected.* I then slipped the phone into the pocket on my cardigan.

Entering the kitchen, I opened the back door to get some fresh air through the stuffy house, noting how everything looked different in the daylight. As light streamed in the windows, the early morning sun warming the cool air, I felt silly thinking about how scared I'd been during the storm.

I jumped as the clock on the wall above the refrigerator struck six. The cuckoo clock in the hall struck six. The dome clock on the mantel above the fire struck six, as did the other nine clocks scattered around the house.

Last night before I'd gone back to bed, I'd wandered around counting them. I'd found twelve. Twelve! Who needed that many clocks? Obviously Great Aunt Matilda had. I retrieved my phone and added *Google how to stop clocks chiming* to my notes. If I didn't turn them off, I'd be deaf before the week ended.

As the last clock played its final note, there was a quiet knock on the open door. Wally stood patiently waiting, his wrinkles scrunching with his smile. "Morning!" he sang. "I wondered if you'd be up yet. I've got some eggs for you."

"Good morning, Wally," I replied, happy to see him.

Other than the morning song of the magpies, the occasional squawk from Polly, and those damned clocks, life on this farm was pretty quiet. Another thing I would have to get used to.

"Matilda's chooks are either too old or too lazy to lay, so these are from our pen." He stepped into the kitchen and placed a basket on the table.

"Thank you so much. But you didn't have to do this. I don't want to leave you short."

"Nah, we've got enough eggs to supply a supermarket. My girls are good layers." He took his hat off and fiddled with it. "I was thinking of doing a deal with you. I'll keep you supplied in eggs, if you keep me supplied in those delicious cupcakes you gave me yesterday." He grinned at me, mischievously.

I grinned back. "That sounds like a good deal."

He nodded.

"Would you like a cup of tea or coffee?" I hoped he'd say yes as I already missed company.

"How could I say no to an offer like that?" He sat himself at the little table. "Ah you found Matilda's hat." He pointed to the hat that had mysteriously appeared on the table during the storm.

"Yes, but it seems more that it found me. Was it missing?"

"Yeah. She wore this hat everywhere. We were going to have it cremated with her, but we couldn't find it."

I stopped, staring at Wally and allowing his words to filter through my mind. How did a lost hat end up on my kitchen table at three in the morning? Did the wind blow it there? And if so, where had it been before that?

Goosebumps broke out at the thoughts and I shook myself before asking, "Are there any recent photos of Matilda about?" I wondered what she would have looked like recently.

"She didn't like having her photo taken too much, but I think we have one Noah took last Christmas. I'll see if I can find it for you."

"Thanks Wally. That's really sweet of you to do that." Touched that he would go out of his way for me, I pulled back the small floral curtain which acted as a cupboard door and studied the contents of the pantry, hoping to find something edible to repay him the favor.

"Did you see what we left in the fridge for you?" Wally asked. "Milk, some butter, fresh bread, that kind of thing. We didn't know what you would bring with you and I didn't like the idea of you not being able to make yourself a cuppa when you woke up this morning."

"I did. Thank you so much, that was lovely of you."

Wally really was the sweetest man I had ever met.

I found a jar of coffee and two cups sitting right alongside another tin of teabags—Matilda had obviously kept these a secret from Noah—and placed them all on the table, pushing the hat to one side. "Do you know where the kettle lives?" I asked.

He shrugged. "Sorry. You're on your own with that one."

After searching for the kettle, I gave up on the coffee, filled the cups with cold milk from the fridge, and opened my container of cupcakes. They made the perfect dinner last night and I didn't see why they couldn't make a good breakfast.

Wally didn't seem to mind as he helped himself to one and smiled.

"I'll need to find a supermarket today. Get some food and supplies," I said, as Wally took a bite of his cake, and washed it down with the milk.

Once he'd wiped the crumbs from his freshly shaved chin, he said, "Closest supermarket is in Westport. But we have the shop in town which sells just about everything we need. They've got a good selection, and the owner, Monty's an alright guy. Are you okay?" Wally asked, his tone showing his concern. "You look a bit pale."

I took a deep breath and allowed the sweetness of the cake to fill my soul. Sugar could fix everything. I was sure of it. "It's all just a bit overwhelming."

"Have you ever even been to a farm before?"

I shook my head.

"I didn't think so. The shoes you were wearing yesterday didn't depict a girl who was prepared for farm life. But don't worry." Wally reached for my hand and gave it a pat. "You'll get the hang of it. I'll help you."

"You don't have to do that." I gave him a weak smile. "I'm sure you have better things to do."

"What could I possibly be doing which would be better than teaching a wonderful young lady how to work a farm?"

I could think of a thousand things, but I chose not to say them as I liked his company. The farm felt a lot less lonely whenever he was around.

When we'd finished our cupcakes and drunk the last of the milk, I dressed in cut off denim shorts and candy pink T-shirt, popped in my contact lenses, and took a minute to examine myself, fluffing my long, dark straight hair and admiring how it was behaving in the dry country air.

I clicked the lid off my eyeliner and used it to frame my eyes, adjusted my push up bra, and slipped on my chai colored Jimmy Choo wedge sandals (knock offs I found on a trip to Bali. $15.99!)

Until I ventured into town, my stiletto's were going to be sitting on the shelf.

"Ready?" Wally asked, as I stepped into the early morning sun.

"As I'll ever be."

To the left of the house was a tall hedge of shrubs protecting it from the winds which picked up over the never-ending fields behind it. Clifford ran ahead as we walked beyond the hedge and crossed the brown grass which now surprisingly held a tinge of green. Last night's storm had cleared the clouds and a sea of blue filled the sky for as far as my eye could see.

"I thought I'd start by showing you your animals." Wally shuffled alongside me. "Come over here and you can meet the chooks. I should warn you, they don't look like much."

We rounded an Oleander bush and stopped in front of a large fenced area sitting beneath a tall gum tree. The tree shaded the ground inside the fence which was mainly dirt, and the sign swinging by one nail above the gate told me this was *The Palace*. Of the three chickens who dashed toward us, one had no feathers, one was missing a leg, and one was wearing a knitted jumper.

Oh geez.

Clifford ran excited laps around the perimeter of the pen as Wally opened the gate and stepped inside.

The chickens immediately moved around his feet, clucking for attention.

"You coming in?" he asked me.

I knew this was something I was going to have to do eventually, but it didn't have to be today. I shook my head.

"Um, Wally…" Growing up in the city, the only chickens I'd ever encountered came from the freezer section at the supermarket. Of course, I knew what real chickens looked like…well, I thought I did. "Are these birds normal?"

"Of course, they are." He lifted the lid off a nearby bucket and sprinkled a handful of pellets around. The birds immediately bounded toward the feed, their frenzied clucking only stopping once they pecked at the ground.

"I've never seen a chicken wear a jumper before."

"Ah, well she is Daisy and she has a skin condition which means her feathers don't grow. The jumper protects her from the weather."

"What about the one with no feathers? Doesn't she need a jumper too?"

"Ethel only lost her feathers a few days ago. None of us around here can knit, so I asked one of the women at the CWA if they could make something for her, but they just said she should be..." He swiped his finger across his neck.

I gasped as I looked at Ethel. "No! You wouldn't do that, would you?"

"Not my place considering she doesn't belong to me. If anyone was to make the decision it would have to be you." He stepped back out of the gate and pulled it closed behind him.

I looked at Ethel as she pecked at a pellet, happy in her own little world and two thoughts ran through my mind. First off, I was going vegetarian. Second, I needed to learn to knit, because there was no way Ethel was being given the chop on my watch.

"Okay then." I pulled my shoulders back. "Where do I buy yarn?"

Wally grinned and slapped me on the shoulder. "That's my girl."

"What's the name of the third chicken?" I asked.

"That's Cottonball."

"What happened to her leg?"

"Last season, the Barrett's decided to do some breeding to increase their stock of laying birds. Cottonball was just a little thing when a Mickey bird got him and tried to pull him from the cage they kept him in. Pulled his leg clean off. Matilda stepped in and saved him. He's a bit slower than the others but he seems to cope alright."

44

"He?"

"Yep. Figured that one out when he started to Cock-A-Doodle-Doo at two in the morning."

"I thought roosters crowed at day break," I said, remembering all my childhood books.

"Cottonball never got that message."

Great.

The brown dead grass had been slightly softened by last night's rain, but it still felt hard beneath my shoes as I followed Wally and Clifford around the grounds, Wally pointing out the few outbuildings and sheds we owned.

"That's one of your buildings over there." He pointed at a small house.

Its stump foundations seemed to have seen better days, giving into the weight of the building. The tiny house leaned precariously to one side, the white walls were stained with the brown dirt from the rains.

"I believe it used to be a workman's cottage," Wally said. "But Matilda used it to store all sorts of odds and ends."

"Is it safe to go inside?" I wondered what sort of treasures it would hold.

"Hmm, I'll check with Noah. Though I don't know why you'd want to go in there. It's only full of rubbish, rats and dead mice."

I shivered despite the hot sun beating down on me.

"Now in that paddock ahead," Wally pointed to a metal fenced area, "You've got Ruby. She's a miniature horse and I should warn you she's a bit neurotic."

"Neurotic?"

"Yep, but don't let her worry you. What you need to watch out for is the cows. You've got four of them. Sirloin, Rump, T-Bone and Chuck. Sirloin's very serious, so don't ever tease her when it comes to food. Rump will give you a nudge if you get too close. T-Bone has a bad attitude and likes to bite. Chuck escapes from her paddock once in a while but she doesn't cause any problems other than sitting in the driveway."

"I think I met her yesterday. I had to drive around her."

"Nah! Just drive up to her. She'll move out of the way."

Remembering that Chuck was heavier than my car, I didn't think I'd ever be testing this theory. "What type of cows are they?"

"Belted Galloways. A neighboring farmer hit hard times a few years ago and was going to shoot them. Matilda got in first."

Wally changed direction and we walked around a group of shrubs, sidestepping a wet patch of green grass.

"Don't want to walk in that," he announced as Clifford ran straight through it, the water splashing up his legs. "It's waste water coming from the house. Thought we might as well use it to water the grass." As he spoke a house just like the one I had dreamed about came into view.

The house was grand, wide verandahs surrounding it. The large oak cased windows reflected the morning, the manicured native gardens blossomed, and the dog sitting contentedly on the top step lifted its head and sniffed in our direction. *Wow.*

"That's our place," Wally said as the black and white Collie stood and casually made its way toward us, happily greeting Clifford in a way that humans never would.

"It's beautiful," I whispered, referring to the house.

Not the dogs. The dogs sniffing each other's backsides was far from beautiful.

"It's been a labor of love for Randall and Noah. Restoring it distracted them both during hard times." Wally's voice cracked and I reached out and touched his arm. He swallowed hard and then patted my hand. "The farm they owned before this one never had a house like this. It's the reason we bought here. Sophie always wanted a white farm house with big verandahs."

"Sophie?"

"My daughter in-law. Randall bought it before she passed

away. Back then, the house didn't look as good as it does now. After Sophie died, Randall and Noah wanted to do it up as a tribute to her." I noted the tears filling behind Wally's lashes before he pulled his face away and swiped at them.

"They've done an amazing job," I kept my tone cheery. It wasn't easy. I was the type to cry at a McDonald's advertisement. Emotion bubbled up and my own tears stung.

"She'd be really proud of what they've done." Wally cleared his throat and gave the Collie a pat.

"That's a gorgeous dog," I said, wanting to move to a less painful subject.

"Sebastian belongs to Noah. He's very intelligent. More than once he's helped me round up Goatie."

"That's the goat you were chasing yesterday, right?"

Wally nodded. "Bloody animal that is. I've no idea what Matilda was thinking when she took that one. Never the less, I'll show you her paddock."

Wally continued to chat about the menagerie which made-up Dun Roamin' as we wandered past some large outbuildings and toward Goatie. The chain holding the gate closed was twisted around the post in a complicated way, but Wally easily managed to open it.

"Will she bite?" I asked, as he pulled up a small stool and sat down alongside Goatie, dropping a bucket beneath her udders.

"Nah, she's a good girl most of the time. You can watch how I milk her, then if you ever need to do it, you'll know how."

Was it something I needed to learn? I sighed and thought it was so much easier when I lived near a supermarket.

"Randall's had eczema lately," Wally said. "Apparently goat milk is good for it. Thought while I'm out here I could get him some."

I hadn't met Randall yet, but looking at the dirt already in the bucket, I really hoped he wasn't drinking the milk.

"Hold onto her collar, will you?" Wally instructed.

I tentatively held out my hand to Goatie, hoping she wouldn't bite me. Up close she was pretty cute. Her brown face had a white streak running from the tip of her head to the point of her little brown nose and then covered the rest of her body. Her hair was rough under my touch, as she squirmed against my grip, and her quiet bleat was music to my ears.

"Who's a pretty girl?" I cooed, pretending to not be scared.

"Hold her still!"

"I'm trying. She's a bit fidgety."

Wally released a breath. "I think she senses your fear. You got to look her in the eye and tell her who's the boss. Like this." He moved to her head, leaned forward, and stared at her daring her to argue his authority. "Got that?" He straightened himself up.

Not really, but I knew that if this was to be my new life, then I had to at least try.

I copied Wally as best as I could, as he moved once again to sit on the stool. I seemed to be doing a pretty good job telling her who was in charge, until he grabbed her udders. As he squeezed, she bucked sideways, her full belly knocking into Wally. The stool wobbled precariously before falling backward and throwing Wally into the mud. Goatie then let out a little bleat, stole Wally's cap that had fallen beside her, and ran to the opposite end of the paddock.

"Bugger!" Wally grunted.

That about summed it up.

Even though Wally cursed Goatie all the way to Polly's cage, thankfully he wasn't hurt.

"Oh geez!" shouted Wally, his hand lifting in the air. "I forgot about passing wind."

I wondered why he had to remember such a thing. Manners kept my bodily functions in check when I wasn't alone, but generally I didn't have to remember to actually do it. It was more of a sudden urge kind of thing. "Don't mind me," I said. "If you feel the need, go right ahead."

His nose scrunched as he turned to face me. "Noah was supposed to remind me, but oh well. I guess I'll move him over later."

Okay, now I was confused. "Move him over?"

"Yeah. Passing Wind is your horse."

Oh, that was a relief.

"He was supposed to be a race horse, but nature had other ideas," Wally continued. "We had him in one of the closer paddocks, but Noah moved him to a more secure yard yesterday. The breeze brought him a whiff of a filly and he was going a bit crazy. We were worried he might break the fence and hurt himself."

"He'd do that?"

"You'd be surprised what he'd do to get to a female. Add that to your list," Wally said. "Get him de-nutted. He won't be a problem if you do that." I retrieved my phone, opened my notes and added *Find a vet* to my ever-growing list.

Walking around the property, I had thought that the sun and fresh air had done wonders to calm me, but I was quickly realizing that I was actually being paralyzed with fear. I had no idea how to look after so many animals.

Wally's feet scuffed against the cracked cement as he stepped onto the path next to Polly's cage.

"Silly bitch," Polly called as I numbly followed Wally toward my back deck and kitchen.

"Don't worry about her. She'll soon get bored of that. I think," he assured me.

"I didn't know birds could swear." The heat of the day caused the sweat beading on my brow to run down my temples. But then again it could be my anxiety at my new life causing that.

"Don't show her fear." Wally pointed to Polly. "You'll never get control of her if you do."

Judging by the way she had her feathers fluffed and her crest standing at full attention, I didn't think control over her was something I would ever have.

"Wally, did Matilda have any animals that didn't have issues?" I asked as Izzy the cat fell from the top step, landing with a *thunk* on her back, two feet from where she had started.

Wally sighed. "No. Matilda only saved animals who were otherwise going to be put to sleep."

What a sweet lady.

I watched Izzy as she righted herself, shook herself off and sat in the dirt where she had landed.

"Izzy has a bit of a balance problem. She belonged to Deidre over on Littlebrook Road, but when Matilda learned she was going to euthanize her, she marched into the vet and demanded they give ownership of the cat to her. She could be fierce when she wanted to be, and Dave wasn't going to argue with her."

"Did she get Polly the same way?"

Polly squawked a four-letter word starting with F at me.

"Polly came from a farmer over on the west side of Dun Roamin'. He'd taught her to swear at his mother-in-law whenever she visited. The mother-in-law didn't like it and Matilda ran to the rescue when his missus was going to have her put down. Polly that is, not the mother-in-law."

"Lucky Polly. Did she swear at Matilda the same way?"

"Only when Matilda got too close to Noah. She has a bit of a crush on him."

So, I'd seen.

5

I pulled the key from my shorts pocket and negotiated the few steps to the back door.

"You don't need to keep doing that," Wally said as I turned the lock. "We're trustworthy people out here."

"Sorry. Habit," I pushed the door open and Clifford ran in ahead of us.

The sound of a car pulling into the gravel driveway filled the morning air.

Wally and I looked at each other. I made my way through the house to the front verandah. I should've walked around the outside, but I forgot about the front steps being unusable.

Stepping on to the timber decking, I noted the sleek black Audi glinting in the mid-morning sun. The driver got out and closed the door behind him, his dark Ray Bans shielding his eyes. His pale blue cotton business shirt, black suit pants, immaculate grooming and perfectly trimmed facial stubble made him look like he was here for a photo shoot for GQ magazine.

"Good morning Tilly," Gregory Blackburn the Third's dimples flashed as he looked up at me and smiled.

"Oh, good morning Mr. Blackburn. This is an unexpected

visit." And it was. I really hadn't thought he would drive all the way here from Westport to see me.

"I hope you don't mind I've arrived unannounced. I've been trying to call you but your phone seems to be switched off." He stopped at the bottom of the steps. I could see his brow furrow as he assessed their condition.

"Is there something wrong?" I knew it. The inheritance was all a mistake. He was here to tell me it was all to go to The Arts Society, just like Matilda's back up plan.

"It's a hot one today. Do you mind if we chat inside?" he asked, as his Ray Ban's fogged up.

Wally stood tall alongside me. I say tall, as he seemed to have pulled himself up to his full height and his chest was much more pronounced than it had been five minutes ago.

I heard his scoff as I told him to go around the back.

"What?" I asked Wally, as we made our way toward the kitchen.

"Nothing."

"It's clearly something."

"He just thinks he's better than the rest of us."

"He's been really nice to me."

"Of course, he has." He stared straight ahead at Gregory Blackburn standing on the threshold.

I moved closer to him. "Mr. Blackburn, I wish I could offer you a coffee but I haven't been into town yet. Sorry." I didn't add I couldn't find the kettle, and Wally and I'd finished off the last of the cupcakes.

"That's perfectly okay. But please call me Greg." He folded the arms on his sunglasses and placed them in the breast pocket of his shirt. "How are you settling in? Enjoying the country life?"

"It's been interesting," I replied. "Do you know Wally?"

Gregory, ummm Greg, nodded politely. "How are you Mr. McKenzie?"

"I'm perfectly well, thank you." Wally grunted. He pulled up the lone chair and sat himself down, obviously here for the long haul.

Greg kept the professional persona in place, but I could swear that I saw the corners of his mouth turn up ever so slightly.

"So, what brings you all the way out here?" I asked.

"It's official business."

"Oh." Anxiety made my voice low and heavy.

"The will stipulated that you had to be living here one week from when we met. I'm just here to check that you have indeed moved in."

"Oh," I repeated, but much more brightly this time. "Yes, I have moved in. Yesterday in fact. Wally can attest to it." I turned to Wally, my look attempting to convey now was the time to speak up. But he just sat there with his arms folded over his chest, glaring at Greg, chunks of dirt falling from his shirt as his dentures rotated in his mouth.

"Can you confirm it, Mr. McKenzie?" Greg asked.

"Of course, I can. I'm still wondering how she got that little car of hers down the driveway, but she did." Wally gave me a big toothy smile, and his top dentures popped out of his mouth. They hit the dusty floor and Clifford ran in and scooped them up. Before I could stop him, he ran between Greg's legs and out the back door.

For a man in his late seventies Wally sure could move fast. He was up and out of his chair before I barely registered what had even happened. Only when he was out of sight did I look Greg in the eye. His face was contorted from the effort of not laughing.

"I should probably go and help him," I said.

"Sure. I'll give you a hand."

Unexpectedly, Greg seemed to know his way around the farm, and within minutes we caught up with Wally near a large open fronted tin clad shed I hadn't come across on our morning walk.

"He's under the tractor." Wally nodded toward a rusty old piece of machinery.

I moved closer to him as I surveyed the contents of the building.

"Whose shed is this?" I asked, coughing against the dust Clifford had stirred up.

"It's yours," Greg answered, before Wally had the chance.

"Great."

It wasn't exactly the highlight of my day. The shed was barely staying upright. The timber support poles looked rotten, the tin was rusty, and the floor was dirt. An old tractor took pride of place amongst the other pieces of equipment I couldn't even name.

Wally knelt down under the back of the tractor. "You rotten bugger, come here!"

Clifford crawled closer to the front wheels, his prize clamped between his jaws.

Greg crouched, attempting to reach Clifford's collar. Clifford, sensing he was outnumbered, took his opportunity and made his escape, running past me to freedom.

He was quick but running was one thing I was good at, and I took off after him before Greg could even stand up. Even though my wedge heels slowed me down, I managed to corner Clifford around the back of the shed.

"You're a naughty boy," I clutched his collar, my legs itching from the tall, dead grass which reached my knees. "Drop!" I didn't know much about dogs, but this was one thing I knew they were trained to do.

Clifford however, hadn't gotten the memo. Instead he spun me in circles as I attempted to hold on to him, until I tripped over my own feet and landed on my backside—which was still bruised from my fall from the front steps. But the upside was I didn't lose my grip, and Clifford eventually gave up and sat.

"I've got him," I called, as Greg and Wally ran toward me.

Wally scowled at Clifford, and after a bit of tugging, Clifford eventually gave up the dentures. Wally shook them off and popped them back in his mouth.

"Wally, don't you think you should wash them first?" I asked, horrified.

"Germs don't pass from a dog's mouth to a human mouth. It's not possible."

That wasn't something I was prepared to take his word on.

After I'd managed to control the gagging, I let go of Clifford's collar and allowed Greg to help me to my feet, his eyes lingering on my dirty butt.

"Close your mouth," I warned Greg. "Flies will go in."

He promptly clamped his lips together.

Wally grunted a goodbye, then headed in the direction of his house, leaving Greg and I alone.

I fiddled with the hem of my T-shirt as my eyes skimmed the bronze colored crop, the mid-morning heat shimmering in the distance, before coming to rest on the shed wall.

The grass tickled the tin as it gently swayed in the breeze. Grass this long freaked me out as it could hide a snake, and I needed to ask Wally where the mower was kept. I knew how to use one of those—thank goodness.

Reaching out and touching the wall, I noted the ugly green paint covering it. I wondered why this wall was painted when the rest of it was just rusty tin.

"So, I own all of this?"

"All yours. Plus, there's two others that go with it," Greg replied.

"Are they as old as this one?"

"Yep," Greg said with an amused smile.

I smiled at him and allowed my gaze to wander back to the fields. The occasional whinnying from the horses and the clucking from the chickens carried on the wind. "It's really beautiful out here," I commented. "Quiet, but beautiful."

"Yeah. It's very different to Westport."

A lump formed in my throat and the emptiness I was struggling to keep at bay, filled my soul. "Have you ever had a feeling that you're drowning yet you're nowhere near water?"

"I have. It's overwhelming."

"Setting up my bakery was the scariest thing I had ever done. Until now, that is."

"You have help?"

I looked at him blankly.

"Family? Friends who will help you?" he continued.

I shook my head and fought back the tears which unexpectedly stung. "My friends are all in Westport." And there was no way I could ask my parents for help again.

"Boyfriend?"

I thought of Warwick. "Sort of. But he's far too busy fighting crime to help with my loneliness." I swallowed hard.

"You understand you don't have to do this, don't you?" His voice was filled with compassion.

"I do have to do it," I replied quietly. "I've failed at just about every little thing I have ever tried in my life. I failed at gymnastics as a kid, I failed my attempt at a university degree, I failed as a photographer."

"That's not true," interrupted Greg. "I've seen your photos."

He had?

"How?"

"Since taking over the business from my grandfather, I've visited Matilda on numerous occasions. She proudly showed me your work, and your photos are amazing, Tilly."

I swallowed hard against the emotion clogging my throat.

"But they didn't pay the rent, did they? I was a driving instructor once, you know. Every student I had loved me, but they all failed their driving tests. Do you know why? Because I failed as their teacher."

"I'm sure that wasn't why they failed."

"I still believe we're all good at something," I continued, lost in my own thoughts. "When I learned to bake, I thought I'd found my thing. The one thing I would succeed at. I know my cupcakes are good. It's my business skills which sucked." Tears once again stung, but I flicked them away at Greg's pained expression. "I can't fail at another thing. And Matilda had a reason for leaving this all to me. I'd be letting her down if I didn't at least try."

Greg let out a soft breath. "You're stronger than you think, Tilly. And remember I'm only a phone call away. If you need anything—just ring. Between me and my secretary we can organize almost anything."

I looked up into his dark eyes and swallowed against the kindness which shone back at me. "You don't know any good plumbers who can install an indoor toilet, do you?" I joked.

"I'll have one here this afternoon." He gave me a smile and my heart beat a happy tune at the news.

Returning to professional mode he pointed out various parts of the farm, as we walked back toward his car. He showed me the other two sheds which I owned, along with the truck.

I use the word 'truck' loosely. Yes, it had four wheels, and yes it looked like a truck, but the rotten timber tray, the rust, and the fact that plants were growing out of the open windows made me question its roadworthiness.

I really hoped the McKenzie's kept renting the land from me because I had no idea what I was doing and I had the impression I didn't have the tools for the job either.

As we rounded the last building and his sleek Audi came into view, he gave a loud guttural moan.

There, standing proudly on the Audi's roof, was Goatie.

I was kind of worried Greg was about to pass out. All the blood appeared to have left his face. His pale color sharply contrasted with the redness of his neck, which shone out against the deep brown of his bulging eyes.

I didn't know what to do. An hour ago, Goatie was in her

fenced paddock. And I *distinctly* remembered double checking I'd closed her gate when Wally and I left her. Wally had given me explicit instructions on how to tie the chain and I followed them to the letter. But none of it changed the fact she was now happily prancing on the spot, seemingly very content with her new vantage point.

Greg sprinted toward his car, his arms flapping, his voice so high I was sure his man parts were somewhere around his navel.

"Shoo! Shoo!" he yelled at Goatie.

She looked disdainfully down her nose at him. "*Baa aaa aa*," she bleated as if to tell him to bugger off.

"Shoo!" He ran in circles around his car, frantically waving his hands. "Don't just stand there!" he screamed to me. "Help me get her down."

"What do I do?" I hurriedly asked.

"I don't know! She's your goat—you tell me," he snapped.

Shit. Did that mean I had to pay for the damages?

I quickly copied Greg and started running around the car waving my arms about, yelling "shoo".

We successfully got her off the roof of the car. But now she was prancing on the bonnet, not very happy with either of us if her stomping was anything to go by. The more she stomped, the more dents she put in the car.

Greg's screams got louder, and I felt the panic take hold in my stomach, working its way up my throat.

When he'd pulled up this morning, this car had looked brand new. Now it looked like it had been through a hail storm.

My panic attack was just taking hold as help wandered toward us.

Noah was a sight for sore eyes. His gait was relaxed, his smile was at full wattage, and in his hands he carried a bundle of hay. Stopping at the Audi's front grille, he held the hay just out of Goatie's reach.

"Come on lovely," he gently coaxed. "You know you want it."

Goatie's nose twitched as she tentatively took her first steps in his direction.

He took a large stride backward, tempting her to follow him. Greg and I both stood holding our breath.

As Noah's plan worked and Goatie leaped off the bonnet, I wasn't sure which one of us wanted to kiss him first. Judging by the look of relief which was now flooding his face, I thought it may just be Greg.

———

Greg's shoulders slumped as he scuffed his feet toward his car, his smile non-existent.

Noah stood alongside me holding Goatie by the collar, as we both watched a broken man getting behind the wheel of his once pristine vehicle.

"I know I closed the gate," I moaned to Noah as the car roared to life. I watched feeling defeated as it then disappeared down the driveway, a cloud of dust billowing in its wake. "I know I did."

"Don't worry about it." Noah adjusted his grip on Goatie's collar, taking a few steps away from me.

I'd originally wondered why she wore a collar, but now I understood.

"She knows how to open the latch when she wants to. I thought we'd sorted the problem, but obviously not." He gave me a dazzling smile, seemingly not bothered by the series of events which had just occurred.

"It's alright for you to say don't worry about it. I'll have to pay to have that car fixed," I whined, following him across the grass. "And I'm sure it's not going to be cheap."

"He already told you he has insurance."

"I have no idea how much the excess is though. And I'm sure he'll never speak to me again."

Any thoughts of using Matilda's money to install a new kitchen had just flown straight out the window.

Noah let out a scoff. "Just send him a batch of cupcakes with the promise to keep them coming and I'm sure he'll forgive and forget."

"Is this how I should also pay you for saving the day?" I asked.

Noah flashed me another smile. "I won't say no."

I followed him back to Goatie's paddock and watched him close the latch in exactly the same way I'd done earlier. Maybe I just hadn't tied it tight enough.

"Thank you, Noah. I don't know what we would have done without you."

"Actually, it's me who should be thanking you."

"No really. I have no idea how we would have got Goatie off the car if you hadn't arrived with that hay." I shuddered at the thought.

Noah chuckled. "Don't mention it," he said. "But I wanted to thank you again for the cupcakes. Dad had one after tea last night, and for the first time in a very long while he genuinely smiled."

"Really?"

"Yeah. Mum used to make red velvet cupcakes. They were her specialty, and they were Dad's favorite. He said that yours reminded him of a happy memory. He's been struggling to remember those, he's just been so focused on her passing away." Sadness flicked through his gorgeous blue eyes, and my heart squeezed.

"I'll bake him some more once I can get a new oven installed. Not sure how long it will be, though."

"You're welcome to come over and use ours at any time. Don't be shy."

"That's very kind of you."

"It'll cost you though." Noah winked.

I knew he was talking about paying him in cupcakes, but my

heart skipped a whole beat. Heat rushed to my face as my thoughts jumped to places they shouldn't go, and I turned away from him grateful he couldn't see the delicious tingle that ran down my spine.

I tried quickly changing the subject. "So, I need to go into town and get some food. Can you give me directions to the shop please?"

"I can do better than that. I'll take you."

"You don't need to do that," I protested.

"Yes, I do. I've seen your car and I'm surprised it got you this far."

n the drive to Littlebrook, I distracted myself from the close proximity to Noah by asking him about Matilda. "So, how well did you know her?"

The dust from the gravel road created a cloud behind us as he drove the Land Cruiser at an alarming speed, negotiating the bumps like a man who'd done it a thousand times.

"As well as anyone could know her, I guess. She was a private woman, not that you'd know it."

"What do you mean?"

"She didn't talk a lot about her life, but she was pretty vocal about a lot of other things. Most people in this area were a little bit afraid of her." Noah's deep gravelly laugh danced across my navel. "She'd put you in your place pretty smartly if she thought you needed it. She was kind though."

"Yeah, I figured that. I've seen the animals she's collected."

Noah's Ute bounced over a pothole which would have swallowed my car. No wonder he didn't want me to drive it here.

"She sure loved them," he continued, completely unfazed by the bump. "And they loved her. It was like they knew what she'd done for them and they were forever grateful for it. Clifford was the one who alerted me to the fact something was wrong the day she died."

"Oh, really? How?"

"Well the day had started normally enough. I'd taken the beer and placed it in her fridge and she seemed fine, but about an hour later I was down the paddock on the tractor when Clifford came. He'd literally run a couple of kilometers to get there. I lifted him into the cab but he was acting really weird, scratching at the door and wanting to get out. So, I let him out. Then he stood staring at me and barking. I eventually got him back into the tractor and drove him home where he then raced toward Matilda's house. I found her on her bed, but it was too late—she was gone."

I blinked away a tear. "So, she died alone."

Noah nodded. "Yeah, but I like to think she died happy. She loved Dun Roamin'."

"Why did she sell part of it off in the first place?"

"She suffered too many dry years without a crop and age was getting the better of her. We've had a lot of small farms selling up to a conglomerate we like to call the Super Farms but she sold it to us because she didn't want to go to the big guns."

"Why didn't she sell you the entire property if she was struggling?"

"I asked her that same question. She just replied she was born and raised here and didn't want to be anywhere else. I did my best to keep things running as well as I could for her. And now, it's yours." He gave me a smile.

"And now it's mine." I sighed.

"Do you know what you plan to do with it once its title is legally transferred to you?"

"I can't think past the next half an hour, let alone know what I'll do in a year's time," I confessed.

Noah nodded. "Well, if you do decide to sell, could you please offer it to us first?"

"Of course."

He negotiated a curve in the road and the town of Littlebrook came into view. When I'd driven in yesterday, my GPS has taken me in the back way and I'd bypassed it. As Noah drove through the town now, I could see I hadn't missed much.

Littlebrook was made up of a smattering of houses, two small churches, a primary school, a police station which according to Noah had a single police officer in attendance, an abandoned railway yard, and a town hall. It had a road in, a road out, and one crossroads, that if the street sign was to be believed, led to Mt Lockhart.

"There's a Mt Lockhart?" I asked in disbelief as he indicated and pulled the Ute to a stop outside the service station, slash post office, slash convenience store.

"Yep. Even though it's not a very big mountain. More of a large hill." He pointed at an elevation in the distance.

"Can you show me how to get there sometime?" Being a Lockhart, I felt it was my duty to at least check out the mountain named after my family.

"Sure. You'll need to wear different shoes if you want to climb it though," Noah teased as he opened the truck and stepped on to the hot bitumen road.

I huffed and followed him toward the cream-colored building with the bright red sign saying 'Monty's'. The outside looked like a regular service station, with one pump for petrol and one for diesel. There was a hose connected to the air pump, a bucket holding a windscreen cleaner, and a sign advising the price of fuel.

"Geez, fuel's expensive," I muttered.

"Monty has his own price guide," Noah replied. "But don't worry. We have a pump on the farm that you can use to fill your car. Even though I recommend you use Matilda's Ute if you want to go anywhere."

"There's a Ute? I didn't see it this morning when Wally gave me a tour."

"He gave you the basic tour, not to overwhelm you. I'll take you around the property again and show you where everything is. I also need to show you how and when all the animals are fed. You're probably keen to start looking after them."

If he said so.

The inside of the store was a lot bigger than I'd given it credit for. I grabbed a basket and made my way around the four aisles selecting the necessities I thought I'd need until I made a trip back to Westport to the supermarket. I also found some pink wool and knitting needles, so I popped them into the basket, thinking I'd check YouTube as soon as I got some internet and figure out how to knit. I wasn't sure if Ethel would like the color, but I didn't have a whole lot to choose from and I guessed she wasn't in the position to be fussy.

Once I was loaded up, I found Noah at the back of the store, his hip causally leaning against the counter marked Take Away Food. This store really did have everything.

"Tilly, I'd like to introduce you to Monty."

I looked to the middle-aged man grinning at me across the counter. "Pleased to meet you."

"The pleasure is all mine." As he offered me his hand to shake, and I accepted his gesture of friendship.

"I was just saying to Noah it'll be good to have a new face around here. There are only thirty-three residents in Littlebrook, half of which are kids, so you get a bit sick of the same old faces, day in and day out." Monty gave me a large smile. I noted his missing front tooth, the scar running from his nose to his ear, and the grim reaper tattoo on his forearm.

"I'm looking forward to getting to know everyone," I replied.

I heard a scoff and spun around to see two late twenty-something girls.

The blonde one looked me up and down, her top lip curling as if she had seen something that disgusted her. She exchanged a grimace with her friend, before giving her full attention to Noah.

65

Her expression immediately changed. Fluttering her fake eyelashes, she widened her gray eyes at him until I thought they may hurt, and pushed her ample chest out until the fabric of her shirt looked like it might tear against the force. "Hi Noah," she purred, stepping past me and ever so lightly running her fingertips over his bare arm.

He gave her a small smile as he looked down at her through his long dark lashes, and her fingers snaked around his arm possessively.

"Janie." He pulled himself away from the counter and stood tall. Next to him, Janie looked tiny. Apart from her boobs, the rest of her was minute. "I'd like to introduce you to Tilly. She's just inherited the farm from Matilda. Tilly, Janie's on the committee for the Littlebrook Arts Society. And this is Eliza."

"My father's the chairman." Janie turned to me as Eliza gave a little wave and fleetingly looked me up and down. "I believe if you don't stay then it becomes ours. Dun Roamin' is quite the handful."

That was one way to describe it.

"Do you have much farming experience?" she asked sweetly, but it sounded like more of a challenge.

"No. This is my first time." I gave her my biggest grin. I'd already gauged her, and I knew instantly that we weren't going to be best buddies. However, if Littlebrook had so few residents, then I couldn't afford to alienate any of them. And if she was Noah's girlfriend, which her body language definitely indicated, then I especially couldn't afford to upset her.

She laughed. "Oh geez. Well, good luck. I guess."

"Thanks," I replied, only she had already moved her attention back to Noah.

"So, Noah, don't forget the town meeting this Friday night." She touched his arm again.

"Town meeting?" I asked.

"It's basically just an excuse to get together and have some fun," Eliza said, giving a little shrug.

Eliza was really pretty, her long auburn hair tumbling over her shoulders. Her large green eyes were framed by long, natural lashes and her skin was like porcelain. "Even though we do cover some very serious topics," Eliza continued. "This month we're discussing the upcoming Craft and Fine Food Fair and the joint shire Amateur Dramatic Society play."

"You should come," Noah suggested. "You're a part of the community now and it would be a great way for you to meet everyone."

"Sounds awesome!" I flashed him a smile.

Daggers were thrown from Janie's eyes directly at my heart, but I ignored them as the ring from my mobile phone which I'd left in the bottom of my handbag, startled me.

Hurriedly retrieving it, I stared at it in disbelief. "I have a signal!"

Noah laughed.

"You need to upgrade your carrier if you don't have phone reception out on the farm," Monty said. "Most of them work here in town, but only one works out there. I can sell you a plan if you like."

I held my finger up to him to say hold that thought, as I swiped the screen. "Hi Warwick!" I was excited to be speaking to someone I knew. At the sound of his familiar reassuring voice, I stepped away from the others and toward the front of the shop.

An older woman stepped behind the counter and stopped next to Monty. I distinctly heard her mutter the words *bloody townie* as I walked away from them.

"Hey, Tilly." Warwick's soothing voice traveled across my skin and into my belly where the anxious butterflies had been zipping around. Hearing his dulcet tones, they settled together and their flapping ceased.

"Hi!" I trilled, stepping out of the store into the heat. "It's so good to hear from you."

"Sorry, I haven't called sooner, but I've been busy. There's some serious stuff happening at work."

"Anything you can talk about?" I asked, enjoying the sense of familiarity he aroused.

His sigh was loud in my ear. "Sarg has us playing bodyguard, but I can't really say much at the moment."

"Oh. But you're okay, right?"

"Yeah, I'm okay. How are you going? How's Dun Roamin'?"

It was my turn to sigh. "Not what I expected." I started to explain my new life, but I could hear voices in the background yelling out to Warwick. The rustling sound of him placing his hand over the microphone crackled in my ear, then his distant voice called out.

"Okay! I'll just be a minute!"

"Is everything alright?" I asked. "Do you have to go?"

"Sorry." He removed his hand, talking to me. His tone was weary and he sounded tired. "Yeah, I have to go. I was on a break but we've just had a call that someone's in trouble. I'll call you later, hey?"

"Sure thing." Disappointment sat heavily on the butterflies in my belly. "I'll get a new number and I'll text it to you."

"Thanks for understanding."

"Of course, I understand! I know how important your job is. My problems are nothing compared to those who are relying on you."

I felt his smile, when he said, "You really are the best."

I blew some kisses down the line to him before ending the call. Sliding my phone back into my bag, I filled my lungs with fresh air, grateful that I didn't need the professional services of the police. Yet as the knot in my stomach tightened, that needy little voice in my head wished, just once, he could find some time to put me first.

I mulled over the morning I'd had and figured I'd schedule in a nanna nap. I was exhausted and it was only lunch time.

Noah had dropped me home vowing he would be over later with some tools to start work on fixing my front steps and to give me the tour he'd promised. To be completely honest, the steps weren't high on my priority list. I would have been far happier if he was installing an inside toilet. Greg had promised to find a plumber but after the whole Goatie incident, I didn't like my chances of it happening.

I'd purchased a new phone plan from Monty, switched out my sim card, and had since messaged everyone in my contact list my new number. I was about to log on to Instagram, when the distinct sound of car wheels on the gravel driveway filled the air.

By the time I made it to the front steps, my second-cousin, Ethan, was sidestepping Clifford.

"Tilly!" He beamed at me. "Hope you don't mind that I popped in unannounced?"

"Ethan! Ummm, G'day."

What the hell was he doing here? I hadn't seen him since the last family reunion and that was over a year ago. Ethan and I were almost the same age, but we weren't what you'd call close. His dad Tony and my dad were cousins. We'd both been educated at Westport's one and only private college and we got along okay.

"Yeah, well I was out this way and I thought I'd say hi." His long legs and lanky frame loped toward me. He gave me a gummy smile. Ethan had teeth, but they were the little ones perched on the end of large gums. "Looks like you've had some visitors already." He nodded toward a cane picnic basket, covered by a pretty pink checked cloth, sitting in the sun on the decking boards.

"Oh! I didn't know it was there." Probably because I was now using the back door and hadn't walked this way since Greg had turned up this morning.

I told Ethan to walk around to the back door and I picked up the basket, the smell of scones floating toward me as I pulled back the covering, making my stomach grumble. I searched the basket for a note as to who left it there, but when I couldn't see one, I made my way back through the house. Placing the basket on the table I met Ethan at the door.

He ran his fingers through his messy strawberry blonde hair, his brown eyes squinting against the glaring sun. His shoulders were tense and the little crease he had between his brows reminded me of the Grand Canyon.

"Come on in." I opened the screen for him and hoped he'd shoo the five flies off his shoulders before stepping inside. He didn't. Humph.

"How are you settling in?" His eyes expertly scanned the room.

"Oh, you know. It's different to town but I'm sure I'll get used to it."

He pulled out the one kitchen chair and sat down, throwing his cap on the table.

A collection of hats was accumulating so I picked up mine and Matilda's and set them onto the hook near the door.

"How did you know I was here?" I asked, wishing the truck containing all my stuff would arrive so I would have a chair to sit on. Furniture would definitely help make it feel more like home.

"News in this family travels pretty fast. When I heard you were moving to a farm, I was worried about you."

I had no idea Ethan cared that much. "Thanks. But really, don't worry about me. I survived my cupcake shop closing down, I'll survive this."

I hoped.

"I was sorry to hear about that. Looks like luck was on your side, though." His eyes roamed the room, taking in every detail, as he rolled his shoulders. "If you still owned the shop you wouldn't have been able to take over all this."

I looked at Clifford, sitting near the table staring into thin air, his tongue hanging happily to the side. "Yeah, lucky me. I'm sure losing my shop was the best thing that ever happened to me." Irritated that he could even presume that had been a blessing in disguise rumbled low in my belly.

"Worse things happen in life Tilly." He shrugged.

"I guess so. And you're right. If our great aunt hadn't left me such an amazing gift, I'm not sure what I'd be doing. Now, would you like some lunch? Freshly made scones by the look of it." So far, I wasn't enjoying the visit, but manners had been drilled into me as a kid.

"They do smell good," Ethan replied, rubbing his belly. "But I'm on a gluten free diet now."

"I can make you a salad."

"Perfect. Sounds great."

Busying myself with plates and cutlery, I was grateful I'd just visited the store. "How are your mum and dad?" I made small talk as I chopped lettuce, tomato and carrots and threw them all into a bowl. Ethan brought me up to date with their up and coming world cruise, and I listened with strained interest as I threw in alfalfa then sprinkled nuts over the salad for good measure. I'd purchased some cooked chicken from the deli, so I sliced it and added to the plate.

Remembering Ethel and Daisy and my new resolve to become vegetarian, I put the chicken from my plate onto Ethan's, then placed it on the table, before moving the scones to the counter.

"That looks really good," Ethan said. "Thanks."

I had no idea what he was doing here, but silence heavily descended between us as he pushed his food around his plate seemingly not overly hungry. An involuntary tick had started under my eye, and I shifted uncomfortably as I leaned against the counter, picking at my own salad.

"How did you know where Dun Roamin' was?" I asked, breaking the silence and getting to the point of why I thought he was here.

"Ah, well my dad spoke to your dad."

"My parents are on the trip they won to Peru. At the moment, they have no signal."

He responded with a shrug and my impatience skyrocketed.

"Ethan, tell me the truth. What are you *really* doing here?" I demanded.

He sighed and put his fork down. "I wanted to see the farm. You said it yourself. Matilda was *our* great aunt. How come she left everything to you and not to me?"

"Well when you figure it out, will you let me know? As it stands, I don't have a clue!" My fork clunked as it hit the plate.

"Matilda was an idiot thinking you'll last this out a year," he spat. "You see nothing all the way through."

His words hit hard like bullets, piercing the armor I'd been trying to hold up.

"I only have fifty-one weeks to go, thank you very much. And I will stick it out!" I turned away so he couldn't see the hurt he'd inflicted.

"Dad's going to contest it," he announced. "We have good grounds to win, so don't get too comfortable."

I prickled at his tone. Pulling my shoulders back I crossed my arms over my chest.

"Matilda had every right to give this to whoever she wanted to. You have no right to say she didn't."

Ethan stood and snatched his hat from the table. "We'll see about that."

"Why do you care? It's not like you need the money."

"I'm entitled to it as much as you are," he spat. His eyes were hard as they narrowed in on me. "I just want what's fair."

"No one ever said life was fair," I countered, thinking of the life I'd left behind in Westport. Tears prickled my eyes and I hurriedly blinked them away not wanting Ethan to see how this conversation was upsetting me.

But he was sharp and barely missed a trick and I knew that he understood the impact of his visit very well.

A hint of a smile played on his lips. "Thanks for the lunch, Tilly. I'll see myself out."

As he stormed out slamming the screen door behind him, I dropped my head to my hands and groaned. As if I didn't have enough to contend with. Now I also had a family feud on my hands.

My appetite had disappeared along with Ethan, so I scraped my plate into the bin. Clearing up his leftovers I remembered the scones. At least someone was thinking nice thoughts about me today.

Turning to the plate that they were placed on, ready to smother my sorrows in butter and jam, I noted there was only one scone left where there had previously been half a dozen.

It looked like Clifford had seen an opportunity when my attention was elsewhere and had taken full advantage of it. I sighed and scraped the last scone in the bin. I mean, if he had gotten hold of the others there was a good chance he'd also licked this one.

7

*A*fter I'd cleaned up the lunch dishes, I decided to make some room in the bedroom for my own possessions which were arriving the next day. I didn't own a lot, but what I had was quality and I was looking forward to sleeping on my queen size mattress and thousand thread count sheets.

Clifford seemed to have made himself comfortable on Matilda's bed for an afternoon nap now his belly was full, so I left him alone and spent an hour or so moving the unnecessary furniture out of my room and placing it all on the back verandah. I'd transport it all to the old house which was already storing Matilda's overflow of possessions as soon as Noah showed me where the Ute lived. I really needed to investigate that house and make sure there was enough room to store everything until I could figure out what I should do with it. Considering the conversation I'd had with Ethan, I probably shouldn't get rid of anything just yet.

I was making my way out of the room with the last of the boxes stored in the wardrobe when a breeze pushed the door to Matilda's room open. I couldn't see a cloud in the sky, but I wondered if an afternoon storm was brewing.

I shivered and looked in on Clifford. "Clifford, you want to come for a walk?"

He jumped off the bed and drool pooled from his mouth as he panted at an alarming rate.

"Clifford, what's wrong buddy?" He heaved and threw up at my feet. When he was done, he sank his bottom to the floor, his eyes large and sad.

"Oh geez!" I scooped him in my arms and made my way through the house, running to the one person I knew who could help. Noah.

Noah was a rock. He immediately laid Clifford on the back seat of his vehicle, instructed me to sit with him, and then drove us to Littlebrook, whereby Dave the vet, took Clifford to a back room and told us to take a seat.

I sank onto the hard timber bench and dropped my elbows to my knees. Taking my head in my hands, I rubbed my eyes and willed the knot in my stomach to go away.

"He's going to be okay, isn't he?" I asked, more to reassure myself than for an actual answer.

Noah sat beside me, and I felt his warmth as he placed his hand on my shoulder, then gently rubbed my back.

"Clifford's a tough boy, and Dave will do everything humanly possible to help him."

I nodded and blinked back the sting in my eyes.

"I don't understand what happened. One minute he was stealing the scones and the next time I saw him he was vomiting. I shouldn't have left them where he could reach them. I'm so sorry."

"Tilly, don't get upset. Clifford's always getting into things he shouldn't. It's not your fault."

"But I should have done something." The familiar feeling of

panic was starting to bubble in my chest, as I wrung my hands together. "I should have prevented it!" I stood abruptly, my legs restless and needing to move. Noah met me and pulled me in close wrapping his arms around my shoulders allowing his heat to soothe the panic.

"You did everything you could."

"But I didn't know what to do! I should know this stuff. I'm responsible for him now. I should know how to help him."

"You did know. You brought him to me and together we helped him. Dave's amazing and he will do whatever is needed. Clifford will be fine."

"How do you know that?" I asked, allowing myself to lean into his chest. His strength helped me regain control of my breath, and I appreciated the comfort he was offering.

"Because he's strong."

Noah allowed me to lean on him until I calmed down. It felt good to be there. Not just because he was helping me with Clifford, but because it had been a long time since a man had stood beside me when I needed his strength. Warwick was a great person, but he was always so busy helping others that it didn't leave a lot of time for me. I knew I shouldn't need a man to be strong, but every now and again it felt nice to be comforted in times of a crisis.

The door to the back room opened and Dave appeared, his brow soft and a small smile tugging at the corners of his lips.

The knot still consuming my stomach released slightly and I stepped out of Noah's arms.

"How is he?" I immediately asked, rushing toward him.

"He's going to be fine. I'm confident he'll make a full recovery."

The knot dissolved and I blinked back tears of relief.

"I'm going to keep him here on a drip for a while," Dave explained.

Noah moved alongside me as I fiddled with the ends of my hair, twirling it around my finger.

"What was wrong with him?" Noah asked. I wanted to ask the same thing but I was afraid of the answer.

"I think it's poison." Dave nodded. "He's displaying enough of the symptoms."

"But he only ate the scones. Are they poisonous to dogs?" I asked.

"Not usually."

"What did you put in them, Tilly?" Noah asked.

"I didn't bake them. They were a gift."

"From who? Maybe you can ask them if there was any unusual ingredient in them."

"I have no idea where they came from." I quickly explained how I'd got them.

Noah scratched his head, deep creases marring his perfect brow. "Was there a note?"

Yes, but I hadn't read it because I was too preoccupied with Ethan.

"Probably from the Country Women's Association ladies," Dave suggested.

Noah's brow creased.

"But you're sure Clifford's going to be okay?" I asked again for reassurance.

Dave nodded again. "Yeah, we've got to him quickly. He's already looking brighter."

"Can I see him?" I asked.

"Sure, just don't get him excited." Dave indicated for us to follow him.

The Littlebrook Veterinary Surgery was pretty small, taking up residence in the front part of an old house. Dave lived at the back which was super convenient.

We followed him through to a room where Clifford was now lying in a cage, a drip connected to his front leg. The room smelled of disinfectant, and I squinted against the glare of the overhead lights bouncing off the stainless-steel benches.

Clifford whined as I stepped closer to him.

"I'm sorry, little man," I pushed my fingers through the wire to stroke his paw. "But you hang in there, okay? I know we've only just met but I've kind of fallen for you already." I kissed my fingertips and pressed them to Clifford's forehead.

He sighed and his head flopped back to his blanket.

"Call me if anything changes, please?" I asked Dave, holding back the tears. "It doesn't matter what time, please just call."

"I will. And you can call me for an update at any time."

Noah was quiet on the way back as we zoomed past acre after acre of copper colored paddocks just like the ones at Dun Roamin'.

"What are they growing?" I asked, noting the pretty color in the late afternoon light.

"Sorghum. It'll be ready to harvest soon. Doesn't look like it'll be getting a very high yield this year."

"What's it used for?"

"Traditionally this area sells for livestock feed, but the last few years it's getting more money for ethanol. Not that we get a lot for it."

"Is that what you're growing?"

Noah nodded.

"Is it a good year for you?"

"It's average. Not good but not bad either. We were lucky because we got rain just at the crucial time. A few properties not that far from us weren't so lucky."

"What happens to them if they don't get a good crop? Is that all they produce?"

"Pretty much. A few irrigated properties are growing cotton and they're doing a lot better financially."

"Are we irrigated?"

Noah once again shook his head. "Not yet. We have a small dam but it's not big enough for what we need. I'm hoping that if we can get a few good years under our belt we may be able to implement one."

The vehicle slowed and we turned into our driveway.

"If you come to the town meeting on Friday, you'll meet our neighbors Don and Margie Barrett," He continued. "A lot of the locals are selling up and moving away."

"Why?"

"The seasons have just been too hard. Plus, they're getting offered some pretty good money and the chance to get out while they can and it is too good to turn down."

"How does that work? If the seasons aren't great, then why are they getting good money for their properties?"

Noah sighed. "The Super farms are gradually buying up Little-brook. It's backed by an overseas conglomerate with a lot of money."

"And people are selling to them?"

"Yep. Most farms are handed down through the generations. People love the land, but farming is getting harder and harder to make a living off of. The money's too good to refuse."

"That's sad."

Noah pulled to a stop outside my house. "It is, but it's the way it is."

"Matilda never considered selling to the Super farms?"

"Nope. She hated them. She believed the land should stay in the family, passed down from generation to generation. I think that's why she left her share to you, not anyone else."

I jolted at his words. "Why do you think that?"

"I think she saw something in you she didn't see in others in her family."

"She didn't think I would sell it?"

"Was she right?"

I looked at the fading sun as it disappeared over the roof, noting the red and pink light reflected from the heavens.

"It really is beautiful out here," I whispered. "I can see how easy it would be to fall in love with the place. I just don't know if I have what it takes. Eventually the inheritance money will run out and I'll need to make a living. How am I going to do that?"

Noah reached across and gently squeezed my hand. Silence surrounded us and I could almost feel his heartbeat echo in the cab.

"You're not alone Tilly. I'll help you any way I can."

My eyes moved to his and for a moment I held his gaze, an unspoken emotion passing between us.

Then an uncomfortable thought prickled me, and I broke his gaze and looked away. "Can you afford to buy me out if I do decide to sell?" I asked, my voice low and quiet.

Noah sighed and moved his hand away from mine.

"I'd certainly try to. I can guarantee the Super farms will make you a good offer, but I'll mortgage everything to match it if I have to. The Mackenzie's aren't going anywhere, no matter how much they offer us." His eyes radiated a fierceness that showed me just what he was made of.

"You're stronger than you think Tilly." He reached out and once again squeezed my hand.

He was the second person to tell me this today, and he was the second person I didn't really believe.

"I hope you're right." I gave him a tight smile then climbed out of the cab, quietly closing the door behind me.

As he drove away a coolness enveloped me, and I rubbed my arms making my way inside. Flipping light switches, I moved toward the front of the house. It felt lonely without Clifford. In the short space of time I'd known him, he'd already become my friend.

When I reached Matilda's room, I stood at the open doorway and looked at her bed, wanting to shy away and close the door behind me. Instead I took some deep calming breaths and stepped inside the room.

"He's going to be okay, Matilda," I whispered. "Dave said we got him there nice and quick. He's going to be home before we know it."

A breeze picked up and swirled around me, causing a note to fall at my feet. It was the note that had accompanied the scones. The words *Welcome to Littlebrook. Enjoy!* danced in front of my eyes and I wondered who had left the scones.

And then I wondered why they made Clifford so sick.

8

a week had passed since Clifford's unexplained illness and I'm pleased to report that he pulled through like a champion. After spending a couple of days with Dave to recover, he was now back home where he belonged, bounding around like a puppy. I'd spent the week giving him extra treats and cooking meals just for him, allowing him to take more than his share of the bed, and indulging in cuddles whenever I could. He accepted every gesture with enthusiasm, his eyes bright and his spirit even brighter.

I was starting to settle into a routine on the farm and had gotten up with the sun every morning, tied my sneakers, and gone for a run around the property. I'd also found a recipe for bird treats and had been sucking up to Polly with the idea that maybe, just maybe she could learn to stop swearing at me.

Noah had been so busy that he hadn't taken me down to the paddocks like he promised, but he had shown me where I would find Matilda's Ute. I just hadn't ventured anywhere in it alone yet.

Warwick had been really quiet. He'd responded to my message about my new number but so far hadn't called. In the early hours of the morning when I found myself counting sheep, I'd sent him a couple of texts telling him about my new home, but all I'd got back was a smiley emoji with the promise he'd call soon. But it was okay. He was busy saving lives.

After my morning run, I would make my way with Wally around the many paddocks and feed all the animals, and wave to Randall as he tended his garden. His absence in day to day farm life was noticeable but when I saw him, I was determined to make him smile. No luck so far, but he also no longer ran inside at the first sight of me, so that was an improvement, right?

The animals scared me no less than they had when I'd arrived, but my confidence was growing every day. Wally was also in the habit of staying for breakfast. I figured he was lonely once Noah went out to work the farm, as from what I had learned Randall didn't chat to him very much either.

"Wally, do I have a mower?" I asked as he helped himself to a breakfast muffin. With the amount of sugar I offered him, I needed to at least give him a healthy start to the day.

"Sure you do," he replied, sipping his hot cup of tea.

Thankfully the truck containing my possessions had arrived and I now had a kettle.

"Oh great. Would you mind showing me where it is, please?"

"I could. It won't do you any good though. It's about a hundred years old. Alright, I'm exaggerating, but I seriously don't think it's seen action since the last war."

"So how did Matilda cut the grass?"

"She let T-Bone do it."

Well that explained the remnants of dried up cow dung around the house.

I hadn't admitted to it out loud, but the cows scared the beejeezus out of me. "Do I have any other options?"

"You could buy a new mower."

"Yeah, only trouble is I don't have any inheritance money yet." Which reminded me I needed to follow it up with Greg. "And the savings I had, paid for the oven and toilet I'm having installed. Could I please borrow yours?"

"You could, only it's being repaired. When I used it last, I may have had a small mishap with it."

I raised my eyebrow.

"I drove it into the dam," he explained quietly. "I didn't mean to. I just had a small error of judgment and hit the accelerator instead of the brake."

"Wally! You're lucky you weren't killed!" I exclaimed, horrified.

"Yeah, that's what Noah said. Among other things. But anyway, all's well that ends well. And the ducks were fine once their feathers grew back."

I sighed. "So, what do I do about the knee-high grass growing around the shed?"

"We could burn it."

"That sounds dangerous."

"Nah! Not if you know what you're doing."

"And therein lies the problem."

Wally grinned, his false teeth precariously protruding. "Well, lucky you have me here then."

"You know what you're doing?" I asked.

"Of course, I do!" he replied, indignantly. "I've been burning grass since long before you were born!"

"Okay, okay," I held my hands up in surrender. "Sorry! I didn't mean to imply anything. I'll just admit I'm out of my depth and a little bit scared by the idea, that's all."

"Well don't be. Come on. We can do it now while there's no wind blowing." Wally stood and shuffled toward the door. I was hesitant to follow him. Fire scared me.

Wally was already out the door and heading to the shed by the time I jumped into action.

"You get the hose." He pointed toward a large water tank perched high on an old timber stand, the grass and weeds surrounding it magnificent and green. "We haven't had a lot of rain for a while, but that tank should still be full. It's not one we use very often." As I headed to the tank, he went to the shed. By the time I'd unraveled the hose, fallen over it three times, and had it in place, Wally emerged holding a small gas tank attached to a metal handle.

"What is that?" I asked.

"It's a flame thrower."

Oh geez. "Is that really necessary?" I croaked.

"Of course, it is."

"Can't we just use a match?"

"Nope. This is much more efficient."

I wiped a bead of sweat from my forehead. "Um...do we have a plan?"

"Sure. I aim this at the grass, we let it burn in the areas that we want it to, and then when it's done its thing, you smother it in water from the hose and put the fire out. Easy."

He did indeed make it sound easy, so why did I have butterflies the size of magpies buzzing around in my belly?

"Ready?" he asked.

Not really, but I nodded and moved closer to the tap.

Holding my breath, I watched as Wally confidently turned a few knobs, pressed a button and a flame erupted from the nozzle. As he lowered it to the dry ground, the heat ignited the grass and within seconds a large fire had started.

Wally strutted around and as the fire grew so did my confidence that this was going to work just as he said it would.

"Go around the other side with the hose," he instructed me. "We don't want it getting too close to the crop."

I was halfway to my spot, when I realized I hadn't turned the water on. Holding the hose, I sprinted back to the tank and turned the tap.

"Quickly!"

I twisted the knob on the tap up to full capacity, yet still no water came gushing out of the nozzle. Panic flipped in my stomach. I stared at Wally.

"What's keeping you?" he yelled to me, as the fire raced over the dead grass, destroying every blade that fell into its path, its girth doubling with every second.

"It's not working!" I shouted.

"Did you turn the tap?"

"Of course, I turned the tap!"

Geez, how stupid did he think I was?

Wally hurriedly shuffled toward me. "Humph, I was sure there was water in this tank," he stated, knocking the sides of it as he spoke. The echoing sounds of tin reverberated back at us. "I'll be buggered."

Wally crossed his arms over his chest, his brows knitted together. For a man who had started a fire which was now dangerously close to the crop, he sure was calm.

I swallowed a very large lump in my throat. *"What do we do? Is there another hose?"*

"Yeah there is. But it's at the other tank near the house."

"Will it reach?"

"Not sure, but I guess it's the only option we have."

As the first flame licked at the green leaf of the sorghum crop, I felt the blood drain from my face. The world swayed for a brief second but I pulled myself together, and sprinted for the house. One of my shoes came flying off as I ran so I kicked off the other one and headed straight for the water tank that serviced my kitchen and bathroom. I felt the needle of every prickle on the dead grass dig into the soft flesh of my feet and wished I could go back in time and start today all over again.

Spotting the ancient looking hose, I turned the tap on, hoping it was long enough to reach. My knees buckled with relief as water spurted from the end of the nozzle. It also spurted from the gazillion other holes dotted along the aged green rubber.

Did anything of Matilda's actually work?

I held the end tight and ran flat out back to Wally, getting drenched from the holes of the hose pipe as I went.

Thankfully the hose was long enough. Just.

As I stopped next to Wally, the flames lapped the back of the shed, bubbling and blackening the paint with every lick. The fire consumed the crops as it spread its wings, gathering momentum with every whisper of breeze.

I felt sick, the urge to throw up made it difficult to move. Still, I pushed the panic and fear aside, and aimed my hose at the monster.

"Wally, call the fire brigade!" I shouted.

As he stared back at me, his eyes huge and bulging, his skin scarily pale, very loud cursing came hard and fast from the side of the shed.

Noah was once again coming to the rescue. Only this time he didn't look amused.

Apparently, the Littlebrook rural fire brigade only had one fire truck. It had responded quickly to Noah's call, but thankfully Noah had most of the fire out by the time they'd arrived.

The upside to the whole incident was that I'd learned a Backhoe was a large piece of machinery which effectively pushed dirt around. And the dirt smothered the flames a heck of a lot more efficiently than my pathetic hose had.

I leaned against the timber poles of Goatie's paddock, pulling prickles from my feet before I pulled my phone from my pocket and added 'hose' to my list of things to buy. My knees felt rubbery, my hair smelled of smoke, and I was soaked.

Monty strode toward me, his wide smile showing his missing tooth to perfection.

"So, you're a fireman as well as a shop owner and service

station owner?" I managed to ask despite being mortified by what had happened.

"Yep. And don't forget I'm the postman. We all have double duties out here."

I absently nodded, not knowing what duties they would all give me.

Monty scratched Goatie behind the ear and Noah stood close by, his hands in his jeans pockets which sat low on his hips, his lips tight, glaring down at Wally. Wally had the grace to look sheepish, kicking his toes in the dirt as they both stood surveying the crop. Or should I say the large mound of dirt Noah had used to smother the crop.

A lone tear slid down my cheek as my breathing shallowed, and a panic attack threatened to take its hold.

"Don't stress about it," said Monty. "Noah's only lost about a quarter of an acre, and you know, the ground loves a good fire once in a while. It's good for the soil."

"But isn't the crop worth a lot of money?" My hand shook as I swiped at the tear and took a deep breath.

"Nah. That sorghum isn't that good. Hardly any head on it. Noah's good stuff is over in the back paddocks."

Well, thank goodness for small mercies.

Noah turned from Wally, and moved toward us, his stride long and purposeful.

"Thanks so much for coming out Monty," he said, his hand outstretched.

Monty accepted it and pumped it vigorously. "No worries. I knew you'd have it all under control. I came mostly to spectate."

I cringed at his words, but stood silently as he said his good-byes and made his way back to the fire truck.

Wally solemnly walked toward his house, his shoulders slumped and his feet almost dragging in the dirt. I knew that Noah had been harsh. Not that I could blame him. The fire could have been so much worse if he hadn't arrived when he did.

"We need to talk," Noah's tone was stern.

Oh geez. "I said I was sorry. And I'll pay for the loss of your crop as soon as I get the inheritance money."

"When did you ever think burning dead grass was a good idea?" He stood tall, his blue eyes boring into mine.

"Well...um...I'm not really sure. It was somewhere around Wally telling me he'd been burning grass since before I was born." I didn't mean to get him into any more trouble than he already was, but hey, those were his words. "You know, he kind of seemed to know what he was doing. And he's like seventy, and been farming and doing this stuff his entire life, so who am I to argue with him?"

"No, he hasn't. The closest thing he has come to burning anything was in the grate of his lounge room fireplace."

"What?"

"And he hasn't been farming his entire life. In fact, until he moved out here a year ago to live with Dad and I, the only time he'd ever set foot on a farm was on the odd occasion he came to visit us."

"But...but, I thought he was a farmer, like you."

"No. Wally was born and raised a city boy."

Shit. "You're kidding me?"

"Nope."

I heaved a big sigh and slumped back against the fence. "I'm really sorry, I had no idea. I just took his word for it."

It was Noah's turn to sigh. "I'm just grateful that neither of you were hurt."

"Listen, I haven't got any money just yet, but as soon as I get some, I will pay you for what you have lost."

"Honestly. Don't worry about it. Just don't fall for any of Gramp's great ideas again, okay?"

I nodded. That was a lesson I'd never forget.

"I should have told you about him before now. He means well, but disaster seems to follow him around."

I almost dragged myself back to the house. The adrenaline I'd had coursing through my veins left me feeling tired, emotional, and overwhelmed. All I wanted to do was have a hot shower.

As I approached the house, I noted that the back door was open and swinging on its hinge. I swallowed the panic, told myself I was overreacting and climbed the couple of steps to the verandah, calling as I went. "Hello! Hello! Is anybody there?"

I strained my hearing for a response, but all I got was silence. Okay, that was good, right?

Stepping into the kitchen, the floor creaked under my weight, the sound making me jump and my heart rate to spike.

"Calm down Tilly," I said to myself. "There's no one here. The wind must have blown the door open."

But how could it? I knew the door had been locked as it was a habit I was having trouble breaking.

I placed my cap on the table and moved down the hallway, keeping my ears strained for anything out of the ordinary.

As a crashing sound came from Matilda's bedroom, I screamed and ran back out of the house.

It took me a whole ten minutes of deep calming breaths before I could go back in and investigate what had made the sound. And that was not before stopping in the kitchen to find the largest of my knives and taking it with me. Just in case.

My blood pressure pounded in my ears as I made my way down the hall.

I wanted to be discreet but considering the amount of groaning and creaking coming underneath me from the floorboards, I decided it wasn't a viable option.

Instead I yelled, "I'm coming and I have a weapon!" at the top of my lungs.

No one came out of the room, but I did hear a lot of heavy thumping.

"Whoever you are, I'm coming in there!"

All the years of living in Westport, and not once had I ever been broken into. I'd always felt safe. And on that note, where was Clifford?

The noise inside Matilda's bedroom was much louder now I was this close.

I held the knife close to my chest, closed my eyes and said a quick prayer. Opening them, about to push the door open and face my assailant, I let out a scream.

There standing silhouetted in the front doorway was Noah.

"Tilly! What are you doing?" His eyes were wide.

"Argh! You scared the crap out of me," I hissed. "What are you doing there?"

"I heard you call out you had a weapon! What on earth is going on?"

"There's someone in there," I whispered, using my knife to point to the bedroom door.

"What do you mean?"

"I mean, there's someone in there!" I hissed again.

"Why are you whispering?"

That was a good question.

"And why do you have a knife?"

"Because someone's broken in and I need to defend myself. How did you even get here?" I asked, remembering the steps were out.

"I jumped."

Wow.

As he moved in close, his scent surrounded me. His clothing had the smell of smoke, but there was also a hint of something much more masculine.

"Ready?" he asked, his hand on the doorknob, his demeanor calm and relaxed. I had no idea how. My heart rate was somewhere in the stroke zone.

I moved in close behind him, holding the knife alongside my leg.

The door silently slid back and I prepared myself to come face to face with whoever was in Matilda's room.

Only I could never have prepared myself for what I saw.

There, laying on the dressing gown which had been pulled from the hook on the wall, was Ruby, the neurotic miniature horse.

oah flashed a megawatt grin. "What are you doing in here, Rubes?" He approached the horse and knelt in front of her.

Seeing Ruby, my heart rate dropped into the 'somewhere above average' range. "She was in her paddock this morning." I watched as Noah's long fingers gently stroked her neck, while he whispered to her. I was sure I heard her purr, but then that could have been coming from me.

"You have to double check the gate," Noah reminded me. "If it's not latched properly, it can come open."

"It was latched properly. I did it exactly as Wally showed me and I even double checked it." After the Goatie incident, I hadn't taken any chances with the gates.

Noah's brow creased. "I'll check it when I take her back."

"I know I have a lot to learn around here, but I can lock a gate." I gave him a wry smile. "I'm still confused about how she got into the house." I looked up the hallway. "I definitely locked the back door when I went out with Wally." I pulled the key from my pocket and waved it toward him.

Noah left Ruby where she was and made his way to the kitchen with me hot on his heels. Stopping to check the lock from both side of the door, he said, "It's broken."

He pointed to the splintered timber where the lock had once been. "Someone or something's rammed the door."

I dropped the knife onto the table and stepped closer to him.

"Did Ruby do that?" I asked, as the hair on the back of my neck rose.

Noah scratched the stubble shadowing his chin. "Maybe. I don't know why she would, though."

I had my back to the hallway, facing Noah as he turned his attention to the door jam, listening as he explained the way the timber had splintered. I was so engrossed in his masculine scent, the deep baritone of his voice and the fact that this close I could see the dark flecks in his gorgeous blue eyes, that I didn't hear the sound of four hooves tap tapping their way toward me. It was only as Ruby head butted me from behind that I squealed and fell forwards. Thankfully, Noah caught me before I landed face first on the floor, but in my panic to save myself I reached out and grabbed anything that would help. It happened to be his shirt and we both heard the sound of fabric ripping as it gave way to my force.

When I regained my composure and straightened myself up, I was faced with very toned pec muscles, Noah's olive suntanned skin glistening in the mid-morning heat. Blood rushed to my face, I just wasn't sure if it was from being mortified I'd torn his shirt, or a hot flush caused from the desire which was now inundating my system. Noah was even sexier without his shirt on. Go figure.

I released the shirt from my hands and did my best to straighten it back up, stroking his chest to put the fabric back into place.

"I only have 351 days to go. In case you're counting."

A soft groan escaped his lips.

Noah eventually removed my hands from his chest (for some reason they didn't want to do it on their own) and then helped me clean up after Ruby.

Ruby was presently back in her paddock (and it seemed the lock on her gate was indeed unlatched—humph). And she had left quite a mess in the bedroom in her wake. A mess I had dry heaved cleaning up.

Noah laughed as I pushed the bedroom windows open and turned the fan up to high.

"How long before I get used to the smell of a farm?" I asked, gagging.

He shrugged. "I was born on a farm, so I honestly can't answer you."

"How did you end up here?" I asked, curious to his story.

"Mum and Dad used to own a property in Victoria. They decided to move to Queensland about ten years ago and purchased a small property on the other side of Mt Lockhart. When they heard Matilda was selling two thousand acres and a house, they jumped at the chance to buy it."

"What happened to the property they had?"

"We still own it. I was supposed to have the house over there but once Mum passed and Dad couldn't cope, I decided I needed to be here. It's pretty much my life now."

"Oh okay." Silence filled the space between us as I studied him.

"Girlfriend?" The word came out just above a whisper.

"Not at the moment." He smiled.

Interesting.

"You?" He tilted his head and gave me a sideways look.

"Nope, no girlfriend."

Noah gave a soft chuckle and my belly flipped. "I mean do you have a boyfriend?"

"It's complicated."

Noah raised an eyebrow.

I sighed. "There is this one guy but he's in the police force and Westport keeps him very busy." I didn't add that I always felt like I was second to his job and he barely had the time to chat let alone have a proper date. Warwick was a good man. He was just dedicated to his profession.

"Not an easy way to keep a relationship going."

I sighed again. "Tell me about it."

"What about your family life?" Noah picked up the bucket that he'd shoveled Ruby's droppings into. "Where did you grow up?"

"Born and raised in Westport."

"Parents?"

"Dad runs a training center for businessmen. And Mum's an interior designer. Both of them are very competitive and successful in what they do," I added. "Which makes it harder for me when everything I've ever tried has failed miserably." I picked Matilda's dressing gown from the floor and opened the dark timber wardrobe. The overwhelming smell of mothballs hit me. I gave the fan a minute to dispel the smothering scent, then looked for a coat hanger.

"Geez Matilda sure did own a lot of clothes." I flipped through the hangers searching for an empty one. I stopped flipping as a pretty pink shirt caught my eye. For a moment the smell of the moth balls was replaced with the fragrance of Chanel number five. I lifted the shirt toward me and inhaled the scent of the woman I never knew.

Noah had stopped in the doorway to the room and I noticed him staring at me in the mirror.

"She smelled nice," I whispered, holding his gaze.

"That's her perfume on the dresser." He nodded toward an

old-fashioned crystal atomizer. I tended to keep my visits into Matilda's room to a minimum as I felt like I was invading her personal space, but on the few occasions I had come in here I'd noticed it but never stopped to study it.

Now curiosity about my great aunt got the better of me, and I placed the shirt back in the wardrobe and picked up the perfume. The sun caught the cut crystal of the bottle and sent prisms of color bounding around the room, as the aroma surrounded me.

Noah moved in close, inhaling deeply. "She once told me that as she aged, she couldn't do much about the way she looked, but she could make sure she smelled bloody good." His grin exploded as he remembered Matilda, and I found myself joining him. The earlier awkwardness caused by the fire had long gone and in its place, I felt the flame of friendship kindle.

"The character trait must run in the family." He smiled.

"Well, if you like the smell of smoke, I smell fabulous right about now!" I laughed.

I placed the atomizer back into its place on the dresser and stepped out of his zone remembering I needed to call Warwick and see exactly where things stood between us.

I went to hang the dressing gown up in the wardrobe when a sparkly box on the floor of the wardrobe caught my eye. I hesitated before picking it up.

"It belongs to you now. Why don't you see what's inside?" Noah suggested.

"It feels like I'm sneaking into her room while she's out."

As I spoke the wind picked up and the clothes on the hangers swayed, revealing more boxes in the wardrobe. They were all about the size of a shoe box, all sparkly pink, and all tied with a white ribbon.

Clifford ran in between us and sniffed at the boxes enthusiastically. Before either of us could stop him, he'd knocked a box onto the bedroom floor, spilling its contents about our feet.

I gasped as about a hundred black and white photos stared back at me.

Noah picked up a photo. "I think this is Matilda when she was younger." His brows furrowed as he studied the image.

Taking the photo from him, I recognized Matilda's smile. "She looks so happy."

"There's writing on the back of it."

Flipping the photo over I read, "New Year's Eve, 1953."

We looked through more of the photos that were scattered across the floorboards.

"She was really beautiful when she was young." Noah flipped another over to see what was written on the back.

"How old would she have been in this photo?" I asked, taking it from him.

"Twenty-nine."

"How do you know that?"

"She was born in 1924."

"I can't believe you knew that."

He nodded. "Her birthday was on the 8th of August."

Shock slapped me hard. "No way!"

"What?"

"That's my birth date."

"Huh. Interesting. So, you share the same name and the same birthday as your great aunt."

I looked over at Noah as he knelt beside me, handfuls of Matilda's photos scattered around him. He had no connection to me or my family, yet he had far more of a connection to Matilda than we'd ever had.

I sat cross legged on the floor mulling this new information over in my head. "A great aunt who I never knew existed, yet she left me an estate worth millions of dollars."

"Are you sure your family maybe have mentioned her and you'd just forgotten?"

"No. When I told my Dad, he said he didn't know her."

Noah scooped up a handful of the photos and placed them back into the box. "I guess stranger things have happened."

I held onto a few photos and looked at them again. "Matilda was wearing a key on a chain around her neck in every one of these photos."

Noah took the photos from me, his nose scrunched. "I remember that key. She never took it off. I asked her about it one day, but she told me to mind my own business."

"What happened to it after she died?"

"I have no idea. When I found her, I called Sergeant Doyle Canon and he came straight over."

"You didn't call an ambulance?" I interrupted.

I know I would have if I was there.

"The closest hospital is in Westport."

"What happens in an emergency?"

"We have a doctor in town and we have Tim. He owns a helicopter and will get you to Westport faster than any ambulance will."

"Oh, well that's good to know. So, what happened after the police got here?"

"Oh, um, Doyle did the official thing and the undertaker eventually turned up and took her away."

"I wish I'd known about her. I would have gone to her funeral," I said, quietly.

"There wasn't one."

Another wave of shock hit me. "So, what happened to her?"

Noah shrugged. "I don't know. She was cremated but other than that you should ask Doyle."

That was a good idea.

Once we'd cleaned everything up and placed the room back the way Matilda had left it, Noah offered to show me around the farm.

"Hop on when you're ready." He handed me a helmet, as he straddled the dusty quad bike.

"Why aren't you wearing a helmet?"

"I'll get helmet hair," he replied with a grin. "Ever been on a bike?"

I used my fingers to pull my hair into a low ponytail. "I once dated a guy who rode a motorbike, but it was a long time ago."

"I'm sure you have a lot of fond memories," Noah coaxed.

"Hmmm, I'm not sure my mum would agree."

"So, your mum didn't like you on a bike, or didn't like the guy who rode the bike?"

"Mum didn't like the fact that I 'borrowed'," I air quoted, "her favorite platform heels and used the exhaust as a footrest. Let's just say that the heels and the exhaust were permanently joined after that ride."

Noah laughed. "I bet the owner of the bike wasn't too happy either."

"Yeah, that was pretty much the end of that relationship. It didn't matter though. Mum grounded me for so long, the guy would have been old and senile before I could have seen him again."

Noah looked at my white strappy sandals with the thin cross strap that curved around my ankle.

"What?" I may have temporarily retired the heels but it didn't mean my shoes needed to be ugly.

"Are they plastic?"

"Nope and anyway I promise to keep them well away from the exhaust."

"Hop on, then."

I climbed on the back of the bike, and with that, Noah hit the start button. The bike roared to life and the vibration traveled through the seat and tickled areas which hadn't been tickled in quite a while.

"Put your arms around me and hang on tight," Noah commanded.

Oh boy!

By the time we'd made it around the perimeter of Dun Roamin', I was one very contented girl. The fact I'd had to keep my arms firmly pressed against Noah's hard abs stirred feelings which could have caused a lot of frustration to a woman who hadn't had male contact in a long time, but the vibration of the quad bike sorted that situation out. I just hoped Noah thought the rose in my cheeks was caused by the wind whipping through my hair.

"So, this um...is the um, dam, is it?" I asked as Noah pulled the bike to a stop and killed the engine. My hands accidentally rode up inside his T-shirt and the heat of his skin zipped all the way to my nether regions. I really wished he would restart the bike up—quickly.

"Sure is," he said, holding out his hand so that I could remove myself from my position in heaven.

Bugger.

Reluctantly accepting his offer and getting off the bike, I removed the helmet and gazed across the water.

To be honest the view didn't compare to the one in Westport where the aqua blue river twinkled its way into the ocean, but considering we were in the middle of acre after acre of black soil with the copper head of the sorghum crop bouncing in the breeze, the water was a welcome sight.

Shame it hadn't been around this morning when I'd needed it to put out a fire.

"Nice spot." I moved to the bench seat beneath the tall paper-bark tree, and plonked my tush on the timber slats.

"I'd often find Matilda out here staring toward the horizon," Noah said, sitting alongside me. "This was one of her favorite places."

"I can see why she liked it here."

"This place gets in your blood."

We fell silent and the sound of nature exhaling danced across the water, leaving ripples where it had touched the surface. A duck slowly glided by, seemingly not having a care in the world. A crow cawed in the distance and the sun settled on my skin, warming me.

"It's so quiet out here. I'm not sure if I'll ever get used to this," I said, my voice just above a whisper.

"You learn to find the peace in it."

I turned to face him, as he looked into the distance. His eyes were soft, a smile playing at the edge of his full lips. I wasn't sure I could ever get used to the quiet, but I sure could get used to the view. And the loneliness disappeared whenever Noah was within my reach.

I jolted at my thoughts, and spun away before he caught me staring at him. I had a lot to deal with in the coming months, adding a man to that equation would only complicate things. No, I just needed to learn to ride a quad bike. That would definitely suffice for now.

"So, tell me about your life before you moved here," Noah prodded.

"I told you earlier."

"No, I want to know more. I've only ever visited Westport for day trips. I want to know what it is you love about the place. I'd love to know why you opened a bakery."

My stomach twisted at the thought of my old life. The life that had changed in such a short space of time. "Okay, but if I tell you, you have to promise you'll tell me all about you."

And that's what we did.

I recounted the years growing up in Westport as an only

child, I told him about my family, my friends and about my hopes and dreams for my bakery. Then I listened with bated breath as he recounted how he too grew up as an only child, I learned about his life on the farm and his dreams for the future.

By the time we had both stopped talking, the sun was starting to set below the crop and my stomach was telling me it was dinner time.

10

*B*efore I knew it, it was Friday night. I had on my best skinny jeans, my pale pink flowy silk blouse, and I'd spent ages getting my make up just right which wasn't easy considering the age of the mirror in the bathroom. It had more chips in it than the chocolate biscuits I'd made Noah as a thank you for showing me around the farm.

I'd straightened my hair, then decided it was too stark, so I quickly spritzed it with some water and hit it with the hot air from my hair dryer to give it some bounce. I generously sprayed myself with Vera Wang's Princess, and slipped on my knock-off Fendi ankle boots with the silver heel over my stockinged feet.

With a box of cupcakes under my arm I waited patiently on the remains of the front steps for Noah to pick me up.

Tonight was the night of the town meeting. Knowing I'd be introduced to many more of Littlebrook's residents and the surrounding farms, I wanted to look my best.

I fiddled with the edge of the cardboard bakery box (leftovers from my shop) which held the cupcakes. I'd spent most of the day playing with the new oven which had been installed, learning how the temperatures worked and if it had any hot spots.

I'm happy to report I'd chosen well and the oven had met my expectations. After I'd baked five batches of cupcakes, I decorated each one with Littlebrook in mind. I'd discovered the local footy team wore red and white, so one batch of lemon raspberry cakes was iced in white with red polka dots. I'd learned the local pub's mascot was a bull terrier so I made some Cookies and Cream cupcakes and decorated them with royal icing which I'd molded into a dog, and I made a replica of the pub (well it looked like an old building so it was close enough, right?) which I placed onto a dozen decadent chocolate cakes. I also had a dozen café mocha cakes with icing cows on them and a dozen vanilla topped ones with icing roses. Noah had told me that only about twenty people (tops), ever turned up to the town meetings, so I chose appropriately and sent the remaining cakes home with him. He hadn't complained.

Now as I waited, I felt anxious about my selections. Would they like my cupcakes? Would they like me?

Clifford seemed to sense my uneasiness. He sat himself down on my foot, every so often licking the leg of my jeans. I appreciated the gesture but I really liked these boots and didn't want Clifford's hair all over them.

As he looked up at me, his deep brown eyes reminding me of a bowl of chocolate ganache, my heart melted. He could sit wherever he wanted to.

"I left your dinner in the kitchen," I told him. "Did you get it?"

Woof!

I took that for a yes.

The sound of tires on gravel grabbed my attention and I looked up to see Noah approaching. As he pulled up in front of me, my heart stuttered.

He leaned across the cab and pushed the door open. "Hop in."

He was dressed in the usual jeans, but this evening he'd accompanied it with a blue cotton shirt. The color accentuated his eyes and the five o'clock stubble accentuated his masculinity.

The scent of fresh shower drifted toward me and I had to take a moment to steady myself.

"You do know you don't have to bring anything tonight, right?" he asked, good humoredly. "The ladies of the CWA already provide tea, coffee and snacks."

"It's rude to turn up empty handed." I smiled.

"Hey, I'm not complaining. I'm more than happy to help myself to them."

I made a new mental list.

1. Don't ever bring baked goods to a town meeting again. The ladies of this particular CWA did not like it. In fact, the way they turned their noses up at me, indicated they were more than a little miffed.
2. Don't ever wear delicately laced, sock high stretch knit boots to a town meeting. People tended to stare as they didn't blend with the worn leather cowboy boots favored by men and women alike.
3. Don't sit next to Monty while wearing a sheer silk blouse, even with a fitted singlet underneath it. He was taller than me and had the perfect viewing position to see what hid inside my Victoria Secrets.
4. Don't wear Victoria Secret. The push up bra made my cleavage look far more impressive than it actually is, and some of the attendees weren't as taken by the lace creation as I was.

Thankfully I'd anticipated a cooler evening and had pushed a light cardigan into my bag. After glaring at Monty to keep his eyes to himself (he at least had the grace to blush), I now had that buttoned to the neck and perspiration dripping down my back.

The room held four rows of chairs, with twenty-two people presently sitting on them, all listening to Blake Emerson profess the virtue of *Agriculture Combined*, a Fortune 500 company that, from what I could make out, scoured the world for farms they could buy to help them dominate the global farming industry.

Noah was right, a lot of locals had sold up to this company which was offering higher than normal prices for the land. And from what I had heard so far, Blake Emerson was an excellent agent for them. He was actually making me believe that I would be doing the planet a favor if I sold to him.

"I know a few of you are reluctant to submit to our proposal." Blake handed out a batch of A4 printed brochures as he spoke. He looked to be in his early thirties. His short, dark hair was tinged with a few gray streaks above his ears. His white shirt and dark jeans blended with almost everyone else's in the room, and his worn leather boots told me he'd been around the traps for quite some time. "But I urge you to consider our points," he continued. "With the funding this company has behind them, they can afford to change the water tables. Littlebrook will flourish once again."

"And what do we do once we've sold?" asked a man with a bushy beard and glasses perched on the end of his hook nose.

"You take the millions of dollars they offer you and enjoy your life," Blake replied confidently.

Murmurs traveled around the room.

"Well, thank you for your input Blake." A gray-haired man stepped up to the front of the room.

Blake stepped aside slightly, smiling assuredly.

"Now I know that has left us all with a lot of thinking to do, but we need to move on to other news." The man frowned as he unfolded a piece of paper and skimmed it until he found what he was looking for. "I have an announcement about this year's joint shires Amateur Dramatic Society production of *The King and I*. As most of the town are involved in one way or another, you've probably already heard that they've moved the date of opening night forward by a month. Those of you who aren't involved, mark your diaries. I hope to see you in the audience." He gave Noah a pointed look before clearing his throat. "Now, I'd like to ask Betsy to step up and tell us all about the upcoming Craft Fair." With that he gave a small smile as a woman, who I assumed to be in mid-sixties, took his place center stage.

"Thank you, Marshall." She returned his smile. "I'd like to announce that the Littlebrook CWA will once again host the Craft and Fine Food Fair." Betsy wore a pink and white striped polo shirt over a denim skirt, and had tied a red scarf around her neck. Her tortoiseshell glasses hung from a chain and her blue eyes sparkled with kindness. Where had she been when the CWA accepted my cupcakes? "We'll be sending out emails shortly to get volunteers and stall holders organized. So, if you've been considering displaying any of your talents, please let us know."

"The arts society will of course support the Fair in any way we can," Marshall announced loudly. "We'll get a display together and also offer a sponsorship."

"Can you afford that?" Someone called out.

He cleared his throat before addressing her. "We may not be in as strong a position financially as we have been in previous years, but we're working on changing that."

I could have been mistaken, but I was sure he flicked a glance my way.

"I'll speak to Barry about getting a stained-glass display. He might even offer a small prize for best new talent if we ask him nicely," a man from behind me called out.

"I'll get the kids from the school to do some creative writing," added a woman who seemed to be about my age. "And I'll talk to Benny about showing his books of poetry. He's been doing quite a bit of work with my students, so I think he'll be happy to oblige."

"I've spoken to a few people from Westport," continued Betsy.

"And I think we've secured Helene Brown. Helene is an excellent musician and will make a lovely addition to the day."

An excited buzz traveled the room.

"I'm hoping to announce it in the next edition of the Littlebrook News."

"There's a Littlebrook News?" I asked Noah quietly.

"Yep," he replied, his mouth close to my ear as the crowd cheered Betsy. "Print edition comes out once a month."

I was impressed an area as small as this one had enough news to fill an entire newspaper.

"Awesome work Betsy!" sang Marshall. "That's quite a coup."

I was about to ask Noah who Helene Brown was, but Janie, the woman from Monty's store, grabbed his arm and pulled him away from me.

My stomach squeezed.

"If you can think of anyone who may be interested in holding a stall, please let me know. I'm very happy to approach people about the opportunity," Betsy announced.

"Whoever made these cupcakes should have a stall," shouted a man from the back of the room. I spun in my seat to see who it was and a twenty-something heart throb with the low-slung jeans and too tight T-shirt winked at me. Well, at least someone appreciated the effort I went to. Even if he was sleazy.

The older CWA member standing next to him was the one who hadn't been happy to receive my cakes. She narrowed her eyes and glared at him, but he didn't seem to notice. Instead he picked up one of my lemon raspberry delights and popped the entire thing in his mouth.

Oh geez.

"Billy behave," the older CWA member loud whispered, slapping the heart throb around the back of the head.

"Come on, Ma." He laughed and cake crumbs shot from his mouth. "They're way better than anything you've ever produced."

Ma positively bubbled with anger. I guessed she was the local bakery queen and didn't like competition. I'd made quite the impression with her already.

"We could have a bake off!" shouted the teacher, standing from her chair to face the crowd. "That would be a great addition to the Fair."

Ma's mouth hung open but before she could speak Billy jumped right in and said, "That's an amazing idea. Ma! Your bakery could sponsor the event."

"I don't know about that," she spat.

"Where did those cupcakes come from?" asked Betsy. "I'll have a chat with the creator and see if they would be interested in a good-natured competition."

I really didn't want to be involved in any sort of competition. I'd come here to make friends not enemies, so I slid down lower in my chair and hoped no one noticed me.

"Tilly baked them," announced Noah, his grin wide and fast.

"Pleased to meet you, Tilly." Billy held another of my cakes in the air, before taking a deliberately seductive bite.

"Ah, Tilly," Marshall said. "I was planning to introduce you to the group just before the meeting wrapped up, but I may as well do it now. Please stand up, Tilly, so everyone can see you."

I had no idea how Marshall knew who I was, but I figured Noah had told him. All eyes fell on me. I cleared my throat and stood, giving the room a small self-conscious wave.

"Everyone, this is Tilly," Marshall announced. "She's taken over Matilda's share of Dun Roamin' so I do hope you will all introduce yourselves and make her welcome."

As I looked around the room, some had warm welcoming smiles and some eyed me with suspicion. What I wasn't expecting was Blake Emerson, agent to the Super farms, to bound across the room and reach across Janie and Noah to enthusiastically pump my hand.

"So pleased to meet you, Tilly," he gushed. His hand was warm and doughy. "It's always good to see a new face in the crowd."

I nodded, as Billy pushed him aside and formally introduced himself. "Hi, Tilly," he drawled. "The pleasure is all mine." He reached for my hand and raised it to his lips, planting a delicate kiss against my fingers.

An uncomfortable shiver grated down my spine, but I managed to smile back at him. I needed all the allies I could get.

Noah and Janie moved out of the way, as one by one the crowd introduced themselves.

Betsy had long lost control of the meeting, and now everyone milled around with cups of tea and eating my cakes. More than one person congratulated me on how good they were.

Ma, aka, Callie Perkins, kept her distance, eyeing me suspiciously across the room. I made a mental note to call in and see if I could mend the fence that I seemingly had already broken.

"Tilly, do you mind if I have a moment?" Blake Emerson asked. He turned to Billy and gave him a 'bugger off' look, but it was only when Callie bellowed at Billy then he slunk off to help her.

"Did you hear my proposal for the community?" Blake got straight to the point.

I nodded.

"Great! What are your thoughts?"

"I don't really have any at this stage."

"Well, then, maybe I could bother you for some time? I can come over tomorrow and give you the full details of my offer." He gave me a charismatic smile, reminding me of all the lessons my dad gave in 'how to get what you want in business'.

"The thing is, Mr.. Emerson," I started.

"Call me Blake," he cooed.

"Sorry. The thing is Blake, I'm pretty sure that me selling the land to a super farm isn't what Matilda would have wanted."

A flash of irritation appeared in his eyes, but he quickly blinked and it was gone, the professional façade sliding back into place. "What Matilda wanted is no longer the issue. The property is yours now and you get to decide its future."

"Not yet it isn't. I don't legally own the property at this stage, so you'd just be wasting your time."

"A minor hiccup." He dismissed my concerns with a wave. "I'll come over tomorrow with the offer. We can get everything into place so that we're ready to strike when you become the legal owner."

Strike was an appropriate word. Blake reminded me of a snake ready to strike at every chance he got.

"Blake why don't you give it up. Dun Roamin' is not for sale, no matter how much money you offer either Tilly or us." Noah appeared beside me again.

"Noah, you know as well as I do, that you're going to say yes eventually, so why not do it now and save us all the heartache?" Blake sneered.

Noah's jaw clenched as his eyes hardened.

"There's only a handful of properties left for us to purchase." Blake stepped closer into Noah's space. "We signed a contract on your neighbors land this afternoon. We now own everything between you and the catchment."

"So what? You can't plant on it."

"We don't need to plant," Blake said with a smirk. "All we need to do is divert the drainage lines and depressions that flow toward your property."

Noah didn't flinch. "Go ahead. We don't need your water. I have plans to extend the dam we have. That'll collect more than enough water for us to irrigate."

"Provided it rains." Blake laughed.

"It's bound to rain eventually," said Noah, his tone clipped. "And we'll be prepared."

"Your father doesn't seem to share your sentiment, Noah." The smile hadn't left Blake's face.

Noah's lips flattened into a thin line. "What?"

Blake laughed. "You haven't spoken to Randall about this, have you? I have and let me tell you he's ready to sign the contracts right now."

"You're a liar. My father would never sell."

"Don't worry, mate," Blake tapped Noah's shoulder. "My relationship with my father is strained at times too. I'm sure you'll work it out."

"My relationship with my father is perfectly fine!" Noah's face reddened.

"Of course, it is. I apologies. I overstepped." Blake held his hands up in surrender, but his eyes gave away his glee.

"Stay away from Dun Roamin'." Noah poked a finger at Blake's chest.

"Everything alright?" A man stepped up behind me and stood between Noah and Blake.

Noah relaxed his shoulders, but he continued to eyeball Blake. "Yeah, everything's fine thanks Doyle."

"It was a pleasure to meet you, Tilly," Blake said, breaking eye contact with Noah. "Doyle." He nodded and stepped away, approaching another couple standing alone by the window.

"That was intense," I muttered, watching him leave.

"Blake causing you any grief?" Doyle asked Noah.

"No more than normal." Noah released a deep breath and turned his attention toward me. "Doyle, have you met Tilly yet?"

"I haven't." Doyle extended his hand to me. "Pleased to meet you, Tilly."

"Tilly's Matilda's great niece," Noah explained. "Tilly, Doyle is the local police officer."

"I'm sorry for your loss, Tilly," Doyle said in a gentle tone.

"Thank you. Are you the policeman who was there the day Matilda passed?"

"Yes that was me. Sad day. Sad, sad day." Doyle's expression was warm and empathetic. He looked to be in his late thirties. He had deep set green eyes and a shaved head, and his belly hung over the waist band of his jeans.

"Can you tell me who you contacted about Matilda's death?" I probed.

Doyle furrowed his brow. "Off the top of my head, I can't remember a name, but he was her next of kin."

"He?"

"Yes. Did your family not inform you?"

"No."

"Well, I can assure you that everything on our end was done according to protocol."

"Oh, I don't doubt it. I'm just trying to work who in the family knew about her and why they never shared the news."

"If you want to call around the station some time, I can dig out the report."

"That would be lovely, thank you. Can I come tomorrow?"

"Of course." Doyle nodded.

I was about to book in a time when a woman tapped on my shoulder. "Excuse me, Tilly. Do you mind if I interrupt for a moment?"

"Sure." I gave her a smile.

"I'm Franny." She held out her hand.

"Nice to meet you Franny."

"I was wondering if I could commission you to bake some cupcakes for my class?" she asked. "I have a set of twins whose birthday is next week. Usually, the mums' bake for their children's birthdays but their mum is sick and can't this time. And I burn water, so I'm no help. But I thought you might be interested?"

"Sure," I found myself saying. It's not like I had anything better to do with my time, so why not? "What did you have in mind?"

"I'm easy. Whatever you think."

I nodded. I already had an idea in mind. "Are there any food intolerances, allergies?" I asked.

"I have two gluten free, one nut free and one dairy free. One is soy free, one is egg intolerant, one can't eat chocolate, and two are sugar free."

"No problem," I said mentally flipping through my recipe book. "How many cakes in total?"

"Twenty-four. That's the entire school. I'm the principal and one and only teacher."

"That's a handful!"

"It is." She smiled, a kind of hysteria settling behind her eyes. "I should ask how much you charge."

"Oh, ummmm..." I used to charge five dollars a cupcake in Westport but it seemed like a lot all the way out here.

"Callie charges seven fifty, if that helps."

No, it didn't help. In fact, it made things harder. There was no way I would charge that much, but if I charged less than Callie, she would think I really was out to take her business.

I looked across the room and caught Callie giving me a death stare and realized, it didn't matter what I charged. Clearly, she's already decided we were enemies.

11

*C*ottonball crowed at two in the morning. He crowed again at three thirty, and he crowed again at eight past five. Sunrise. At least he got it right on the last attempt.

I rolled over and stretched my arms and legs to the four corners of my queen size bed, enjoying the feel of the sheets against my skin. My head sank deeper into the pillow and I wondered how long I could sleep this morning.

Clifford, feeling my movement, jumped off the bed, shook himself and ran to the door, lightly scratching at the paint.

I ignored him, rolling onto my side and snuggled deeper into the pillow.

Woof!

"Can't we just have five more minutes?" I opened one eye and glared at him.

Woof, woof!

Ugh!

I hadn't slept well and not just because of Cottonball's crowing and Polly's squawking in between times. The dynamic in the town hall had been so diverse it had left me in a spin. It had been a restless sleep filled with strange dreams and tangled sheets.

I rubbed my eyes, reluctantly threw back the doona and padded my way to the door to let Clifford out. He immediately bolted for the kitchen, dancing in circles as he waited for me to let him into the fresh air. Noah had fixed a new lock into place and I pulled back the latch enjoying the clunk of safety it made.

Letting Clifford into the sunshine I took a deep breath and enjoyed the crisp morning air as it filled my lungs. I still had a lot of adjusting to do to my new life, but one of the things I already loved about Dun Roamin' was the mornings. As the earth released the last of yesterday's warmth, the new day started full of fresh beginnings and adventures.

A loud wolf whistle from Polly echoed in the silence, startling me. As Polly hadn't yet succumbed to my bribery she still only whistled whenever Noah was around.

"Tilly!" he called urgently, his long stride purposeful as he crossed the yard.

Damn it. I tugged on the hem of my silky singlet, really wishing that I'd pulled the matching shorts on before I opened the door. Oh well, at least I had undies on.

"Morning," I mumbled, my cheeks now matching the color of the sky as the sun breached the horizon.

"Polly loves Noah!" Polly called, as Noah continued past her cage toward me. "Polly loves Noah!"

"Are you okay?" I could see the concern etched into his eyes.

"Um, yes. I'm fine! Thanks for asking."

I held the door open for him as he stepped into the kitchen, his breathing ragged and his jaw tense.

My breath disappeared as his gaze stopped on the bottom hem of my singlet and the corner of his lip turned up in a small smile.

"You know it's Saturday, right?" he asked.

Last year for Christmas, my mum had purchased me a set of

undies with the days of the week written across them, and today I was wearing my Tuesday undies.

"Thank you for the reminder," I replied, pulling my shoulders straight and tossing my hair over my shoulder. Dad's advice ran through my mind—when you're wrong footed, bluff. "I wasn't expecting company." I grabbed my hat from the table and used it to cover my girl bits.

"I was about to go out on the tractor when I noticed your house," Noah's eyes returned to mine.

"Yes, well, the house has been here for a long time now. I do believe it's over a hundred years old. Very observant of you to notice it." I gave him a wry smile.

"No, well, yes. The house has been here for a long time, but that's not what I noticed. Have you been outside yet?"

"No."

"I think you should come and have a look."

Something in his tone made my skin prickle, and not in a good way. "What is it?" My breath hitched.

"Just come and have a look," he replied, his voice soft.

"Let me grab some pants." That was a sentence I never thought I'd say out loud to someone at quarter past five in the morning.

I jogged to the bedroom and grabbed the jeans I had worn last night from the laundry basket, hurriedly pulling them on. I noted my hands shook as I attempted to do up the button, but I was unsure whether that was because of the effect Noah had on me, the fact I'd been caught in my not-so-sexy undies, or the fact that something about the house had upset Noah enough for him to bother me at such an early hour.

Once dressed, I took a quick look in the mirror, wiped the dried dribble from my chin and attempted to detangle my hair.

When I went back out to him, Noah was sitting on the kitchen chair, his head in his hands.

"Ready?" I asked.

He looked up, a vulnerability shone back at me, and my breath hitched again.

I thought it must be really unhealthy for a woman my age to stop breathing as many times as I had this morning, but I pushed all of it aside as Noah stood and I followed him to the side of the house, ignoring Polly cursing at me as I passed.

Noah stopped and pointed to the side wall. I gasped and the heart palpitations started.

"Who wrote that?" I choked.

The words *GO HOME OR ELSE!* were graffitied approximately two feet high. The red spray-painted letters were jagged, and uneven, looking like they had been put there in a hurry, and the sting of the threat hit me hard.

"I don't know. I've already called Doyle. Did you hear anything throughout the night?"

"No. Nothing apart from Cottonball being unusually noisy." I rubbed my arms where goose bumps had appeared.

"Clifford didn't stir at any point?"

I thought of the number of times I'd nudged Clifford to stop him snoring. "No."

We both stood staring at the graffiti, silent in our own thoughts.

It was Wally walking up behind us who broke the silence. "What the heck?" he cursed. "What the bloody hell happened here?" His hands rested on his hips, a familiar red G-string dangling from his fingers contrasted against his dark jeans.

Noah's gaze flipped to the flimsy briefs. "Gramps did you hear anyone around the house last night or early this morning?"

"No, but I didn't have my hearing aid in."

Noah sighed.

"I did hear Polly stir at one point," I said, remembering.

"What time was that?"

"Um, around three. I'd only just gotten back to sleep before Cottonball woke me. That was three forty-five."

Noah considered this, before striding toward Polly.

She immediately started her routine of wolf whistles followed by her chant, "Polly loves Noah." Her glorious yellow crest rose and fell as she bobbed on her perch.

Noah's long fingers stretched toward her as he lovingly stroked her feathers and I was sure I heard her purr.

"Polly, was someone here last night?" Noah asked.

She nodded and bounced on her branch.

"Was it a man? Or was it a woman?" he asked.

"She's a bird," I reminded Noah. "I don't think she can actually tell you who was here."

With that, Polly ran toward me, stuck her tail feathers in the air, and showed me the moon, all the while singing, "You're an idiot. You're an idiot." Well, that was nothing new.

Noah flashed me a grin. "She's smarter than you think."

Obviously.

"So, Polly." He opened the door to the aviary. She immediately jumped on his arm and then moved to his shoulder, where she fluffed her chest feathers, and lifted her crest, excitedly dancing up and down.

"She reminds me of Janie," I mumbled thinking of the display I'd seen the night before.

"What's that?" Noah asked.

"Nothing. I just think Polly is a bit of a floozy in the way she flirts with you."

"Polly loves Noah," she sang, spinning in circles.

I sighed and crossed my arms, a headache starting behind my eyes. "I haven't even had my morning coffee yet," I complained.

"Polly did you see a man here last night?" Noah asked her.

"Nut-uh."

"Did you see a woman here?"

"Nut-uh."

"Did you see anyone here?"

"Polly loves Noah," she cooed, nuzzling his ear.

I'd heard enough. I spun on my heel and made my way back into the kitchen, flicking the kettle on as I went in.

The others followed me in.

"Gramps, is there a reason you're carrying a G-string around with you?" Noah asked as Wally dropped the garment on the table.

"Yeah, I wrestled them from Goatie this morning. I figured they belonged to Tilly as they didn't look your size."

Noah laughed as I blushed, rushing to the table to scoop the briefs and shoved them into my jeans pocket.

Bloody Goatie.

"You need to peg your underwear nice and high on the clothesline where she can't reach them," Wally explained.

"They weren't on the line. I haven't done any washing yet so last I knew they were still in the basket."

Wally grimaced, rolling his teeth. "Excuse me a minute," he mumbled and wandered to the kitchen sink and gave his hands a thorough wash.

If you could die from embarrassment, they'd be zipping up my body bag.

"Do you think the writing on the house was just a prank?" I asked Noah, desperate to move away from the topic of my knickers.

He shrugged and rubbed his face. "Maybe. I just don't know who would have done it."

"I pretty much met the entire district last night." I handed him my favorite cup filled to the brim with the heady scent of coffee. "Janie has already taken a dislike to me."

"Janie isn't a fan of anyone's," he replied.

"She's a fan of yours."

He flashed a grin, before hiding it behind his cup and taking a sip of coffee.

"It's not the first weird thing to happen since I've been here," I continued. "There was the radio going off, the mysterious basket of scones, Ruby somehow getting into Matilda's bedroom." I counted off my fingers as I spoke.

"The radio thing?" Noah asked.

"Yeah. The first night I stayed here we had that storm. The radio came on all on its own. Oh, and then Matilda's hat appeared."

"Hat?"

"Yep." I quickly explained what happened that night.

When I finished Noah stared into his cup, lost in thought.

"Well, the radio could be explained by a power surge during the storm. But the hat?" He scratched his head. "The wind, maybe? Perhaps a draft blew it there? As for the rest of it, yeah it might just be someone playing a joke. I just don't know why."

Wally dried his hands and re-joined the conversation. "It might be a joke, or maybe someone actually does want Tilly to leave." He accepted the cup I held out to him. "I could name more than one person who would have a motive for that."

"Motive for what?" came a deep voice from the doorway.

I spun to see Doyle frowning at us.

Geez, this man had a habit of creeping up on me.

"Doyle," Noah said, standing. "Sorry, mate. Didn't hear you pull up."

"I see the front steps are out of action." Doyle was in full police uniform, complete with a gun belt and Taser. "I wondered how long the old timber would hold out for."

"Fixing them is on my to do list," Noah said, thankfully not mentioning how they broke.

My tail bone still ached at the memory.

"Would you like a coffee?"

"That would be lovely."

I left Noah and Wally to show him the graffiti while I made more coffee and found a container of cupcakes to offer them. I didn't bother to take it outside, instead I used the time before they reappeared to hurriedly get dressed properly and slap on some make up.

The bathroom window opened to the side of the house they were looking at, and as I quickly brushed my teeth, I heard their murmurs over who could have done it. Wally mentioned Marshall, the head of the Arts Society, and Noah mentioned Blake Emerson. I wiped my face on my plush pink towel, pushed the window all the way open and suggested Janie. Again. And I also reminded them that Callie hadn't seemed all that impressed that another baker was in town.

Thinking about the list depressed me. I'd only been here a short period of time and already four people could have potentially vandalized my house in order to get me to leave. What exactly had I done wrong for this to happen?

"Hey guys," I called. All three turned to look at me as I stuck my head out of the window. "I can understand Marshall having a reason to see me gone, but why would Blake?"

"It's no secret that Blake and Marshall are friends," replied Noah.

"Really?" I asked, surprised. "Marshall didn't seem so keen on Blake's proposal at the meeting last night."

"Don't be fooled by Marshall. He's a player who will say and do whatever it takes to get what he wants."

"Even if what he wants is mine?" I asked, gulping. My opinion of Marshall had taken a sudden turn south.

"Well now, Marshall has never done anything illegal," added Doyle, his feet kicking up a small cloud of dust.

"He's just never been caught," snarled Wally.

"And if they are friends?" I asked Noah. "Why would Blake want to write that on my wall?"

"Marshall knows that if you renege on the agreement of Matilda's will, then the Arts Society benefit. They need the money. They'd sell this place in a heartbeat."

"And Blake wants the commission from the sale," I finished.

That was a pretty big motive to want me gone.

"Now Noah, you can't go around making assumptions like that," Doyle cut in.

"Hey, it's just my opinion, and last time I checked an opinion wasn't illegal," Noah replied.

"You're not denying that Noah could be right, though," Wally countered.

Doyle sighed loudly. "Look, I'll ask around. See what I can find out. But my guess is someone's just messing with Tilly. That it's just a harmless prank."

I hoped he was right, because the thought that someone out there wanted me gone, was a little bit scary for a woman trying her hardest to stick out this new life.

12

*A*fter Doyle left, Noah disappeared up one of the back paddocks, saying he needed to check on the crops.

"What does he check for?" I asked Wally.

"We've been having a few issues lately with some cows. Noah found them in one of the paddocks happily eating away."

"Do they just wander in?"

"Yeah, well that's the thing. The cows belonged to the Carlson's and they live on the other side of Mt Lockhart."

"So how did they get here?"

Wally shrugged as if he had no idea, but his eyes told a different story.

I opened the container of cupcakes and held them in front of him, my eyebrows raised. As he lifted his hand to take one, I pulled the container away.

"Spill the beans," I teased.

"You play hard ball." He eyed off the red velvet delight just out of his reach and sighed. "When Noah rounded those cows up and took them back to the Carlson's, they said they knew they were short on stock but had no idea what had happened to them. I would have thought if any of their stock was missing, they might have called Doyle about it. Cattle rustling is a serious charge."

"So why didn't they?"

"Well, it's just a theory but Noah's worried they were planted here to ruin his crop."

I gasped. "How many cows were there?" I had a lot to learn but I already had a gauge on how much my four bovines ate.

"Twenty."

"I'm sure he's got it under control," I said, hoping to allay Wally's concerns.

"He's a capable boy. He'll sort it out." Having earned his way to a cupcake, Wally dove into the container and chose the biggest of the batch. "Anyway, what are you doing today?"

"Well I'm trialing some recipes I want to make for the school order, and then it looks like I'll be washing red paint off the side of my house." I took a cake myself and pulled back the silver foil wrapper.

Wally grinned and rubbed his belly. "If you need someone to taste test, look no further, but you're on your own as far as the house washing goes."

"What? You won't hold the ladder for me?" I teased.

Wally grinned, his pearly whites precariously protruding as he waggled his eyebrows. "I think that might be a job for Noah."

As I thought of Noah standing at the bottom of the ladder looking up, I made a second mental note to shave my legs.

"Hey, before you start cooking," Wally said, "I wanted to show you something around the back of the old shed."

"Sure. Do you want to go now? I can feed the animals on the way."

By the time I'd fed the animals, had a quick chat with them, and double-checked Ruby's gate was locked, the sun was heating the ground and I was starting to sweat. I adjusted my cap, making sure my ponytail was secure and keeping my hair off my neck, and followed Wally as we made our way toward the outbuilding in question.

I would have been grateful for the breeze if it hadn't been carrying the smell of charred sorghum. Instead guilt swamped me as I turned to face the shed, really wishing I could turn back time.

But all I could do was to move forward and learn from my mistakes.

Wally stood and looked at the building, its paint now peeling and the back wall burned to a crisp. He moved closer and pulled at the toasted timber and it fell in chunks of blackened char, revealing another layer beneath. "So, I thought I'd come and access the damage. See if I could fix it."

"I wouldn't worry," I told him. "It was pretty old."

"But that's the thing. It's older than me. It's withstood drought and storms and everything nature could throw at it."

Until we came along.

"I don't have a lot of skills," Wally faced me. "And I never mean to cause any harm. Disaster seems to just follow me around." His shoulders slumped and his features drooped, and a vertical crease between his eyebrows deepened.

My heart squeezed. "I'm as responsible for this mess as you are, Wally."

"But I led you into it. Noah's right. I could have gotten us both killed. I'm real sorry for that." Before I had a chance to respond, he straightened his back and continued, "Anyway, I decided that maybe I could fix what I broke and help you out along the way. So yesterday I came out here to take a look. And that's when I noticed this."

Using both hands and a lot of force he started to pull at chunks of the scarred timber. Age had had its effects on the wall and it didn't take much for it to start groaning.

"I don't think that's a good idea," I cried, waving my hand in the stop position.

"Nah, it's fine. I just want to show you what I found. Look!" Wally yelled excitedly, using his weight as he heaved against the planks.

He had more strength than I gave him credit for, as moments later the air filled with the sound of splintering timber and the entire back wall succumbed to age and deterioration, and fell away.

I screamed and grabbed for Wally, pulling him to safety just in time, as a blanket of charcoal and dust surrounded us. I held my breath as large particles of soot waltzed on the breeze, and a momentary quiet enveloped us before the sounds of the roof supports creaking and groaning filled the silence.

"Wally, I think we need to move!" I yelled, pulling his arm.

His pupils were dilated like large black pools, his skin was as white as snow, and his feet were glued to the ground, but I dragged him to safety just in time, as the upright supports of the old shed gave up on life and crashed to the ground, the rusty tin roof following them.

I coughed. The soil, cinders and rust billowed like a nuclear cloud, the sound thundering through the peace. My blood ran cold at the thought of Noah seeing what we had done this time.

As peace settled with the debris, I heard Wally mutter, "Bugger."

Not the word I was thinking, but close enough.

We stood in silence for ages, watching the sunlight beam down on the fragments which fluttered down like rain. Only once the last particle had settled did Wally droop his head and kick his toe in the dirt. A large breath escaped his lips. "Oh, geez."

"It's okay, Wally. I'm sure it's not as bad as it looks." No sooner had the last syllable left my lips when a familiar groan sounded behind us.

I shivered despite the hot dry air, as I turned to face Noah.

He didn't say a word, instead looked stone faced at the mess.

"You'll need a good dentist if you keep grinding your teeth like that," I quipped.

"Blood pressure medication is what I need," he hissed, staring straight at Wally.

Wally nervously fiddled with his wedding ring, his eyes darting from Noah to the fallen building.

He looked skeptical as his gaze flicked between us, but I didn't stop. An overwhelming sense of protection consumed me as I stepped in front of Wally and closer to Noah. "It was my fault!" I blurted before Noah could say another word.

"Yep, me. All me!" I proclaimed, waving my arms toward the destruction. "Not that I did anything." I pulled slightly back as Noah's eyes narrowed, locking onto mine. "It just kind of fell," I lied. "It was an act of God, actually. Yep, we were just looking at it and poof! It fell down." Problem was, I was a quick thinker, not a quick liar, so coming up with a convincing lie on short notice was always going to be difficult.

Wally opened his mouth to protest, but I shushed him with a glare and spun back to Noah, flicking my pony tail over my shoulder and sticking my chest out just a little bit further than normal. Putting on that 'tough guy' persona with a formidable posture was a tactic my dad had taught me to use whenever I needed to get attention in the boardroom. Not that I was ever in a boardroom, but it had helped me on more than one occasion while running my own business. With my shoulders pulled back, I stared Noah down, feeling none of the confidence I was putting out there.

I gave him my most convincing and dazzling smile and the corners of his mouth turned up ever so slightly.

Phew.

"So, it just *fell?*" he asked.

"Uh-uh!"

"Why do I have trouble believing that?" His voice was deep and husky as he held my gaze.

I had to look away. Body parts were heating up and I didn't think it had much to do with the wreckage only meters away from me.

Noah surveyed the rubble which once was my shed. Somewhere in the middle of the pile stood the old tractor, but I wasn't worried. It was decrepit before a building fell on top of it.

"I'm sorry Noah," Wally said. "I'm really sorry."

Noah released a sigh and stood with his hands on his hips. "It appears there's no stopping you now you have a partner in crime." He flashed me a quick smile, and Wally's shoulders relaxed.

"What were you trying to do, anyway?" Noah asked.

"I wanted to show Tilly what I found."

"And that was?"

"There was a painting. Under the old wooden wall. I could see some of the colors when the sun hit it," Wally explained.

Noah looked even more skeptical than when I told him I was to blame, but Wally wasn't deterred. He hurried toward the pile of timber and tin and started to pull back years of neglect. He removed several pieces of broken wood, and my heart jumped as a bright flash of yellow caught the sunlight.

I dashed toward him, ready to help him uncover a secret. Noah helped us too until we had the sheet of old corrugated iron laying on the grass.

It was blackened and bent but I rubbed away the soot.

As more colors revealed themselves, Noah went in search of a hose and some old cloths.

"I knew I'd seen something." Wally grinned brightly.

"It's a mural," I commented, as a picture started to form with Noah hosing it down and us scrubbing the dirt away.

"Part of one," Wally added. "That looks like another piece over there." He pointed to a spot in the rubble where the corner of the metal was peeking out.

"You keep washing," Noah told him. "I'm going to see if I can find the rest of it."

It took us a few hours, but by the time we'd finished we were staring at a picture that would have covered most of the shed wall. It was battered and scratched and patches of paint were missing, but we could clearly make out the dam, a duck regally gliding on the sparkling water, the tall paperbark tree shading the bench seat below it. Dangling ethereally from the backrest of the seat was a chain holding a gold key that sparkled in the light.

"Wow." I sighed. "This is really beautiful."

"Isn't that the key Matilda's wearing in all the photos we've found of her?" Noah asked,

Squinting my eyes against the glare of the sun hitting the tin, I nodded. "Yeah. I think you're right."

"Who would have painted it?" Wally asked.

"Someone signed it." Noah pointed at the remains of the signature scrawled in the right-hand corner.

"Can you make out what it says?" I asked him.

Crouching, he used a rag to gently rub the dirt away from the writing. "It's hard to read, but I think it says Archie. Can't read a surname though."

"Why was it hidden beneath the timber sheeting?" I wondered aloud.

"If it hadn't been for the fire, we may never have found it," Wally said with glee dancing in his eyes.

Judging by his expression I didn't think Noah shared Wally's enthusiasm for the fire.

"Maybe Matilda didn't like it," suggested Noah, standing shoulder to shoulder with me, his eyes never leaving the mural.

"I don't know why she wouldn't have. It's stunning," I replied, ignoring the warmth that was flooding my body from his touch.

"What do you want to do with it?" Wally asked.

"I'll move it over to the house," I replied. "Maybe I can build a frame for it and display it somewhere."

"You know how to build frames, do you?" Noah turned to face me, his eyebrows raised, a mischievous grin playing on his lips.

"Okay. I'll ask you nicely if you'll build a frame for it." I grinned. I knew my skills and woodwork was not among them. "I'll trade you for cupcakes."

---

13

*N*oah had moved the mural to the house and had built a beautiful frame for it from some old pallets he had in one of the sheds. It was presently leaning against the outhouse and I had an amazing view of it every time I pulled back the curtains and looked out of the kitchen window.

I'd been gradually making changes around the house, replacing Matilda's possessions with my own, but there were a few things I had trouble parting with. Even though the curtains were not my style, they fitted with the kitchen and I knew they had to stay.

I wanted to thank Noah and the McKenzie men for everything they had done for me, and I wanted to meet Randall properly. Other than the odd quick hello when I'd seen him wandering around the vegetable patch, we hadn't had a proper chance to get to know each other. Whenever he saw me approach, he retreated into his house. Which left me obsessing about how I could help him, which then led me to the wonderful idea of inviting them to dinner.

Well, it had seemed like a good idea at the time.

Now I was sweating and my stress levels were in the danger

zone. I didn't really understand why. I'd cooked dinner many times before today, but this one seemed special. I liked the McKenzies and I wanted them to like me. And my mum had always told me that the way to a man's heart was via his stomach. In my late teens and early twenties, I had disagreed with her conclusions, having a completely different idea on how to reach a man's heart. It was only after having my own heartbroken on more than one occasion I quickly realized it wasn't the man's heart I was satisfying and that only led to disaster. So today I was giving Mum's advice a go.

A roast was always a hit, but after my decision to go vegetarian I wondered what the men would think of the lentil roast with balsamic onion gravy I'd painstakingly made.

To be honest, it didn't look quite like the picture Google had shown me. Nope instead of a nice meatloaf dish, mine resembled more of meatloaf disaster. It didn't help that my loaf tin was still in my parent's garage, nor that I'd substituted eggplant for the mushrooms, but it sure smelled good, so fingers crossed the men would like it.

Clifford had already given his woof of approval once I'd given him the scraps.

I'd cleaned the back verandah and laid the table for four, finding Matilda's best crockery hidden in one of the kitchen cupboards. I was going to use my own crockery but the tiny blue flowers and gold trim on the plates was breath taking, and I wondered why she kept it hidden. I knew from now on, I'd be using it for every special occasion I could. It took me hours to clean her silver cutlery set, and wash the crystal glasses, but it was worth the effort.

The gardens were pretty sparse of flowers so I wandered down to one of the paddocks and picked a couple of sorghum heads, making an arrangement in a tall glass vase that I'd long ago found in an op shop.

I was just standing back admiring my handy work when I heard the crunch of tires on the gravel.

Less than a minute later, Polly squawked something beginning with f, and Janie's high-pitched squeal pierced my ears.

"*Janie?*" What the heck? What was she doing here? She was the last person I wanted or expected to see on the back verandah. Especially considering the time of day.

"Urgh! What is that *smell*?" Her tiny nose was screwed up in disgust as she stopped in front of me.

Ignoring her lack of manners, I said, "That would be dinner. I'm cooking for the McKenzies."

"Oh. Is Noah going to be here? He never mentioned it to me."

"Yep. All of them are coming."

"Even Randall?"

"Yep." I kept my sigh low and long. "Is there something I can help you with?"

"I'm looking for Noah."

"Then you'll probably find him at his house. He's not due here for another half an hour." Even though I wished he'd get here earlier.

Janie huffed and her keen eye roamed my table.

"Looks like you're trying to impress someone," she scoffed, her nose tilted.

"I just thought it would be fun to set a pretty table."

"Well, it's wasted on those men. Noah doesn't like fancy things, you'll be lucky if Randall even bothers to turn up, and who cares what Wally thinks?"

She really knew how to press my buttons. "I care what Wally thinks."

She spun to face me, her eyes narrowed. "Don't get comfortable here," she warned. "And you might want to stay away from Noah."

"Is this what you really came here to tell me?" I matched her stance.

"Noah's mine. Stay away from him!" She stabbed a red painted fingernail at my chest.

"Sorry, I didn't realize he was taken. He never mentioned it." I pushed her hand away. What I really wanted to do was to rub where she had stabbed, but I didn't want to give her the satisfaction of knowing she'd hurt me.

Red flashed her cheeks. She shifted uncomfortably. "Don't say you weren't warned."

"What exactly do you mean by that?" I asked, placing my hands on my hips.

"I mean what I say. You've been warned. Go back to where you belong. Everyone will be so much better off without you here."

I was about to respond when footsteps echoed loud on the steps.

Janie spun toward Noah, a dazzling smile replacing her scowl. "Oh, just the man I was looking for," she trilled, rushing toward him and placing her hands protectively on his chest.

"Janie," he replied, surprised. "What are you doing here?"

"Well, I was looking for you, silly."

"Why would you be doing that?" Wally stepped up behind Noah.

Janie gave him a quick irritated look, but she didn't let the façade drop. "Because we were supposed to be going out tonight."

"We were?" Noah asked, the adorable crease on his brow deepening.

"Yes. I told you I'd pick you up. Remember? Billy's having drinks to celebrate his new job. You said you'd come."

Noah removed her hands from his chest, then scratched the back of his neck, a grimace forming. "Sorry, I forgot. But tell Billy that I'll have a drink with him next week."

Janie's face was pinched as she crossed her arms. "But you promised, Noah. You can't just go around breaking promises."

"I'm sorry, Janie. Another time." He led her by the arm toward the back stairs.

Before she left, she looked back at me over her shoulder and if looks could kill, I'd be dead.

Randall was a good six inches shorter than Noah, his hair was dark and his eyes were green. I figured him to be in his fifties, but tonight he looked closer to Wally's age. Once he'd warmed to me, he loosened up and I discovered he actually had a great sense of humor, which I hadn't been expecting,

"What exactly is this?" Wally asked, forking at his no-meat meatloaf.

"It's a disaster," I explained.

"It tastes pretty good," said Randall after swallowing his first mouthful. "I remember when Sophie made her first ever meat-loaf. It resembled something like this."

Noah and Wally both stopped breathing at the mention of her name, and turned their attention to Randall.

"Did it taste good?" I asked, unsure what else to say.

Randall's smile was bright and fast. "Nope. Can't say it did."

"It can't be any worse than the first meat loaf I ever made," I said, laughing. "I tried to feed it to my parents but they both threw it in the bin behind my back. I found a dead rat laying on top of it the following morning. Poor thing. It never did deserve a fate like that."

Three men stared back at me, probably wondering if they were going to suffer the same fate.

"Lucky I found sugar," I continued. "What I lack in cooking skills I make up for in baking skills."

Noah's gaze fell between me and his father, and the emotion that burned bright in his eyes nearly took my breath away.

"Is that dessert I saw in the fridge?" Wally asked.

"Yep. Sticky date pudding." A smug smile played at my lips. "You do like sticky date pudding, right?"

"Can't wait," said Wally, scooping up a forkful of potato.

"I think you've done a wonderful job Tilly," said Randall. "The meal may not look magazine worthy, but it sure tastes good."

I held my breath as Noah picked up his fork and tasted my cooking. After a few mouthfuls, he grinned at me and oxygen once again filled my lungs.

After that I relaxed and enjoyed the banter between the men. Randall was slow to add to the conversation, but the more he ate, the more he too, relaxed.

By the time I was collecting the plates, ready for dessert, I knew the evening had been a success.

"Let me help you with that," said Noah, taking the stack of plates from me.

"Thanks." I followed him to the kitchen, enjoying his company as well as the help.

"Blake stopped by today," I said, by way of conversation.

"What did he want?" Noah placed the crockery on the sink and attempted to act casual, but he wasn't really pulling it off.

"He brought me the offer he'd promised. I have no idea of land prices but it was more money than I'd ever seen. Don't worry. I sent him packing," I finished. "Told him I wasn't interested in selling." At least not to him.

Noah nodded, but his gaze flipped toward the door and to Randall. He looked tortured.

"Are you okay?" I filled the sink with hot water to soak the plates.

"Yeah. Blake's comment about Dad wanting to sell still bothers me, that's all."

"Did you ask Randall about it?"

Noah shook his head. "He's like a bear with a sore head whenever I try to ask him anything about the farm."

"He seems relaxed tonight," I commented as Randall's laugh drifted in through the open door.

Noah gave me a small smile. "Thanks for that. It's been a very long time since I've seen him smile, let alone laugh."

"Maybe he just really likes meatloaf."

"No, I think it's just that he really likes you."

"Oh! That's really nice." A prickle of happiness bubbled behind my breastbone.

Noah's expression softened as his eyes moved to mine. "And he enjoys your cupcakes."

The sounds of the evening stilled as Noah handed me a plate and his fingers touched mine. The electricity between us was palpable and I jumped at the sensation but didn't move my hand away. Instead I held his gaze. "What about you?"

"I enjoy your cupcakes too," he replied, and a small thrill ran all the way to my hoohah.

14

The farm had kept Noah busy in the last few days. So much so that other than a passing wave I hadn't seen him since our dinner.

Even though I hadn't known him for long, I missed his company. To top that off it was that time of the month and I was hormonal. My emotions were running high and nostalgia pangs hit hard.

Thoughts of my shop kept sneaking into my conscious, reminding me of what I'd lost. Not just my business, but my friends, family and those regular customers who had grown to be more than that. I missed people, the sounds of the city, and even traffic.

I pushed the last tray of cupcakes into the oven when my phone rang causing me to jump. A ringing phone was a rarity these days and was another thing I missed. Catching it before it vibrated off the table, I swiped to answer, seeing the strong handsome face of Warwick. This was the first call I'd had from him since buying my new phone and joy mixed with sadness, swirling with some nerves and regret, all leaving me feeling a little bit unwell.

"Hello," I trilled, a fake smile in my voice.

I listened as Warwick's deep soothing voice boomed into my ear and I waited for the thrill I should feel upon hearing it. I liked Warwick. In fact, I liked him a lot, but recently I realized liking someone wasn't enough. I wanted more.

Like the sizzle my brain feels whenever I see Noah?

"Hey Tilly." He sounded as if the happiness in his voice was fake too. "How's life at Dun Roamin'?"

"It's been interesting." I brought him up to date with all my latest dramas. He oohed and aahed in all the right places, and I began to think that maybe thrills were overrated. "How's life in Westport?" I asked.

I heard his sigh loud in my ear. "I'm sorry I haven't called for a while." His tone was heavy. "But I've been in hospital."

I sucked in a fast breath. "Why? What's wrong?" Warwick and I may not have been close recently, but he was a good guy and I hated the thought that anything bad had happened to him.

"I'm sorry to tell you like this, Tilly, but...I've been shot," he said, quietly.

Shock shook me all the way to my toes. *"What? How?"*

"Calm down. I'm okay. Well...I will be."

"What happened? Tell me!"

"You know how I told you Sarg had us playing bodyguard?"

"Uh-huh."

"Well, turns out it wasn't unfounded. The guy was a psychopath and got the better of me."

"Are you really okay, though? Where did you get hurt?"

"I was lucky. He shot me in the stomach, but none of my vital organs were damaged. I'll live."

"You don't sound okay to me, Warwick," I said gently.

He took a moment to reply. "It's just, well...if the bullet had been another inch to the left it would have been a different story. I'm happy it wasn't," he quickly added, "but an inch isn't a lot. I know this job comes with danger, but I never really thought I would come this close to..." He didn't finish.

"I'm really sorry this happened to you." I held back the tears. "Is there anything I can do?"

"No. I'm just having a hard time reconciling it all. We train for this stuff, but you know, when it happens...it's a whole different thing."

I could imagine.

"I should be released tomorrow. Doctors are happy with my progress, but the psychologists are saying I need some more work." He gave a hollow laugh.

"I'll come and visit you! I'll bring you a batch of your favorite cherry ripe cupcakes."

"No! Please don't!" he almost shouted. "I'm sorry Tilly. My head isn't in a good place at the moment. I don't want to pull you into this."

"Okay," I whispered.

"I am sorry. I've been thinking a lot these last few days. I've been thinking a lot about us." He paused. "I think we should take a break for a while. I really do have feelings for you, Tilly, but this has been life changing for me. I'm not even sure if I want to return to the police force or whether I want to buy a plane ticket and go and live on a desert island somewhere. I have no idea how long it will take me to feel normal again. Until I do, I can't even think of a relationship, and you deserve better than that."

I gulped. "You've been through a lot. You just need to take your time and not rush any decisions."

"You sound like my psychologist," he replied, with a sad sounding chuckle.

"She must be a sensible woman then." I smiled despite the fact I was being dumped.

"Are you okay?" he asked me.

"You're the one who's been shot!"

"But right now, you're the one I'm worried about."

"I'll be fine. I mean, don't get me wrong. After we end this call, I will cry my heart out and eat chocolate and cupcakes, but otherwise I'll be fine." I was going for upbeat. Warwick had enough to worry about.

"You're a star. Thanks, Tilly." He sounded genuine.

I sighed. Even though I hadn't been feeling the thrill a love affair should give, he was a good person and I would miss his company. "Can we stay friends?" I asked.

"I'd love that."

We stayed on the line chatting for another five minutes, and even though I left Warwick laughing, I knew inside he was a different man. I just didn't know what I could do to help him, other than bow out of the relationship gracefully.

After we said our goodbyes, I pulled my feet up under me on the chair and hugged my knees. A sadness settled into my heart, but at the same time I felt a lightness, a freeness, and guilt for feeling those last two things. Loss and loneliness competed for attention, and despite the hot air I felt cold. Unexpected tears prickled and my nose started to tingle. Indulging in a moment of self-pity I allowed the tears to turn to sobs as anxiety and remorse consumed me.

It was the buzzer on the oven dinging that reminded me of the time. I straightened my back, held my head high, found the tissues, and swiped at my tears

"That's enough Tilly," I told myself, blowing my nose. "It's time to pull yourself together." Yeah, well that was easier said than done.

I'd only just turned off the oven to save the delicious smelling cakes from the heat, when there was a knock on the door.

I turned to see Noah, his hands shoved into his pockets, his forehead wrinkled as he cleared his throat.

"Are you okay, Tilly?"

"Oh, I'm fine," I waved my hand dismissively and did my best to sniff discreetly.

"You sure?" Noah studied my face. "You seem upset."

I sighed. "Warwick got shot," I blurted. *And dumped me*, but I didn't add that.

Noah raised his eyebrows. "Whoa." He dropped his hat on the table, and ran his fingers through his hair, pushing a lock of golden blonde strands from his forehead.

A butterfly emerged from its cocoon in my stomach.

I willed the butterfly to leave the rest of his family safely at home, but I could feel them twitching, wanting to make their escape, and adding desire to my already overloaded emotions was not a good idea.

Distracted, my mind a mess, I forgot the oven mitt as I lifted a hot tray from the rack. *"Ouch!"* I screamed as the heat seared its way into my skin.

Noah rushed closer, taking my hand in his and led me to the sink. Turning the cold tap on, he pushed my hand under the water. "Keep it under the running water," he said, gently stroking my wrist. My emotions went into overload as his thumb left a soothing trail.

"I'm s...s...sorry," I stammered, holding back the tears. "That was stupid of me." I sniffed. "Just me racking up another notch on the list of stupid things Tilly does."

"You'd just had a shock. It's understandable." His fingers curled around mine as he removed the cool pack. "Let's see what the damage is, hey?" Already the skin was red and aggravated, and I knew it would blister.

He inhaled at the sight of it. "I think you should see the doctor about this, Tilly."

"It'll be okay," I replied, gently pulling my hand from his. "It's not the first time I've burned myself." I was going to add *it probably wouldn't be the last*, but I didn't need to fuel his perception of my ineptitude.

"First time or not, we're going," he replied adamantly.

"We?"

"Do you know where the doctor is?"

I shook my head. "I don't need to know though. My hand is fine." My hand was stinging beyond belief.

"You know it's important to get a burn looked at as quickly as possible, so come on. Don't argue."

I opened my mouth to do just that, but Noah quietened me with just one word. "Please."

"I need to go to Westport soon," I said to Noah as we patiently sat in the surgery waiting room.

"Why's that?"

"I need some cake decorating supplies that Monty doesn't have, plus I want to get some things I've stored in Mum's garage. And I need more wool for Ethel's jumper because I've decided to get creative. Monty only has the one color."

"If you can wait until tomorrow, I'll go with you. Gramps has an appointment with the specialist."

My heart gave a jump. "Is he okay?"

"Yeah. He's due for his two-year colonoscopy." He pulled a face. "Doctors don't get paid enough if you ask me."

I was just thinking about what kind of doctor signed up for that job when the doctor I was waiting for called my name.

"Do you want me to come in with you?" Noah asked.

"I'll be fine," I replied and the receptionist gave me a huge smile. Judging by the wide eyes and dreamy expression her teenage eyes held, she was enjoying staring at Noah.

"Hello Tilly." The doctor held his hand out. "I'm Doctor Drew Collins." His hair was disheveled and his shirt was untucked, and I figured his morning so far had been a hard one.

"Pleased to meet you," I said. "And I'm sorry to be wasting your time. Noah just overreacted to a burn I gave myself."

"Well, you let me be the judge of that," he replied kindly,

leading the way to a treatment room. "Take a seat and let me have a looksee."

His salt and pepper hair fringe flopped over his eye as he bent to look at my left hand.

"Ooh you've done a good job on that, haven't you?" He winced. "I'm going to cover it up for you with these medicated strips," he said as he reached into a drawer. "They'll make the burn heal faster. Have some Panadol when you get home. It'll take the edge off the pain."

I flinched as he dressed the burn.

"How are you finding life on the farm?" he asked as he worked.

"It's okay. Some days are better than others."

"It was a sad day when I got the call from Noah about Matilda."

"Did you know her well?"

"Oh yes. Not that she frequented my surgery often. She kept herself pretty healthy."

"What did she die from then?"

"The body just wears out, Tilly. One day it just had enough. It was Matilda's time." He covered my hand with a bandage.

"Doctor Drew, do you believe in ghosts?" I asked him when he was all done.

"Not the kind that haunts houses and hurts people no, but I do believe that the spirit can remain in a place they loved for some time. Why do you ask?"

"I feel her. In the house. Mostly in her room and Clifford has the awful habit of sitting in front of the kitchen sink staring into thin air, wagging his tail."

"Does it bother you?"

I had to think about my reply. "I guess not. Not now. It did at first, but I'm kind of getting used to it."

"She'll move on. When she's ready, she'll move on. If she's still there she has a reason. Knowing Matilda, it'll be to make sure you're feeding all the animals properly. You are doing that, aren't you?"

"Yes. Wally helps me."

Doctor Drew chuckled. "So, I've heard."

I chose not to question exactly what he had heard about Wally's and my misadventures. Instead, I thanked him profusely for his time and made my way back to Noah.

15

On the way home, my phone rang. The bandage made it awkward to dig the phone from my bag, and swipe to answer it. "Hello Greg."

"Hi Tilly. How's life on the farm?"

"Eventful."

Considering everything which had happened so far, I felt that about summed it up.

"Is everything okay?"

I quickly brought him up to date.

"The shed fell down?" he asked, shocked.

"Uh-huh. And then I burned my hand."

"It sounds like Dun Roamin' isn't good for you."

"I don't know about that. I was pretty clumsy before I moved out here."

"But a shed fell on you! You could have been killed."

"Let's not exaggerate, hey."

"I'm not. Wally is a menace. That farm is a menace. Someone could get hurt."

"I never knew you cared so much," I replied, completely aware of Noah overhearing this entire conversation. I didn't want him to think he had supporters in the *Tilly is a walking disaster* campaign.

"Is there something I can do for you?" I continued.

"I wanted to let you know the first installment of money has been transferred to your nominated account."

My day was taking a turn for the better.

"Thank goodness," I replied. "That'll make my life a whole lot easier."

His quiet chuckle echoed toward me. "I thought it might. Now if you need anything else, please feel free to call."

I considered his offer. "Well, I do need a carpenter to fix my front steps."

"Sure thing. I'll make some calls and see what I can do."

A happy dance started in my stomach until I remembered the last time he said he'd get me a plumber. It had been Noah who had recommended Dave to install my inside toilet.

"Seriously?" I asked.

"Of course. I'll look into this immediately."

"Awesome. Thank you." I smiled. "Hey Greg, while I've got you on the phone, who was the executor of Matilda's will?" It was a question which was bothering me for some time.

"Oh, it was a friend of hers. Bronwyn Brown. She should have been at the reading of the will but she was in hospital at the time."

I quickly jotted the name down, making a mental note to find her and have a chat.

"Thanks Greg."

"No worries. And remember if you need anything, anything at all, just call me."

"I will, thanks."

I dropped the phone back into my bag as Noah shifted uncomfortably in his seat. "I'm um, happy to fix those stairs," he said, concentrating on the road ahead. "I've just been busy and haven't gotten over there yet."

"Oh, that's okay. Greg offered, so..."

Why did I suddenly feel disappointed though that Noah wasn't the one doing it?

An awkward silence filled the air between us, before I found some common ground which wouldn't get me into any more trouble than I already was. "The Littlebrook Craft and Fine Food Fair will be here before we know it," I mused.

"It will. Are you going to have a stall selling cupcakes?"

"I was thinking about it, but I guess I'll have to see how well I can manage with my hand bandaged." I sighed. "I'm a bit concerned about the order for Franny at the school. She needs them by tomorrow and I still have a couple of batches to decorate."

"I can help if you like."

"Really?"

"Sure. You can tell me what to do and I will try and follow instructions. I reckon between us we'd manage."

"That's an amazing offer, but I'm sure you're far too busy to decorate cupcakes."

"I'm never too busy to help you, Tilly."

Noah pulled to a stop outside my house and turned to face me. My insides were doing all sorts of gymnastics at the thought of being in the kitchen alone with him, but I covered my suddenly shaky breath with a cough, and opened the car door.

Once inside I busied myself with the now cold cupcakes which were left on the bench, checking that they were okay.

"Where do I start?" Noah asked, washing his hands in the sink and then moving in alongside me.

"Well, ummm..." The idea of working so closely with him caused my heart to pound and a tiny bead of perspiration broke out along my hairline.

"Could you take those cakes out of the baking pan and put them on that rack for me, please."

He grinned and nodded. "So far not too difficult." He chuckled as he worked and a thrill ran all the way to my hoohah.

Noah was a good listener, and an even better apprentice. He mixed the icing and offered me his hands when I struggled with only one. I knew it was only cake decorating, but something about it felt very sensual. And watching Noah's large masculine hands fumble with the exacting details was mesmerizing.

Not once did he get impatient. Instead he accepted instruction, doing exactly what I asked, his humor and good nature melting into my heart.

When the last cupcake was decorated, he stood back and beamed. "That was fun!"

It sure was.

I'd just handed the last container of cupcakes to Noah so he could load them into his Ute, when Doyle called.

"Hey Tilly," he almost sang.

"Hi Doyle. How are you today?"

"Fair to middle. Fair to middle. Been up to my eyeballs investigating how cows from the other side of Mt Lockhart keep ending in Noah's paddock eating his sorghum, but I'm sure I'll get to the bottom of it."

"Is it still happening?" I asked, horrified no one from Dun Roamin' had mentioned that fact to me.

"Yep. I know they didn't walk, but no one has seen any trucks which could move a cow in either location. It's like aliens have picked them up and placed them there."

"Well, if they can build the pyramids, I'm sure they can move cattle," I said with a smile.

"As much as I want this mystery solved, I really hope there's another explanation." Doyle laughed. "Anyway, I've got the information you wanted about who was informed of Matilda's death."

I leaned against the kitchen bench, absently plucking the blackened wick from my scented candle, my hearing switched to high alert as he muttered, "Ah, here it is. Paul Lockhart. 76 Ivy Road, Westport. Matilda had listed him as her next of kin."

I gasped, my hand slapping the bench. "Are you sure?"

"Yep. I spoke to him over the phone, before he came out here for a visit."

So, my dad was informed, yet he'd told me he'd never heard of Matilda. Why did he lie?

I instinctively looked at the date on the calendar Matilda had left hanging on the side of the fridge. Dad would be somewhere around South America on his cruise today. When he came home next week, I had some serious questions for him.

"Tilly, are you okay?"

"Yes, thanks Doyle. Paul's my dad and he never mentioned it to me."

"Oh, I see."

"Anyway, thanks for getting back to me about it."

"Anytime."

"Oh also," I added before he could hang up. "Do you know anything about a gold chain and key Matilda always wore around her neck? She should have been wearing it when she died."

Doyle was silent for a beat. "Sorry Tilly. Don't know anything about it."

Once the call finished, I took a moment to consider this new information. Why was Dad so secretive about it all? Did Mum know the truth? I dropped the phone into the pocket of my skirt and thought they had exactly one week and then I would be getting some answers.

Pushing all thoughts of Mum and Dad to the back of my mind I thought over the day ahead. Once we'd dropped the cupcakes off to Franny at the school, we would be on our way into Westport as Wally was booked for his procedure. Actually, he was booked in for tomorrow but because of the preparation involved the doctors wanted to admit him a day early. I decided no matter how bad my day got, it was going to be better than Wally's.

"Everything okay?" Noah asked, entering the kitchen.

"Yeah. Just a strange conversation I had with Doyle. I'll fill you in on the trip. I just need to grab my bag and change my shoes and then I'm ready."

I'd taken to wearing my low-heeled sandals around the farm, but for the trip into town today, I slid my feet into my very-much-like Kate Spade hot pink sling backs with the satin bow. I paired them with my black halter top and high waisted flared skirt, gave my lips a second coat of pink lipstick and upped the mascara to balance it all out. It felt good to be dressed up again, and my smile reflected it, even though my insides were doing all sorts of tricks as my mind churned.

"I've labeled all the cupcakes so you don't get them muddled up," I explained to an ecstatic Franny. "If you read the flags I've stuck in them you'll know which is which."

"You have no idea how happy this makes me," she replied, smiling widely.

"These are for you." I held up two Bailey's chocolate cupcakes, topped with white chocolate ganache and drizzled with dark chocolate sauce. "The alcohol content is minimal, so you can still teach." I laughed.

Franny licked her lips, her eyes huge as if she was looking at heaven in a patty pan. Which quite possibly she was.

"They look divine," Judy, the teacher's aide, drooled.

I felt the familiar glow behind my breastbone I got when people liked my baking. I may not have been great at a lot of things but I knew my cupcakes made people happy. That in turn made me happy and I glowed with pride.

"I'm having a high tea for my mother's birthday next week," Judy said. "These would be perfect! Can I place an order please?" she asked me, with a hopeful look.

I laughed. "Of course. Exactly like these?"

"Yes please," She licked her lips. "And a dozen of those, too if you don't mind." She pointed to a sweet vanilla I had decorated with pink icing topped with a white bow. "My mum and her friends have weekly high teas but they normally order from Callie. Mum's going to be so happy when I show her a photo of what I've just ordered."

My heart clenched at Callie's name. "I don't want to cause any problems."

"With Callie?" Judy asked, a small crease appearing between her brows.

"Yeah. She probably won't like someone taking her orders."

"Don't worry about her." Franny dismissed my concerns with a wave of her hand. "Her pies are delicious, but you have it in spades when it comes to cupcakes."

"Franny told me you're entering the baking comp at the Littlebrook Craft and Fine Food Fair," Judy added. "That's so good! It's been a long time since Callie had any competition. It'll do her good."

"Not to mention the publicity it's going to give you," Franny said.

"Publicity?"

"For your business." She pointed to the cupcakes.

"Oh, I'm not starting a business," I quickly explained. "These were to just...well, you know. To help."

"If these are as good as they look, I guarantee when Mum and her friends taste them, you're going to have orders up to your ears."

I gulped, my emotions conflicted.

On one hand, I loved the idea of baking as a business again. Lately the McKenzies were the ones to consume my overflow of which there was quite a lot (did I mention I baked when I was stressed?). On the other hand, I sucked at business and didn't want to go through the pain of losing yet another one.

The school bell rang signaling the end of little lunch. I thanked the ladies for their confidence in me and made my way back to Noah's Ute, wondering just how mad Callie would be if I did go ahead with the idea.

As I approached the car, I saw Janie leaning into Noah's window, her shirt unbuttoned just enough to give Wally a heart attack.

"Hi Janie." I walked past her and opened the rear car door.

"Oh, hello. You look…nice." Her curled lip told me it wasn't really a compliment.

"Janie was walking past when she saw my Ute," Noah explained.

"I just had to say hi." She gave him the full effect of her wide, kohl rimmed eyes and demure smile.

"How lovely!" I upped my smile to match hers.

"So lovely I might just wet myself," Wally muttered.

Janie turned her attention to him and her smile turned into a grimace. "Would he really do that?" she whispered to Noah.

Noah coughed. "You just never know with Gramps."

"Yes, well…I'll leave you to it then," she finished, eyeing Wally suspiciously.

After we'd dropped Wally off at the hospital, Noah had taken me to all the places I needed to go, stopping at mum and dads to collect some boxes I still had there, and then going to the store to grab some supplies I didn't have. We even stopped at Café by the River for a steaming hot cappuccino, just one of the few things I truly missed about Westport.

Noah was a lot of fun and surprisingly tolerant with my shopping and I now had the back seat piled with boxes and bags. I promised him a cake for his trouble, which seemed to please him immensely.

"What are you smiling at?" he asked, while we stopped at a red light.

I couldn't tell him I was smiling at how easily he could be bought, so instead, I said, "Just remembering some good times I had with the residents of Price Lane."

Noah nodded. "Do you want a drive by and pay them a visit?"

My foot jiggled up and down as I considered his offer. It would be nice to see some of those people again. I missed Isaac and Adam, Chloe and Brody, and I even missed my daily visits from Mr. White. I hadn't seen any of them since the 'Foreclosed' sign went on the door and I would love to know how they were all doing. But seeing my shop would bring back a whole barrage of unwanted emotions. Did I want to do that to myself?

Before I could say no, the light changed and Noah moved through the intersection, changing direction at the next side street and performing a U-turn, heading toward Price Lane.

The closer we got the tighter the knot in my stomach became. I fiddled with the hem of my skirt and bit the inside of my cheek as Noah covered the few short kilometers to what used to be my home.

Pulling the Ute to a stop outside of what was once *All Things Nice* I strangled a cry in my throat. A new couple had moved into my apartment above the shop, the signwriting across the glass windows advising that a take away shop will be opening soon.

I watched as the woman cleaned the glass, her smile large and full of hope and I remembered exactly how I had felt.

Through the window I could see that my chalk menu board had been replaced with a tacky white plastic one, the antique glass cabinets were now modern and stainless-steel, and the retro bar stools had gone, high backed shabby timber chairs taking their place.

My breathing kicked up a notch as memories danced and a longing ached in my chest.

"Do you want to visit your friends?" Noah's eyes rested on mine.

"No. Can we go please?" I asked quietly, swallowing back my emotions.

"Sure. I'm sorry." He gulped then pulled away from the curb in a hurry. "I didn't mean to upset you." His hand reached over to cover mine, and his thumb traced a small line across my wrist. I allowed him to squeeze comfort and soothe the ache I felt in my soul.

"It's okay. It's the first time I've been back here and I didn't realize it would feel quite so painful."

Noah kept his grip, using his free hand to turn the steering wheel. Only when he needed to change the gear did he let go, a coolness replacing his warmth.

I swallowed hard. "I need to see Warwick," I explained, thinking of the cupcakes I had for him on the back seat, and wanting to do anything but think about the shop.

Noah jolted, his jaw clenched. After a moment of silence, I wondered if he had heard me.

"What's the address?" he finally asked.

16

I nervously reapplied another coat of lipstick, adjusted my top, and checked my reflection in the visor mirror. Nervous butterflies flitted around in my stomach. Smoothing a few stray hairs, I took a deep calming breath and released it slowly.

Warwick had told me to stay away, but I was never good at doing what I was told.

Noah's gaze flicked to me as he pulled his Ute up to the curb. "You look...amazing. I'm sure Warwick will agree," he said with a tight smile. In the last ten minutes his mood had taken a turn for the worse.

"I'm sorry I'm mucking you about today, Noah. I'll be quick and then we can head home."

"It's fine." He pushed his hair back from his face. "I don't mind. It's been nice." He turned to me, his eyes full of vulnerability.

My stomach flipped. "I've really enjoyed today. Thank you."

I opened the car door, the cupcake box already in my hand.

"Do you want me to leave you here for a while?" He looked down at his knuckles as they gripped the steering wheel.

"No, it's okay. I'll be quick," I promised, hopping off the seat and closing the door behind me. I noted Noah's gaze as I tucked a stray hair behind my ear and straightened my skirt with my free hand, then nervously made my way down the path.

Warwick stood over a foot taller than me, his hair and his eyes were dark, and as he opened the door, they matched his expression.

"Tilly?" His frown faded the second we made eye contact. I'd been concerned that things between us would feel weird after our break up, but his smile settled the jiggling nerves.

"Before you say anything, I know I shouldn't be here, but I wanted you to have these." I pushed the box toward him.

"Always thinking of someone else." His eyes were soft as he looked down at me.

I smiled. "I thought they'd make you feel better, even just for a little while."

"They've already made me feel better. Do you want to come in?" He pushed the door all the way open.

"No sorry. I got a lift today." I pointed toward Noah's Ute with my bandaged hand.

"What happened to your hand?" he asked, his fingers reaching to gently grasp mine.

"Oh, nothing much. Just burned it." I explained, waving my hand in front of me dismissively.

"It's not serious, though? Will you be alright?"

"Sure will. Look, it's almost better already. I can wave and everything." I demonstrated continuing to wave like a mad person. "What's more important is how are you doing?"

"Better now that I have these cupcakes." He grinned. "Are you sure you don't want to come in? I know I told you to stay away, but..."

"I know," I replied, completely understanding his unspoken words. "We said we'd still be friends, right?"

"Always." We stared at each other in silence and genuine disappointment sat heavy in my gut.

"Are you sure you don't want to come in?" he asked, breaking the silence.

"I'd better not," I said, once again glancing toward Noah, only this time I remembered the shift in his mood and I didn't want to annoy him anymore than I already had. "Maybe another time." We both knew they were empty words.

Warwick smiled sheepishly. "Well, thanks for these. I will love them and enjoy every crumb." Placing the box on a stand he had inside his door, he gently took my hand and pulled me in close. "I'm sorry things didn't work out for us," he whispered.

"Me too."

His fingertip gently pushed a hair from my eye. "You really are beautiful. Inside and out." With that he lowered his head, and his lips found mine in a tender kiss goodbye.

The trip back to the farm was a silent one. Noah concentrated on the road and I didn't want to press him with annoying questions, so I listened to the country tune playing on the radio and thought about the theme I wanted to create for the Littlebrook Craft and Fine Food Fair.

When we reached Littlebrook, Noah pulled to a stop outside Monty's. "I'm just getting a pie for tea. Do you want anything?"

A pie sounded good. It was now just after 5.30, it would serve as my dinner.

Noah was striding across the road before I could even close my door.

"Noah, what can I get you?" Monty's voice boomed toward me.

I bustled between the grocery aisles toward them, my shoes not made for wonky timber floors. My heel got caught in a crevice between the boards and stuck. Trouble was I had momentum on my side and I lost my balance, falling into one of the metal shelves. Tins of tomatoes, vegetables and spam, clashed against glass jars of jam, relish and tomato paste, some of which hit my foot before rolling onto the floor with a giant smash.

I heard Monty's quiet curse as Noah sighed. To add to my embarrassment, Janie just happened to be there to witness the entire thing. She sneered gleefully as tomato paste dripped all over the bow of my not-quite-Kate-Spade's, ruining them.

I stifled a cry at my now throbbing toe and straightened myself up.

Monty strode toward me, scratching the back of his neck as he snapped, "Leave it!"

I stepped back as if I was scalded. "I'm sorry," I muttered, hanging my head low, unable to look him in the eye. "I'm really sorry."

"Just...just leave it."

Janie stepped up to Noah and whispered something in his ear. He gave her a small smile, and my throat bobbed as unexpected tears stung.

Callie stepped up behind them both, her nose crinkled with disgust. "Some people shouldn't be let off the chain," she sneered.

Janie stifled a laugh, and anger pushed my humiliation aside. Sure, I'd made a mess, but that didn't mean they could treat me like that.

I bit my retort as Monty stepped behind the counter to get something to clean the mess up with and I heard him mutter, "Take her home, Noah."

I gulped and pushed past Noah. "I said I was sorry and I meant it. I'll pay for everything that I've broken." My glance flicked to Janie and Callie. "And I'll bake you as many cupcakes you want as my way of apologizing." That seemed to satisfy Monty, so I tossed my hair over my shoulder and strutted out of the store, careful to avoid aisle two.

I heard Noah's footsteps as he crossed the road, but I was unable to make eye contact with him as I slipped my shoes off before getting into his Ute, not wanting to spread the tomato paste any further than I already had.

As soon as he closed the car door, he broke into fits of laughter.

"What's so funny?" I asked, still mortified by humiliation.

He had trouble responding as tears spilled from the crinkles around his eyes. "You never cease to make life interesting," he said once the laughter had finally died down.

Was that a compliment?

Whatever it was, his laughter had definitely lightened my mood.

A week later I kept my promise to Judy, the teacher's aide, and made her the two dozen cupcakes she had ordered which was easy now that the large bandage on my hand had been replaced with a smaller one.

Noah had given me directions on how to find Judy's property and I had Wally along for company. The news from Wally's procedure was all good, and he happily reported a clean bill of health, with insides as clean as a whistle.

"Wally, I think I'm lost." I stopped Matilda's Ute in the middle of the road. There were no cars as far as the eye could see, so it didn't pose a problem.

"No, you're not. Noah said to turn at the Pepperina tree and travel west for two kilometers."

"And therein lies the problem."

"Which bit?"

"First of all, what does a Pepperina tree look like? And second, which way is west?"

"West is the way the sun sets."

"Well, I know that, but as it's nearly lunchtime, that's not really helping me right now."

Wally sighed.

"Well, which way is it?" I asked him, slumping back against the vinyl seat with defeat.

"Let me just get my bearings," he mused, winding his window down.

Three flies flew straight in and I silently cursed him. Okay, it wasn't silent. "Wally, shut your window!"

"I need the window down to see what I'm looking for," he explained.

I stared through the insect splattered windscreen. The straight bitumen road leading ahead cut through acre upon acre of corn crops which gently swayed in the hot breeze. "What exactly are you looking for, Wally?" I asked, after a minute of silence.

"The Pepperina tree."

That made sense, I guess. "What does it look like?"

"It's tall and droops a bit."

There weren't any trees as far as my eye could see. "So, I should keep driving along this road?"

"Sure. Why not?"

I followed Wally's suggestion and after only three more wrong turns, we found what we were looking for. This would never happen in Westport where street signs existed.

Judy's mum, Rae, and her friends loved the cakes almost as much as they loved Wally.

When they asked us to stay for a cup of tea, he jumped at the chance. "What?" he asked me, shuffling his way into the lounge room. "Can't an old man have a few pleasures in his life?"

I rolled my eyes and reluctantly followed him. Turned out it was a good move. The cupcakes with Irish cream were a hit, and every one of the ten women in attendance placed orders. By the time tea was served I had a recurring order for two dozen cupcakes every Thursday for the next three months. I bit my lip and considered whether I should accept it, still unsure about starting back up in business.

"How's the farm going without Matilda?" Rae asked me.

I placed my cup in its saucer and nodded. "Clifford misses her but I believe she's still around."

"How so?"

"Have you ever had the feeling someone is standing behind you and looking over your shoulder?" I asked. When a few of the women nodded, I continued. "I get that feeling a lot when I'm in the house. I keep waking up feeling like someone is watching me sleep. It's not creepy, though. It feels reassuring."

Rae's friend Eileen patted my hand, her smile encouraging. "I believe those who love us stay around for a while to make sure we're okay."

"But that's just it. I don't know why Matilda loved me. I didn't know her."

"She obviously had her reasons," Eileen replied.

"Do any of you know Bronwyn Brown?" I asked, thinking of the executor of Matilda's estate, and how I really should connect with her.

"Oh yes. She lives in Westport now. Moved in with her daughter a few years ago."

"Do you know how I could contact her?"

They shook their heads.

"Matilda was as close to her as she was to anyone around here," Rae said. "Matilda never had too many close friends. She was a hard lady to figure out. One minute she would be yelling at Monty for not ordering the right brand of tea, and the next she's picking up every stray animal she could find."

"Yeah, she was cantankerous, but she had a heart of gold," Wally said.

I smiled at him. I liked that description.

"Every year she would donate a crocheted blanket for the

large raffle we held to raise money for the children's hospital. Excellent work she did. I've never seen anyone who could produce quality like she could."

"Oh, and she loved art," said Eileen. "For the last twenty years I've been on the committee at the arts society, and every Wednesday Matilda would line up at the hall to collect her pension at the mobile bank that arrived, then make her way out to us and spend a good hour in the art museum just looking at the paintings."

"Did she like some more than others?" I asked, intrigued.

"Oh yes. We have a local artist Lester Montgomery. She loved his work. She would study it for hours. One year the arts society produced a book of local artists and Lester was on the cover. Matilda was the first one there to buy her copy."

"What happened to him? Is he still in the area?"

"He lives in a nursing home in Westport now," Eileen said. "But if you're interested it should be easy to find information about him. His family is very prominent and influential in the Littlebrook area. He did a lot for the farmers back in the day."

"It was because of him the railway line came to town," added Rae.

"Tragic what happened to his family," Eileen tutted.

"Awful," Rae added.

Seeing my quizzical expression, Eileen elaborated. "His only child died about twenty years ago from cancer, his wife died from a broken heart, and then both of his grandchildren, along with their partners were killed in a car crash on the highway about fifteen years ago. They'd been at a wedding for the day and on the way home a drunk driver swerved across the road and hit them. Thankfully the great grandchildren weren't in the car, but it left Lester to raise them."

I gulped as a sadness for Lester and his family hit me.

"He only moved to Westport once he could no longer look after the property," Eileen finished.

"If I remember rightly," Rae said, "Matilda was the one who set up the memorial on the highway for his family. Before you make the turn off for Littlebrook, you can see it on the side of the road."

I did remember seeing that memorial and had wondered about it at the time.

Lost in thought as the women continued to chat about Lester Montgomery's family, I digested what they said about Matilda. I wondered what her connection to Lester was and why she loved his work so much. I thought after this I would get Wally to show me where the arts museum was, as I wouldn't mind having a look at Lester's work. And maybe I could even learn something about Archie, the man who painted the mural.

"Do any of you know why Matilda always wore a key on a chain around her neck?" I asked, interrupting their discussion about which of Lester's grandchildren worked where.

Eleven sets of eyes stared back at me blankly.

Hmmm, well that wasn't much help.

hankfully the only plans Wally had today was Family Feud at five o'clock, so until then we had all the time in the world. The clock had just passed two in the afternoon when we waved the ladies goodbye and hit the road.

Even though I had a headache pounding behind my eyes, I still wanted to visit the arts society museum. Two reasons: to see who would inherit the farm if I failed in my twelve-month stint, and to check out the work of Lester Montgomery.

Trouble was Wally's sense of direction was no better than mine, but eventually we found it.

It wasn't like the art museums in Westport. This one was housed in an old farm shed on a hill in a part of the area known as Iron Gate. Wally informed me that many, many years ago the entire area of Littlebrook was one massive farm and Iron Gate was the entrance. I thought of the super farm people who were trying to buy up all the land and figured if it was up to them, then Iron Gate could very well revisit its heritage.

Pushing all thoughts of Super farms aside, I concentrated on the task at hand, and kept stride with Wally across the gravel driveway.

A bell jingled as I pushed the door and stepped inside. The hum of an old wall mounted air conditioner rattled through the silence, and the scent of moth balls made my sinuses stir. Wally followed me as my footsteps tapped against the vinyl flooring and I made my way across the large room toward a desk on the far wall.

I jumped as a side door swung open and Marshall Berring appeared.

"Ah, I was wondering how long it would be before you paid us a visit." His chest puffed as he removed his glasses and pushed them into the pocket of his red shirt. "Have you come to advise us of our inheritance?" He laughed.

I was glad he thought he was funny.

"Marshall," Wally spat, by way of acknowledgment.

My glance flicked to Wally. It was unlike him to be rude, so there must be a history there I knew nothing about. "We're actually here to look at the art, if that's okay," I said.

"Of course," Marshall replied, glaring at Wally. "Visitors are always welcome. It's $5 each for entry and if you don't mind, I'll get you to sign the visitor's book, too."

I paid the fee and signed both our names, noting that the last visitor had been Matilda. And if I had my dates correct, she'd been here the day before she died. Quickly scanning the book, I saw that Rae, Eileen and her friends had been correct. Matilda visited here on a regular basis.

"Marshall, which paintings are Lester Montgomery's?" I asked.

Marshall's eyebrows raised almost imperceptibly. "Of course, may I ask why?"

"I was told that my aunt liked to study his work."

"Indeed, she did. Quite obsessed with it, if I might add."

"So, I'm hearing. Do you know why?"

"I have no idea."

"That's interesting. I thought you might have asked her, considering she was here so often."

"Follow me." He turned his back on us without answering.

Wally and I followed Marshall who led us through another door and down a long hallway decorated with drawings, some good and some not so good. At the end of the hallway, Marshall pushed back a door and led the way into a small room. "Matilda would come here every week and just sit in this room, lost in these paintings," he explained. "I asked her why once but she told me in no uncertain terms to mind my own business."

As I stood in the middle of the room and looked around me, I understood why Matilda spent so much time looking at them. They were incredible. The walls must have held about forty artworks of varying sizes. The landscapes were vibrant, vivid and electrifying. A thrill ran down my spine as I stared at them.

Wally too must have felt the same sense of awe. He stood alongside me with a slack jaw and wide eyes. After a few moments of silence, he let out a low whistle, "Wow."

That was a great word for it.

"Every time I look at them, I'm in awe of Montgomery's use of light," Marshall explained as the sweeping plain of Littlebrook rolled out in front of me, the fields full of golden sunflowers dancing in the sunlight. The white fluffy clouds drifted by on the breeze and I could almost smell the hot summer air which caused the mirage to shimmer in the distance.

My eyes were drawn to the next painting. This one was of an afternoon storm with dark clouds swirling ominously over a graveled laneway. The fence posts looked scarred, poised for the downpour to begin as lightening surged through the vapor. I could feel the air pressure low and intense and I instinctively wrapped my arms around myself.

A painting almost as tall as the wall towered over me of a windmill standing proud as the sunset bathed the fields in its orange glow.

On another canvas the morning fog hovered over a dam, misting the reflection of the trees which sat along its bank. Something about this painting stirred a memory. I moved closer, studying the brushwork, wondering what it was.

Wally followed me prompting me to move from one painting to the next. All of them were just as mesmerizing as the one before it.

"He's incredible," I whispered.

"He truly is," agreed Marshall.

"Does he still paint?" I asked.

"No. Sadly not. He stopped painting when he was in his twenties."

I spun to Marshall who held his hand out in a stop sign to halt the question which was on my lips. "Before you ask, yes I asked him why he stopped. He just said he lost the passion."

"That's such a shame," I replied.

"It is. To think God gave a man a talent such as this and then the Universe gave him a reason to not use it."

What did Marshall mean by that? His expression told me not to ask.

Long after we'd left the gallery, Marshall's words played on my mind. Why did we have a talent if we let them go to waste? I thought of my baking and how I knew it cheered people, and in that moment, I made a decision.

Tilly was back in business.

Happily, I got Wally home just in time for Family Feud.

"That was close," said Noah, his hands in his pockets as he rocked back on his heels, showing his megawatt grin.

"Tell me about it. He nagged me to drive faster the entire way."

Noah's dog Sebastian wound himself around my legs, as I held my hand out to pat him.

"He never misses an episode."

"Why does he like it so much? I mean, it's a fun show and all, but he's pretty obsessed."

"He used to watch it with Gran. I think he feels like she's still here when he's watching it."

My heart squeezed and I said a silent thank you to the Universe that I'd made it back in time for Wally to enjoy his special TV show. "That's so sweet."

"Yeah. They were a sweet couple."

"What was she like, your gran?"

"Patient." Noah laughed. "No, seriously, she was a beautiful soul. Always thinking of others, helping them out in any way she could. She was pretty special." Noah gulped and the grin disappeared as a sadness came over him.

"So, you're a lot like her then," I said, quietly.

Noah's gaze fell to mine and for a moment the air around us changed. It felt like the world stopped spinning. His eyes held mine in a way that made it hard to think of anything else, the intensity of the moment stole my breath.

Only when I could no longer handle the intensity, did I break the spell and looked away.

Noah cleared his throat. Maybe I wasn't the only one who felt that?

"I'm more like Wally than I care to admit," Noah said, his voice slightly cracking.

"It must be wonderful having a family like yours."

"You have a good family too, don't you, though?" he asked.

I sighed. "My mum and dad do love me, but we're not that close. I've never really felt like I fit in with my family."

"That must be tough."

"It has its moments, but mostly we've all learned to tolerate each other." I laughed at Noah's expression. "It's okay. I know one day I'll find my fit."

"I'm sure you fit with Warwick perfectly," Noah said, his voice low as he looked at Sebastian.

"Warwick?" I asked, surprised. "Why would you say that?"

"The way he looked at you the day you took him the cupcakes."

"How's that?"

"Like he loves you," Noah replied, his eyes dulling as his hand dropped to his side, clicking his fingers to call for the dog.

I took a second to gather my racing thoughts before responding.

"Warwick doesn't love me."

"Really?"

"If he did, he wouldn't have dumped me."

Noah's wide eyes shot up to mine. "What? When?"

"When he called the other day to tell me he'd been shot."

Sebastian suddenly became very interesting, and I gave him my full attention as humiliation bubbled in my throat.

"But...but I saw him kiss you."

So, Noah was watching that, was he?

"It was a goodbye kiss," I explained. "We're just going to be friends from now on."

"Oh."

An awkward silence sat in the air between us and a tightness grabbed my chest.

"What are you doing tonight?" I asked, hoping I could pluck up the courage to cook him dinner. I mean, what did I have to lose other than my dignity?

Noah's eyes momentarily widened before he dropped his head. "I'm um, going out. To the pub. With...Janie," he fumbled.

I froze.

He fiddled with Sebastian's collar.

I stole a glance at him. His tall stance and broad shoulders, coupled with his slim hips made him extremely sexy, yet his soft eyes and gorgeous soul took him beyond that. He was fun and easy to be with, was instinctively there when I needed him, and always a gentleman. My mind stuttered as he licked his dry lips. He was out of my league. My feelings were just setting me up for a broken heart.

"Then I should be leaving you to get ready," I said. "Have a great night!" I pushed my feet in the direction of home before he could see my tears.

"Tilly!" he called after me.

"Sorry Noah. I just remembered that I...I have to make a phone call. Sorry!" I sprinted away from him as fast as my wedged heels would carry me.

Leaving Noah in my dust, I made the rounds of the animals making sure they had food and water where needed and their paddock gates were locked and secure. The chore gave my mind time to settle and I was grateful for Clifford's company as it took the loneliness away. A deep sigh rattled my chest as I checked that Goatie was safe, and then whistled to Clifford before we made our way toward the house.

The sun was setting low on the horizon and I flipped the light switch as I stepped into the kitchen. The house felt still and eerie and I wished the presence of Matilda would appear on my shoulder, reassuring me to go forward.

But it seemed that tonight, she had somewhere else to be.

Before moving here I'd always imagined life on a farm to be peaceful and country air made you sleep better than you had ever slept. Boy, was I wrong.

The last three hours had been spent tossing and turning, my sleep filled with dreams of Matilda, Goatie eating my underwear, and Noah looking at Janie with his soulful eyes. If that wasn't bad enough, Clifford had upped the snoring to freight train level, and Polly and Cottonball were competing for who could make the most noise.

I gave up on sleep, flipped the hall light on, and padded my way to the kitchen to make a hot chocolate and watch the sunrise.

Only as I passed it, the room with the piano caught my attention for a moment. I stopped and studied it trying to figure out what was out of place. The metal cabinet in the corner, the one holding the guns, was now open. A cold chill danced across my skin.

Tentatively I stepped toward it, its door creaking wide as the floorboards moved with my weight. I'd never opened this cupboard, but I knew it was kept locked. The key which was now dangling in the lock, was usually kept in the top drawer of Matilda's bedside table and I for one, had never wanted to remove it because guns scared me as much as cows did.

My trembling fingers clenched the cold door and pushed it all the way back. The cupboard was empty. Apprehension gripped me by the throat. I knew for certain there used to be a gun in there. Greg had told me that the license had been transferred to me with the inheritance, but I should make myself familiar with the law surrounding it before I took it out. I hadn't bothered learning the laws about gun ownership though, because I'd decided I wasn't taking it out—ever. And now someone else had.

"Oh my…"

The clock on the mantle told me it was too early to call Noah to see if he'd taken it, so I tried to push all my fears aside, drew my jumper closer around me and whistled for Clifford. We sat together on the back verandah watching the day break the horizon and listened for the clock to strike five. Only then did I send Noah a message asking him to please stop by.

Within seconds my phone rang in my lap.

I snatched it, swiping fast to answer the call. "Hi."

"Hey, Tilly. Is everything okay?"

"Sorry to bother you so early, Noah." My words sounded rushed so I sucked air into my lungs and tried to slow my breathing. "But do you know if Matilda actually had a gun in her gun cupboard?"

"Yeah, she had a 30-30. Why? Do you need it?"

"No. It's missing."

"Say again."

I quickly explained what had happened.

"Look, I'm not home at the moment," Noah said as I heard a female giggle in the background. "But as soon as I get back, I'll come over. In the meantime, call Doyle. If the gun's been taken it needs to be reported."

Janie's unmistakable voice cackled down the line. "Noah, hurry up. I'm waiting."

Her voice slapped me hard.

"Tilly?"

I tried to respond, but all the air in my lungs had vanished.

"Tilly are you there? Are you okay?"

"Yep. Just shaken up a bit that's all." I managed and pressed 'end call'.

My stomach contracted and burning started in my chest. I dropped the phone into my lap and put my head in my hands, rubbing my eyes.

I needed to get a grip. Noah wasn't mine and he could date whoever he wanted. I had no right to feel this way. Yet that meant nothing to my tangled emotions as visions of Janie and Noah together caused the bile to rise into my throat.

I stood and paced the room, shaking the thoughts away. Only when I had some self-control did I pick up my phone again to call Doyle. The call had just connected when the sound of tires on my gravel driveway caught my attention.

Ending the call, I went outside, to find Doyle striding toward me, looking very official in his navy-blue uniform.

"Good morning, Tilly." His smile was tight, his tone official.

"Geez, you were quick." I smiled. "I hadn't even dialed your number yet and already here you are."

His puzzled look told me it was too early in the morning for jokes.

"I'm sorry, Tilly, I'm not sure what you mean."

My stomach cramped and I wondered if a girl could get ulcers at my age.

"Is everything okay?"

Doyle's brows shadowed his eyes. "Tilly, I need to see your gun cupboard, and then I'll need you to accompany me to the station."

Okay, my stomach did a complete flip as his intense look took my breath away. I'd never been asked to the station before, unless you considered a naughty night when Warwick had turned up at my apartment in his uniform, pretending to arrest me, but I didn't think Doyle had the same thing in mind. At least I hoped he didn't.

The grinding of his jaw indicated he meant business.

I went to reply, but words momentarily disappeared from my brain. Instead I allowed him to push past me into the house. He went straight to the gun cupboard and only when he pulled on the rubber gloves, did my brain kick into gear.

"I was about to call you," I explained. "When I got up this morning, I found it like this."

I think part of the police academy training involved cop face, as Doyle was giving me the perfect example. His eyes were hard, giving nothing away, his mouth was firm in a tight line, and his gaze was intimidating.

"You found it just like this?" he asked.

I nodded.

He opened and closed it a couple of times, his brows low and his eyes sharp.

"No matter how many times you do that, the gun doesn't magically reappear," I said. "I know. I've tried."

"I have your gun at the station."

"Whoa. *What?* How do you know it's mine?"

"I checked the serial number with the register."

"But I've only just noticed it missing."

"It turned up this morning after causing quite a bit of damage. When did you last check this cupboard for the weapon?"

"Never. Guns scare me."

"Where did you keep the key?" he asked.

"Matilda kept it in her bedside table. I never moved it."

"Was this cupboard kept locked?"

"Yes."

"And you're positive it was locked last night?"

"I think so." I nodded. "I mean, I haven't checked it, but it was the first thing I noticed today."

"I need you to get dressed and then come with me to the station. I need to finger print you."

"Wait a minute," I demanded. "Is this about the gun? Because I'm telling you that cupboard was locked when I went to bed last night."

Doyle pushed past me, heading back to the kitchen. I followed him.

Only after he had inspected the back door did he turn toward me. "Was this locked?"

I nodded.

He released a deep breath, his gaze moving up the hall. I could almost read his thoughts as they danced across his face, and knew before he moved that he was heading to the front door to check its lock as well.

I held my breath as he stopped next to the front door.

"Did you lock this, too?" He looked to me.

I nodded quickly.

He turned the handle. The door swung open and the breeze raced toward me.

"If you locked that door why is this one open?" He stormed back down the hall.

"It was locked," I protested. "I check it every night before I go to bed."

"And you checked it last night?"

"Yes. Has the lock been broken?"

"No."

Someone had a key. They'd been in my home while I slept and not a single animal had made a sound.

But hang on. Polly had been very vocal. And so was Cottonball. Had someone disturbed them?

The tremble started at my knees and worked its way up to my hands. "Oh my God."

18

*T*he Littlebrook police station was quite different to those in Westport which were large, made of brick and extremely busy. This one was housed in a small demountable building. Inside was a messy desk, a metal filing cabinet and a smattering of chairs. The floors were linoleum, the walls were covered with flyers advising me to dial triple zero in an emergency, what things the state emergency services did, and alerting me to the dates of the Littlebrook Craft and Fine Food Fair and the production of The King and I. Among other things.

Doyle had taken my statement, had done the whole finger print thing, and explained what exactly my gun had done last night.

Somehow it had made it from my house to the other side of Mt Lockhart where it blew quite a number of holes in a farmer's shed, destroying more than one piece of equipment. And as I had no alibi other than I was asleep alone, Doyle needed to question me, and then dust the weapon for my finger prints. We already knew they were all over the gun cupboard, but I relaxed knowing there was no way in hell they were on the weapon itself.

Doyle did inform me that familiarizing myself with the laws

surrounding weapons in Queensland was a good idea, then offered me a lift home. That was before he got a call from Callie saying that Billy was once again drunk and causing a commotion and she needed Doyle to sort him out. The perils of being a country cop.

This left me stranded at the station. I wished I could call Wally to come and get me, but knew he'd handed his license in a few years ago. The only other person I knew who could give me a lift was Noah.

I sighed and dialed his number, really hoping he had left Janie's place by now.

"Hey Tilly," he answered. "How did you go? Did you get onto Doyle?"

"Funny story," I started. By the time I'd finished explaining my morning, I could hear Noah start his car.

"So, you're at the station now?" he asked.

"I am. Listen, I'm sorry to bother you, but is there any way you could give me a lift? It's just too far to walk."

"Of course, I'm just around the corner from you. Hang on, I'll be there in a second."

It was actually more like thirty seconds, but who was counting.

"Thanks," I said, getting myself into the cab and allowing my hair to fall over my face. Doyle had given me time to get dressed but he hadn't given me time to put on any make up. Hence, I was not looking my best.

Noah wasn't looking his best either. His hair was messy, he had dark rings under his eyes and looked like he hadn't slept a wink.

"Don't worry about the gun," he said kindly. "Doyle'll sort it out. He knows you didn't do anything."

It wasn't that I was worried about.

"Thanks." I didn't know what else to say, so I sat awkwardly picking at the skin around my nails. Only when I drew blood did I look up to see Noah studying me.

I felt myself turning red under his stare, so I quickly looked for something to say. "Do you know who would have had keys to Matilda's house?"

"To be honest I was surprised Matilda still had keys herself. As you know, we never lock our houses."

"Funny, because all the years I've lived in Westport and not once have I been broken into."

"What can I say? It's rare."

"You should check your guns too, make sure they haven't been taken as well."

"I will," he said, turning into our driveway. "But Dad hasn't called me this morning, so I would guess everything is as it should be."

I sucked the blood that was now trickling down my finger. "How was your date?" I whispered, plucking up the courage to ask. Part of me wanted the answer and part of me didn't.

"It was a good night. I ran into an old buddy who left the farm years ago. We had a few too many drinks and I crashed on his parents' couch."

My head shot toward him so fast I kinked my neck. Ouch! "So, you didn't stay with Janie last night?"

Noah turned toward me, a small grin playing on his lips. "No. Well, not technically. She stayed on another couch but that was it. Why? Were you worried I did?"

"Of course not!" I gave a loud false burst of laughter, turning away so he couldn't see my lie. "You can sleep with whoever you want. It's no business of mine."

Thankfully Noah's attention was diverted as he pulled the car to a stop outside my house.

"Well, thanks for the lift," I trilled, opening the car door and almost launching myself out of the cab, waving like a maniac.

"My pleasure, Tilly," he replied, his grin upping to maximum wattage.

After a quick shower, I got dressed in cut off denim shorts and a black T-shirt, upped the make-up and stepped out into the morning air to feed the animals.

To say they weren't happy about a late breakfast was an understatement, but they quickly shut up once food was placed in their bowls. And for the first time Polly didn't curse at me.

"Hey Ethel," I called as she pecked at the ground. "You and me need to set up a time for a fitting. I've just about finished your jumper," I announced, proudly. True the jumper didn't look quite as good as the tutorial on YouTube had, but I was still happy with my first attempt at knitting.

Ethel didn't appear anywhere near as grateful as I thought she should, but maybe she would be happier once it was on. I sighed wondering how the heck I would manage that feat. Maybe Wally would know the best way to put on a jumper on a chicken.

Making my way toward Ruby, ready to get the hose and fill her water bucket, I noticed the man in question in the vegetable patch.

"Hi Wally!" I called out.

He nearly jumped out of his skin. "Cripes girl. You can give a man a heart attack if you're not careful."

"Sorry. I didn't mean to scare you. Are you planting those cabbages?" I asked quizzically as I moved in closer.

"Shh," Wally scolded. "Keep your voice down." His eyes darted from left to right. "I don't want Noah to know."

"Know what?"

He kicked the dirt with his toe. "I must have forgotten to close Goatie's gate last night. Even though I was positive I had. Anyway, she got into Noah's cabbages and ate them. I thought if I could quickly stick these ones into the ground then Noah wouldn't know the difference."

"Where did you get them from?"

"Monty. I purchased every one he had."

"Wally! There must be twenty cabbages there!"

"Keep your voice down," he hissed, his eyes once again swiveling in every direction. "And I know how many bloody cabbages there are. I bought 'em!"

I tried my best to hide my smile but failed and burst out laughing.

"Don't laugh at me, young lady." He pointed a wobbly finger at me. "If Noah finds out, I'm history."

"I think you're over exaggerating just a bit."

"Maybe. But he won't be happy. And my track record's not great of late."

His down-turned mouth tugged on my heart strings. "Alright. How can I help?"

"You can start by pulling out the ones that Goatie nibbled on. I'll come behind you and plant these," he explained, his mood taking a turn for the better.

I got to work pulling the half-eaten vegetables from the soil.

"How are you going to explain the growth spurt these have had?" I asked, hating the feeling of dirt under my nails. Next time at Monty's I would buy some gloves.

"I won't. As far as Noah's concerned, I was never here. And if you've got any sense, you'll do the same."

Wise words if ever I'd heard them.

I was just dropping the last cabbage into the bag Wally had brought along when I heard Noah whistling. He was getting closer by the second.

Uh-oh!

"Bugger!" Wally hurriedly shoved the last full-grown cabbage into the ground. "Quick hide the bag!"

"Where exactly am I going to put it?" I asked, frantically

looking around. "There aren't any hiding places for a big plastic bag in the middle of a veggie patch!"

Wally looked more alarmed than I felt.

Panicking, I threw the bag at him. "Take this and hide it behind your back."

His eyebrows shot up to where his hairline had once lived. "I don't think that's going to work," he hissed.

"It will if I distract him."

The whistled tune of 'It's a happy day today' echoed through the warm morning air.

Wally's eyes were wide as he took the bag and did as I asked.

As Noah rounded the corner, his happy face stilled and the whistling stopped as he saw us standing in the middle of his (albeit very large) cabbages.

Panic now effervescing over the top, I did the only thing I could think of. I took my top off.

"Geez, it's *so* hot this morning!" I called loudly, allowing my T-shirt to fly free and throwing my arms in the air.

For a moment a second wave of panic hit and I had a super-fast look just to double check that I had indeed put on my lacy red Victoria Secret and not gone all Suffragette and was braless. After all, it wouldn't be the first time I'd let the girls fly free.

Bra—check. Phew!

My trick worked a treat. Both Noah and Wally could look at nothing but my lacy red VS bra.

Within seconds of Noah's eyes making contact with my skin, the color of my cheeks matched my underwear.

Noah appeared to not know where to look. Ever the gentleman he tried his best to divert his stare, but I did (quite happily) note that his eyes kept coming back to my bra.

As Wally's eyes bulged, I had a moment of thinking this may not have been a good idea, but it was too late. *In for a penny, in for a pound* as my gran used to say. I pushed my chest out as far as the fabric would allow, held my head high and stepped over row after row of cabbages until I was face to face with Noah.

"Beautiful day," I cooed at him, sashaying my backside toward home and crossing my fingers that he would be too stunned to even notice Wally making his escape with the dug-up cabbages.

Oh God. Did that work? I'd never done anything brazen like that before.

My knees shook and my legs felt rubbery. I could feel Noah's eyes on my back and just as I was rounding an Oleander, I glanced over my shoulder, noting Wally scuttling for the side of the house, cabbages in hand, and Noah's smile in full wattage.

19

*I*t had been a good week since I'd seen Noah. I mean, I'd seen him around the farm and given him a wave, but I hadn't had any eye to eye contact with him. Which was a good thing because my level of embarrassment was still extreme after my display in the veggie patch.

I'm pleased to report, though, that my tactic worked and Wally disposed of the evidence without Noah being any the wiser.

Doyle had returned my gun a few days prior and it was now safely locked back in its cupboard. The key was hidden in my underwear drawer never to be used again, if I had my way.

I'd been kept busy rearranging furniture, adding to the pile that still needed to be moved to the workers hut for storage, and constantly checking Pinterest for ideas on how to redecorate my bedroom. Sure, the farm wasn't legally mine for quite some time, but I figured painting my room wouldn't hurt anyone. I'd also fixed the sign on the chook pen, given Clifford a bath (he wasn't overly impressed and after rolling immediately in the dirt I decided that was the last blow dry I was ever giving him), and baked Polly a month's worth of treats.

In amongst that I also got my recipes ready for the Fair and I was happy with what I'd chosen. So were Wally and Randall. Every day I'd experimented with different recipes until I'd settled on my selections. I'd played with the decoration until I'd found a style I was happy with, and then I'd taken them over to the McKenzie house for the men to critique. Randall opened up more to me with every visit, and if his smile when he greeted me was anything to go by, then I could tell he did indeed look forward to seeing me. And I liked to think it was for more than my cupcakes.

Today was the day of the Littlebrook Craft and Fine Food Fair. The majority of stalls were set up inside the Littlebrook Hall and I'd be lying if I said I wasn't nervous as I set up my table, covering it with Matilda's embroidery Anglaise table cloth. Adding timber stands and glass domes filled with assorted cupcakes decorated with roses, pastel quilted icing, edible pearls and gold scrolls all wrapped up in white and pale pink wrappers, I made a stand of vintage cake tins I had found in the kitchen at Dun Roamin' and softened the look with some pastel napkins. I filled Matilda's fine china teapots with pink peonies, placed a small stack of handmade business cards at the front, and stood back to run anxious eyes over it all. Happy with what I saw, I thought the effect was soft, feminine and absolutely freaking awesome.

It had been a while since I'd spread my creative wings and a passion in me had rekindled. I just hoped the Littlebrook and surrounding community liked what they saw too, because when I expressed myself through my work, I was calm, at peace and happy.

"You all set up and ready?" Wally asked, eyeing my wares.

"Those are for selling," I reminded him. "I have yours back here." I reached for a container behind the table and handed it to him.

"Aw, you're going to make someone a great wife one day."

Make them a great wife or a diabetic? I had an inkling to which one would come first.

He smiled. "Hey, have you given your entry to Betsy yet so that the judges can pronounce you the winner?"

"I love your faith in me, Wally, but the judges may not agree with you," I reminded him, but secretly wished they would.

"Pfft, of course they will. Look at this." He waved his hand over my display. "You've got this in the bag."

A warm fuzzy feeling erupted behind my breast bone. I couldn't remember the last time anyone had shown this much blind faith in me. My parents both loved me, but they were naturally cautious and were always quick for me not to get my hopes up.

On impulse, I gave Wally a hug. "Thank you," I whispered, unexpected tears stinging.

"No need to get emotional about it," he chastised, yet his eyes betrayed just how happy he felt.

Composing myself, I refocused on the task at hand. The show would open within the next ten minutes, so I didn't have a lot of time. "Wally, would you mind watching the table while I move the Ute to the car park?"

"Sure. Take as long as you need." He opened the lid of the cupcake container I'd set aside for him and peered inside.

A feeling of contentment shifted the nerves slightly as I jumped up into the Ute. It coughed and spluttered but valiantly came to life, and I ground the gears, shifting it into first. Hmmm, maybe I should buy a new Ute with the next installment of inheritance money.

The crowd of stall holders had built over the last hour, and I waved to a few as I slowly drove toward the car park. If I sold enough today, I was going to use some of the profit to stop by their tables and purchase a few of the goodies I'd already spied on my way out the door. Like the candles, and the soaps. Oh yeah, they were going in my bathroom tonight.

Callie was parking her car alongside mine, a sour expression her accessory of choice. I gave her a little wave to say 'no hard feelings' and hopped out of the Ute.

Habit had me attempting to lock it behind me, but it appeared that the mechanism had been broken a long time ago. I had nothing valuable inside, so I shrugged and made my way back toward the building, ducking between the neat rows of parked four-wheel drives.

Mother nature had turned on the charm today, and even though we needed the rain, it was a godsend. I'd been told that visitors from over a hundred kilometers away made it all the way here for this Fair. Why I'd never heard of it before, was a mystery. I guessed I just never read the country newspaper.

I joined the queue of stall holders who were jostling to get the last of their wares in the door and I took a moment to look around. The groundskeeper had left no stone unturned for the event, the dead grass around the hall was freshly mowed, the weeds growing up the wire fencing had been whipper snipped, and the paths were swept. A banner hung above the door, and the little plaque sitting in amongst the dozen flowering pansies stood proud.

I hadn't noticed the plaque earlier so I took a moment and read who it was dedicated to.

Littlebrook Community Hall
   Proudly opened and presented to the community
   by Lester Archibald Montgomery
   on March 23rd 1943.

The painter who Matilda liked so much. I wondered how prestigious you needed to be in an area to open a hall and have a plaque with your name on it. When I had some spare time on my hands, I'd look into his history just a little bit more. Maybe I'd learn why he stopped painting when he did.

I took a second look at his name, Lester *Archibald* Montgomery. Could he be the same Archie who painted the mural? I knew the town's population was now only thirty people, but I didn't think it had ever been a metropolis. Archibald wasn't exactly a common name. Surely the odds of more than one painter in this tiny town called Archie were pretty slim. Interestingly, I'd felt the same emotion when looking at Lester's work I'd felt when I'd seen the mural.

My heart rate had picked up considerably as the crowd moved and I made my way back into the hall, heading straight toward Wally. "Wally! Wally! I know who he is!"

Well, at least I thought I did. How I would prove it was a whole other story.

"Who, who is?" He looked at me like I was a mad woman.

"I think Lester, the artist with the painting at the art museum, is the one who painted Matilda's mural."

Wally looked none the wiser, so I explained what I'd found. By the time I'd finished he was scratching his chin, his mouth screwed up in concentration.

"Huh. I'll be buggered. Well, I wonder why she covered it up?"

I shrugged. I could only solve one mystery a day.

It was lunchtime before I was able to relax and started to enjoy myself. My cupcakes were a hit. A lot of women had taken my cards and if they were to be believed, I will be getting a lot of business in the near future.

Callie had decided to pretend I didn't exist. Which was fine by me.

I hummed with happiness as I left Wally in charge and took a break to wander and enjoy the other displays and stalls. I now had money in my pocket so I thought I'd do some shopping before the stalls sold out.

I was paying for a glorious bar of lavender scented soap (thanks to Matilda I had come to love the scent), when I heard my name being called.

I turned and saw Noah jogging toward me. It was the first I'd seen of him all day. Wally told me Noah was staying on the farm this morning fixing gates.

"Hi. Got everything done?" I asked.

His relaxed smile crinkled his eyes. "Surely did. Chuck will be getting out no more."

"Thank you for doing it. I wouldn't have even known where to start."

Since Goatie had gotten out, a host of other animals had also managed the same feat. I had no idea how they were doing it and both Wally and I swore we had been closing and locking the gates securely.

"If they get out after this, then I'm installing CCTV," he announced, his step falling in with mine. "How's your morning been going, anyway?"

"Amazing, but I need food. Real food. Something to balance the sugar out." I smiled, as I spied a hot dog stand outside the door. There was real food if ever I'd seen it.

"Sounds like a plan."

After we had both loaded up on hot dogs and soft drink, Noah stayed with me while I wandered the remaining stalls. There were some talented people around. The pottery, the food, and the dress making were all exceptional, and, after a chat with a talented wedding cake designer, I even had the possibility of more business.

Her clients often wanted cupcakes instead of a traditional cake and she didn't have the time to make them. She said she'd stop by my table later and check out my work after I'd shown her the Instagram account I had for my old shop. I'd never had the heart to close the account down and thought it was good for my resume if ever I tried to get a job in a bakery. Looked like keeping the account open may have paid off.

Noah and I were meandering through the tables, when Janie noticed him. Rushing forwards, her false eye lashes weighing her eyelids down, she possessively grabbed his arm, pulling him toward her.

"Noah, there you are! I've been looking *everywhere* for you," she purred.

"Well, I've been right here." He allowed her to pull him a good meter away from me.

"I have something for you," she said, sliding her fingers slowly up and down his arm. "Come and see, you'll love it."

Nausea rumbled and I threw the remains of my soft drink in the nearest bin.

"See you soon Tilly," Noah called, his fake grimace making me smile.

I kept walking around the stalls, but no longer with a feeling of joy and elation when a large framed picture caught my eye. I instinctively moved closer to it.

"Hello." A woman stepped out from behind the frame.

I instantly recognized her as Eliza, the woman I'd met at Monty's store when I'd first moved to town. Today her long hair was tied in an elegant ponytail at the nape of her neck, her dress was as pretty as a picture, and her skin held a dewy softness any model would kill for.

"You're Janie's friend, right?" My shoulders tightened.

She gave me a half smile. "Kind of. I give her art lessons."

"This is beautiful." I gasped at her beautiful art work. Thousands of tiny hand cut, painted pieces of paper glued to a canvas created a picture of an antique china tea pot with pink peonies cascading over the side. "That's almost exactly the same as what I have on my table today," I commented.

"Really? What a coincidence." She smiled. "The teapot I copied this from is a family antique and I've always loved peonies."

"They're my favorite flower too. That's probably why I was drawn to this piece."

"I've had a couple of offers on it today, but I just haven't been able to let it go. Which is ridiculous. I mean I came here to sell my art!" A giggle escaped her lips.

"How much would you need to let it go?"

She gave me a figure which almost made me choke.

I sighed. "I'm waiting for some money to come through to me and when it does, I'd love to buy it. If you still have it by then."

It was only money and exchanging it for things we love is what it was made for, right?

"You're Matilda's niece, right?" she asked, her perfectly shaped eyebrow arched.

I nodded, my fingers straying to the business cards she had scattered about her table. The scrolled writing told me her business name was *Blossom*, and she was Eliza Montgomery.

"Montgomery?" I lifted a card for a closer look. "Are there many Montgomery's in this area?"

"Not so many anymore. My great grandfather is pretty well known around these parts, but he moved into Westport a few years ago." A tightness appeared around her lips, and I remembered Rae telling me the story of how Lester's grandchildren had died in a car accident and he'd been left to look after his only two great grandchildren.

"Is he the artist?"

"He was once," she said, gulping. "But he gave it up when his business boomed. He said he didn't have a lot of time for dilly dallying. His priorities were really his family and his work kept. He was an amazing artist, though."

"I guess it explains your talent, then," I said.

"Thank you." A smile replaced the tightness "It's time consuming but I love what I do. Hey, that cupcake that's entered in the baking competition which looks like a watering can with flowers, you baked it, didn't you?"

"I did."

"Wow, it looks divine."

"Thank you." I blushed. "I hope the judges like it. Do you have an entry in, yourself?"

"I do. It's a smaller version of this but with the cup and saucer to match the teapot."

A commotion in the far corner pulled my attention from Eliza and we both spun to see what was happening.

There were a lot of gasps, squeals and yelling, but it was a very red faced and flustered looking Betsy who tottered toward me, yellow icing smeared over the front of her dress which took my breath away.

"Ah Tilly!" she squeaked, her voice high on the octave register. "Yes, just the woman I needed to see."

I felt the blood drain from my face at the resemblance of the yellow icing to the one I'd used on my entry.

"Yes?" I replied hesitantly.

"There's been a slight mishap," she said, breathing hard. "Yes. A mishap. That's what it was."

Eliza slunk backward away from us.

My eyes grew wide. "What kind of mishap?" I asked through clenched teeth.

"Hmm, how do I put this?" She looked down at her cake smeared dress. Her fingers absently swiped some of the frosting. "You see, the thing is, we were in the middle of judging. And I must say your entry did catch my attention." She licked her fingers. "Mmm, delicious."

I waited.

"I'm not sure how it happened, but someone bumped Callie who bumped Wally, who then bumped Monty. Monty fell onto Janie who fell onto me and then I, well...I fell...onto your cake. Yes. I'm so sorry, but it's ruined. Quite ruined." She blinked.

"I see," I said, censoring myself.

"I'm sorry."

"Did it at least get judged first?"

"No. Not all jurors had a chance to examine it."

"Oh. Okay. Were any of the other entries destroyed as well?"

"No. Alice's apple pie miraculously survived and so did Joanie's custard tart. Yours was the only one ruined. In fact, Callie's entry, which was right next to yours, was quite fine."

"Lucky them." I sighed.

"I hope you can accept my apologies, Tilly. We've never had anything like this happen before. But I can highly recommend your baking. It really is delicious!" She licked some more icing off her dress.

As she walked away, I scuffed after her, my shoulders slumped.

When I reached my table, Wally was sitting on the stool, his head hung low.

"Care to tell me why you left the table when you were supposed to be watching it?" I gave him my filthiest stare.

"Aw, Tilly. I'm sorry. What happened wasn't my fault though. Someone knocked Callie and she fell into me, you see. I just wanted to make sure the judging was fair. And I did ask Janie to ask you if you'd come back to the table for a bit."

"I never got that message," I snapped.

But Wally looked so sad, I couldn't stay mad at him. "Look, don't worry about it." I rubbed his arm. "It was just a cake after all."

"It should have won!" he spat.

"There's always next year," I said, surprising myself. This was the first time I had considered myself being here in a year.

"Ugh, just when I thought the day couldn't get any worse," Wally muttered.

I followed his gaze as Blake Emerson sauntered toward me, my cousin Ethan by his side.

"What are you doing here?" I asked Ethan, stunned.

"Thought I'd come and see what the commotion was all about." He jutted his jaw forwards.

"We were just talking about you, Tilly," Blake added, his charming smile firmly in place. "Ethan was explaining that he's a part owner of Dun Roamin', too."

"No, you're not!" I shot at Ethan.

"It's just a matter of time," he replied. "And I was discussing a very good deal with Blake. One that you should listen to."

"I don't want a deal. I want to keep Dun Roamin'."

Since when had I become so passionate about this place?

Ethan laughed. "You can have it. If you can match the price Blake is willing to pay, then it's all yours."

"Hold on a moment there, Ethan," said Blake, his smile slipping momentarily. "You shook my hand saying you'd sell to my buyer."

"I have to give Tilly a chance. She is family, after all," Ethan replied.

What a hero.

Wally stood shoulder to shoulder with me, as Noah stepped up behind Ethan.

Ethan never was the tallest kid around, and Noah towered over him. Noah's expression was dark, and I for one would have hightailed it out of there quick smart if I was Ethan.

"Everything okay?" Noah moved around the table until our skin touched.

A jolt traveled up my arm and stopped in my chest, and a feeling of belonging settled where it landed.

"Yeah, everything is great," I told him, then turned my attention to the men in front of me. "I'm sorry Blake, but it appears Ethan is having a laugh with you. Dun Roamin' is mine. At least half mine. But that half is not for sale. Not now, not ever."

"If that's how you want it, Tilly," Ethan sneered. "Don't say I didn't play fair."

"Even if you do get half of my inheritance, you still can't sell," I reminded him.

"I can sell what I own," Ethan fired back, "which will make farming for the McKenzie's very difficult. At the moment they rent our two thousand acres. I know they want access to the dam so they can extend it, making it useful irrigated land, but if I sell that plot, there's nothing any of you can do about it."

I gulped. We all knew what Ethan was saying was correct.

"Get out of here Blake," Noah warned, his tone low, and his stance rigid.

Blake shifted uncomfortably. "I'm sorry about what happened to your cupcake entry Tilly. It looked delicious," he said, before turning on his heel.

Ethan cheerily called over his shoulder, "See you at Mum's birthday party next weekend, Tilly!"

Ugh! I'd forgotten about that.

"He won't get the farm. I promise," I told Noah, thinking I really shouldn't make promises I couldn't keep and making a mental note to call Greg about Ethan's threats. "When Dad gets back from Peru, I'll talk to him about Matilda and find out why she left this to me. If I can find that out, maybe I can stop Ethan from contesting her will."

Noah placed his arm around my shoulder. His warmth combined with the scent of his masculinity was almost over-whelming and the urge to turn toward him and bury my face into his chest was almost too hard to resist. Luckily, I didn't have to.

He pulled me in tight until my cheek was resting against his shirt, then his head dipped to mine as he kissed the top of my head. My hand moved to his stomach as I inhaled deeply, a feeling of calm enveloped me, my yearning for this man almost painful.

As he released his hold, I raised my eyes to his, noting the intensity of their color. His fingers gently smoothed a hair from my forehead and with my body pressed against his, a thrill ran down to my hoohah. Oh boy!

The day had been long and exhausting but I'd had so much fun too.

I'd sold the majority of my cakes and handed out all of my business cards. I was also excited by the promise of a new friendship blossoming with Eliza, she seemed really nice and we'd started following each other on Instagram.

Noah had offered to stay and help me pack up the table, so we'd sent Wally home with Randall as the day had taken a toll on him.

Noah already had the table loaded on to the back of the Ute and I had my box filled with cake stands and containers. Hot air blasted me as I opened the door, and I was about to put the box on the passenger seat ready to open the windows when something shiny and metallic caught my attention. I dropped the box and leaned across the seat to see what it was.

I was no expert, but I'd watched enough cops shows to know a cartridge that belonged to a gun when I saw one. And this particular one was accompanied by a note.

The next one's for you!

*T*he note rattled in my shaking hand, my knees almost giving out on me. I'd never been threatened like this before and it scared me more than I cared to admit.

I spun on my heel, searching for who could have left it, but other than a handful of stall holders, no one was there. But then the heat of the cartridge told me it had been on my seat for quite some time.

I sat heavily on the foot ledge of the Ute, stared at the ground, and considered what to do.

"What've you got there?" Noah's dirty work boots filled my line of vision.

I had no words. Instead I lifted my head and dropped the note and the cartridge into his outstretched hand.

As the brass casing glistened against his skin, his eyes widened.

"We need to find Doyle," he replied, his tone clipped. "Come on." Grabbing my hand, he pulled me to my feet. I was grateful for the warmth of his touch.

Minutes later we marched into the police station to find

Doyle munching on one of my cupcakes. Seeing us, he brushed the crumbs from his shirt, as pink butter frosting tinted his grin.

"Hey Noah, Tilly. I heard about the commotion at the Fair today. Sorry about your entry. I'm sure you would have won." He scraped his chair backward as he stood to greet us. Seeing Noah's tight expression, his smile faded. "Everything okay?"

"Someone's trying to scare her off, aren't they?" Noah demanded, dropping the cartridge and note onto his desk. "Doyle, so far you've written everything off as a prank. Don't tell me you think this is another one." His tone was non-negotiable.

Doyle read the note and released a deep sigh. "This definitely isn't harmless." He rubbed his face with his hands, his happy demeanor disappearing. Hearing Doyle's words of agreement, I instinctively move closer to Noah's side. He instantly reached for my hand. I held on tight wanting his strength.

To be honest I was hoping it was just a prank. At least I'd be able to sleep tonight. "No one would really shoot me, would they?" I bit my bottom lip to stop the quivering.

He didn't answer, instead he picked up a notebook and sat back down, indicating to us that we should do the same.

Only once Doyle had taken my statement and placed the cartridge into an evidence bag, did Noah speak up again. "Doyle, someone wants her gone. How can you guarantee her safety?"

"Of course, I'm going to ensure her safety, but do you really believe this is about getting Tilly to leave?"

"What else could it be about?" I asked. "I don't know anyone well enough to have upset them."

"First there was the poisoned scones," Noah said. "We thought it was a mistake that Clifford got sick, but whoever left those had intended Tilly to eat them. And do you know how many times animals are being let out of our paddocks?" He didn't wait for Doyle to answer. "That can't be a coincidence. And how did Ruby get into the house? And what about the graffiti? That was a threat. 'Go home or else!'. Plus, the fact that her house was broken into and her gun was stolen which was then used to destroy property, setting her up to take the fall."

"If we assume that someone is after Tilly, then who do you think is behind it?" Doyle looked intently at Noah.

"Blake Emerson. And Marshall Berring. Between the two of them, they've hatched a plan to push her out." Noah said without hesitation.

I didn't like the sound of that.

"It could be Callie," I interrupted. "Or Janie. They'd like me gone."

"I don't think either of them would go to this length." Noah pointed to the bullet in the evidence bag.

"Look, let me investigate this," Doyle said in a low voice. "I'll ask around and see if anyone was seen around Tilly's Ute. This town is small enough that I'm positive I'll find who's responsible before the night's out."

"Good." Noah nodded.

"I just suggest you don't stay alone tonight, Tilly. Just to be on the safe side," Doyle added.

Noah seemed to calm down after that, but for some reason my anxiety only spiked.

"You're not really going to shoot someone with that, are you?" My eyes bulged at the sight of Noah's rifle leaning up against my kitchen wall.

"No, of course not."

"Okay. So...why do you have it?"

"Just in case."

"In case what?"

"In case someone breaks in and tries to hurt you."

Alright, good to know his intentions.

"But they won't," he said quickly when he saw my expression. "I'm here just in case."

"So...?" My next question hung awkwardly.

"I'll sleep on the couch," he replied, knowingly.

The only couch in the house was out on the verandah and I didn't like the idea of him sleeping out there.

"There's Matilda's bed," I offered.

Noah wandered down the hall toward the room in question. He pushed the door back and we both stared at the bed, the room cold and uncomfortable.

I wasn't sure if Noah believed in ghosts, but either way the room wasn't that welcoming tonight.

"I think the verandah is a better offer," Noah spoke in barely above a whisper. "But I'll never hear an intruder from back there."

"You can sleep with me," I offered.

His eyebrows shot up near his hairline.

"I mean, you can share my bed," I added quickly. "We'll make you a pillow fort."

"I don't need a pillow fort. I can control myself." He laughed.

It wasn't him I was worried about.

After heading back to the kitchen and making us both a salad for tea, I made the bed 'Noah safe'.

"What's this?" he asked, holding up my now completed knitting project.

"Ethel's new jumper."

"Is that the Nike logo?" He pointed to the large tick I had sewn over the wool.

"I thought it might help her run faster. She needs all the help she can get beating Cottonball to the food in the mornings. For a chicken with one leg he sure can move fast."

Noah's megawatt grin flashed. "You never cease to amaze me."

"Is that a good or bad thing?" I found my ugliest pajamas and threw them over my arm.

MATILDA'S WISH

"Don't worry. It's a good thing."

"I'm going for a shower."

A cold one, but thankfully I didn't say that out loud.

———

It had been a long time since I had spent the entire night with a man in my bed. On the odd occasion Warwick had slept over, he was always called into work at some ungodly hour, leaving me spread eagled on the bed all by myself.

Thankfully Noah didn't snore, but he took up way more space than I had anticipated, which left me clinging to the edge of the mattress, willing my self-control to be strong.

Clifford was banished to somewhere near my feet.

"Are you okay?" Noah's voice was husky in the darkness as he rolled onto his side, facing me.

Even with the pillow fort, his face was now only inches from mine, and the scent of his minty breath washed over me as I inhaled deeply.

"Sorry. I'm just a bit fidgety tonight. I think it's the thought of someone wanting to shoot me."

It wasn't a complete lie. I was worried about it. It's just that I was more worried about giving into desire, climbing the pillow fort, and jumping him.

The sheets rustled as his hand reached across and found mine. Our fingers intertwined, and my desire heightened.

"This is just a precaution," he said, adjusting his head on his pillow, his voice groggy with sleep. "Doyle will have this sorted by daylight. I'm sure of it."

I kind of wished Doyle would never get it sorted.

As Noah drifted back to sleep, his breathing once again slowed and became more regular.

His fingers held mine and it filled me with a sense of calm. In my new place in heaven, I clung tightly to Noah's rough hand and smiled. My head sank deeply into my own pillow, my soul content.

I'd never met anyone quite like him. He was strong, dependable, a gentleman, and kind. He was earth shatteringly good looking, and sexy as hell. But he seemed to have no real sexual interest in me and just cared for me as a friend.

I held my breath as the moonlit night peaked in from behind the curtains, illuminating Noah as he slept.

His features were relaxed, his lips turned up into a small smile, and his hair had fallen over his forehead. I itched to reach out and push it back and my body ached in places it shouldn't.

His lips parted and he whispered something in his sleep. Adjusting my position so I could hear him better, I kept one hand holding his and propped myself up onto my elbow, looking down at him in the semi darkness.

He whispered again, and a small laugh escaped his full lips. Whatever he was dreaming about sure was entertaining him.

Completely mesmerized, I couldn't take my eyes off him. Unconsciously, my head moved closer to his until my ear hovered just above his mouth. At this distance, his warmth radiated into me, his breath tickled my skin, and I may or may not have had a small orgasm. Okay, I'll admit it. I did have one.

"Tilly, what are you doing?" he asked, loudly. I squealed and jumped back to my side of the bed. "If you want to lay on me, you only had to say." He laughed, rolling onto his back, pulling the doona with him as he moved.

"Geez, you scared me," I hissed, my hand moving to my chest hoping to slow my erratic heartbeat.

But hang on. What did he just say?

I was about to get him to clarify when the startling loud bang of a gunshot broke the night air. Clifford jumped off the bed, his bark insistent and ear piercing as the sound echoed. Polly started to squawk and Cottonball crowed.

Noah was out of bed, his hand on his rifle before my mind could even catch up.

"What the...?"

He was out the door before I even had the chance to flip the lamp on.

Clifford ran behind him as the door slammed shut, leaving me inside suddenly feeling cold and alone.

With no idea what was going on, I sat back on the bed and tried to get my thoughts together. I knew I should stay put, but I didn't like hiding like a scared rabbit. Which I was, but I just didn't like to admit it.

So, I crept out of bed, pulled back the curtain just enough to see what was out there. Moonlight flooded the grounds with its soft glow and I could make out the silhouette of a large man jogging under the canopy of the Jacaranda tree.

"Noah!" I whispered loudly through the fly screen. "Is that you?"

The man froze for a second, turned toward me and raised his rifle.

I squealed and sank to the floor, waiting for the gun shot to ring through the still air.

I covered my hands over my ears and squeezed my eyes tight, my mind racing over thoughts of how thick the walls were. Was I protected inside? Or would the bullet pierce the timber and lodge itself into my heart?

Only as silence echoed around me did I think the gunman had changed his mind.

The silhouette had looked familiar. Why? Who was it? What was it that I recognized? The way he ran? The way he stood? Or was it the way he held the rifle?

Argh! This was no use. My brain hadn't had enough sleep to function properly and added to the adrenaline and fear that was now coursing through me, I had no chance of thinking straight. Instead of torturing myself further, I filled my lungs with much needed oxygen, slowed my breathing and plucked up the courage to look out of the window again.

Only this time, the figure had disappeared into the night. But had he gone for good? Was he circling around to come in the back door? Or was he now hunting Noah?

Noah. The idea of him out there alone looking for a crazed gunman scared me as much as the gunman himself. If he got killed protecting me, I couldn't live with myself. The grief losing him would cause Wally and Randall was unbearable, and thinking about it had me rushing from the room.

I needed to help him anyway that I could.

Without a weapon, I crept down the hallway, my legs shaking with every step. My heart hammered in my ears and stars danced in my vision. Floorboards creaked beneath me alerting anyone to my presence and in the darkness every shadow felt like the enemy.

Oh God! Please don't let there be anyone there!

As I reached the kitchen, I found the carving knife and stepped outside into the darkness.

The sounds of the night had ceased, leaving an eerie stillness. My eyes darted from one side to the other, searching for any possible threat as I kept close to the house. The cool early morning air chilled my skin causing goose bumps to break out where it touched, and my heart pounded in my ears, obliterating any other sounds that I was straining for. The thought that this was not a good idea kept running through my mind, but I couldn't stay in the bedroom. Not if Noah could be in danger.

A noise around the chicken coop caused me to jump and drop the knife, and I covered my mouth against my squeal.

The chickens startled, their clucks loud and distressed, and as Clifford appeared from the side of the house, barking loudly, a figure ran toward the fields, the crop swallowing them from view.

Clifford followed, but as my legs gave out and I sank to the grass I called him. Only Clifford had other ideas. His bark was ferocious as he covered the ground effortlessly, racing after the assailant.

I wanted the gunman caught, but I wanted Clifford safe more. I searched the ground for my dropped knife, almost cutting myself as my hand grazed the blade. Gripping the handle tight, I stood and ran after Clifford.

"Tilly!" Noah's voice was loud behind me. "Get back!" He sped after Clifford and as the crop swallowed them both, helplessness filled my soul.

It felt like eternity as I held my breath and waited for them to return. Clifford was the first to reappear, Noah closely on his heels.

"Tilly! I told you to wait inside," he hissed.

"I thought you might need help." My blood pressure dropped into an above normal range, and I fought back tears of relief.

"And how exactly were you planning to help me?"

I waved my knife in the air as Wally and Randall bounded across the lawn, both with rifles in their hands.

Looking at Wally, I gasped. He was a danger without a gun, with one who knew what could happen.

Noah must have had the same thought, because as they approached, he gently took the weapon from him. "Thanks Gramps."

"What happened?" Randall asked, his lips pursed.

"Someone shot out a tire on Tilly's car," Noah explained.

"*What?*" Even though I hadn't driven the car in a while, I still loved it. "Oh my God!"

"Did you see who it was?" Randall asked.

"No. I lost them in the crop. Dad, can you take Tilly inside please? I'm going to drive around and see if I can find him."

"That's not a good idea," I warned. "What if he shoots you?"

"I'll be careful, I promise."

Randall interrupted before Noah could say anymore. "I'm

coming with you, Noah. Dad you take Tilly inside and lock the door until we get there. And call the police."

"Come on then, Tilly," Wally took my arm. "Grab Clifford and let's go."

It had been a long night. Even though Noah and Randall had declared that whoever had fired the shot was nowhere to be seen, Doyle had decided it was for the best if he stood guard on my house. Only then had Randall taken Wally home and Noah and I had gone back to my bed.

Even with the help of hot cocoa and the calming scent of my lavender candle I still tossed and turned. In the end I gave up and took one of the sleeping pills the doctor had prescribed for me after I lost my shop. It knocked me out so well, I could have been mistaken for dead.

However, it didn't stop me dreaming, and what a glorious dream it was. Noah was in my bed and my hands were all over him. His abs contracted against my touch, hard and arousing. I lowered my lips to his bare chest, my tongue trailing a path only stopping momentarily to play with the smattering of hair which traced the way toward the unknown. I wound my leg around his and felt his leg hair tickle me. Every nerve ending was on full alert and my brain flashed with desire. I groaned.

My fantasy however, was rudely interrupted by Cottonball's loud and obnoxious crowing. I fluttered my eyelids, willing my brain to go back to where I'd been, when the sight of male arousal brought me to full consciousness.

Hang on. That *was* a dream. Wasn't it?

My lips were met by the warmth of skin and the crowing was drowned by deep groaning.

My eyelids shot fully open, and the vision of Noah's glorious naked stomach greeted me good morning.

My heart jumped as I realized my fingers were lifting the band of his boxers. Embarrassment swamped me.

"Well, good morning, Tilly." Noah grinned.

I squealed and sat up straight, releasing my grip on his boxers as a trickle of sweat dripped from my temple. "Oh my God!" I whispered. "I'm sorry. I was dreaming. I must have...Oh my God!" I covered my face with my hands wanting to block any vision of him and his gorgeous grin.

"That must have been some dream," Noah said huskily.

"Did I...?"

I pointed to his man business.

"Nearly."

"Argh!" I lifted the pillow and flung it over my head, flopping backward against the mattress, memories of the dream filling my mind.

The feel of his skin, the hardness of his abs, the distance my hand was from his...*did I really do that?*

Peeking out from under the pillow, I saw that Noah was raised on his elbow smiling down at me. Well, at least he was smiling.

"I'm sorry," I mumbled through the fabric.

His deep throaty laugh did nothing for my hormones.

"Don't be," he said. "I enjoyed every second of it." Slapping a kiss on my forehead, he threw back the covers and I was thanked with the glorious view of his back as he made his way toward the bathroom.

21

*E*very day that I spent at Dun Roamin' the place worked its way further into my heart. I found a contentment chatting to the chickens, companionship with Clifford, and a lasting friendship with the McKenzie men. Even Polly was changing her attitude toward me. I wouldn't say I was becoming a country girl, but I was no longer a city girl either. In fact, being back in Westport felt strange. It felt like home yet it didn't. As I made my way through the streets toward Tony and Christine's, everything felt different but nothing here had changed. What had changed was inside me. Something in me now craved the wide-open spaces, the clean air, Clifford wagging his tail as he sat under the Jacaranda tree waiting to greet me, and Noah's...well best not think about that.

We'd all been summonsed tonight to celebrate Christine's fiftieth birthday. Family gossip had it that she'd actually turned fifty quite a few years ago, but between surgery and Botox she didn't look a day over thirty-five, much to my mum's disgust. She and Christine were mortal enemies hiding behind the illusion of relatives of the year.

The grand event was being held at Tony and Christine's

house. Or should I say estate. The five acres of manicured gardens surrounded the Spanish style home which had featured in more than one design magazine. But it felt unfriendly, the large shuttered windows frowned down on me as I stopped in front of the valet parking attendants who were hired for the occasion.

Stepping into the evening, the fairy lights twinkled in the breeze, and the sounds of laughter and clinking glasses filled the air. The atmosphere was festive, yet a weight sat in my chest, as my feet dragged me toward the door.

"Happy birthday." I smiled as Christine greeted me with air kisses.

The smothering flowery scent of her perfume nearly choked me.

"Tilly. How lovely you could make it." She expertly scanned my outfit, her lips pursing. Clearly it didn't meet her expectations.

I'd chosen my royal blue dress with the high neck and short hem which I'd paired with my gold glitter Jimmy Choo pumps (surely even her expert eye couldn't tell they were knock offs). I'd tied my long hair into an elegant bun and upped the make-up for maximum effect. "Thank you for inviting me. It's lovely to be here," I lied.

"You came alone?" A small smile played on her lips. "I did add a plus one to your invitation."

"Yes, I saw that and thank you, but it's just me tonight."

Her tinkling laugh grated on my nerves. "I was so looking forward to meeting your man, Tilly."

I didn't bother to tell her that my man was no longer my man as I didn't think she really cared that much. Instead I lifted a glass of sparkling wine from a tray a passing waiter was carrying and excused myself as I spotted my mum across the room. "How are you holding up?" I asked Mum, before kissing her cheek.

It was the first time I'd seen either of my parents since they'd returned from their travels. Apparently, Peru hadn't agreed with them and Dad had to be carried off the Machu Picchu trail. I pitied the Inca's who did the carrying.

"Where's Dad?" I had a few questions to ask him, and this party gave me the safe zone to do it. He couldn't yell at me in public.

"He's nowhere to be seen." She sighed. "I think he's avoiding Tony. They did Machu Picchu a few years ago and loved it. I don't think your father's ready to answer questions about it, so he's in hiding."

"You're not alone. I'm here now." As far as I knew Mum was as innocent in the whole Matilda secret as I was.

"Thank you, Tilly. I know you didn't want to come any more than we did, but I appreciate you doing so."

"That's okay. I didn't want you to have *all* the fun. Your hair looks pretty, have you just had it done again?"

I think by birth she had mousy brown hair, but in all honesty, I'd never seen its natural color. I'd only ever known her to have it highlighted with different colored foils, shining under any lighting conditions and not a single hair daring to move from where she had set it. I had no understanding as to why she felt inadequate around Christine, because for a woman just shy of fifty, she was stunning.

Mum nodded before turning her designer eye to me. "Are they knock offs?" She looked at my shoes. As an interior designer, she'd always had an eye for detail.

"Of course. I can't afford the real thing. Unless you want to add a pair to my Christmas list?" I asked hopefully.

She shot me down with a glare.

No harm in trying, right?

"I've been listening to Tony talking about your inheritance," she said. "I want you to watch yourself around Ethan. That boy thinks he's entitled to everything and he will stop at nothing to get what he wants."

All the bad things which had been happening at Dun Roamin' flipped through my mind.

"What do you mean?" I asked her. "Surely all he can do is to go through the legal channels?"

Mum sighed. "Just don't get too comfortable out there. If he can, he'll be taking what's his and that farm will be sold. Unless you can afford to buy it, you'll have no option but to sell with him. Which is something you should consider. I worry about you all the way out there."

"I'm fine," I assured her, but my heart sank with her words. I stared across the room to Ethan talking with his father, Tony, and I thought of Clifford and Goatie, of Ruby, Polly, the cows, Passing Wind, and the chooks. What would happen to all of them if Ethan got his way?

My thoughts also flipped to Noah and my heart squeezed. I knew he couldn't afford to buy me out, yet how would he manage if the Super farms held half my share?

I had to do everything I could to stop Ethan. But how? How could I fight the law?

A lump formed in my throat and I blinked back the tears that stung. Gulping what was left in my glass, I took some deep breaths and marched across the room.

May as well grab the bull by the horns and see what Ethan and Tony were really thinking.

"Hi Tony, Ethan," I said, stepping up to them, a fake smile plastered on my lips.

"Tilly," Tony replied coldly. "How's life on the farm going?"

"It's going okay. I'm learning a lot," I replied, snatching a second glass of sparkling wine from a passing tray.

"We have our lawyers ready to contest that will you know." He stared me down.

Ethan laughed. "They're the best at what they do. So far they're not even sure the will's legal considering the solicitor and the agent are life partners and they'll both benefit if you fail."

"What are you talking about?" I frowned.

"The solicitor Gregory Blackburn and the real estate agent." Ethan grinned.

"What about them?" I asked.

"Don't tell me you didn't know?" Ethan rocked back on his heels, his self-satisfied smirk reminding me of the Joker.

I released a hard breath blowing a few stray hairs from my face and attempted to calm my emotions. "Know what, Ethan?"

"Blake Emerson and Gregory Blackburn the Third are partners. Life partners." Ethan looked at me like I was an idiot.

Which to be fair, I probably was because I had no idea about the relationship between those men.

"How do you know this?" I demanded.

Ethan pulled his phone from his pocket and swiped open his photos. "I snapped this shot of the two of them at a function I was at last week." Greg's smile was large as he held Blake in an embrace, the two of them looking very much like a couple.

Humph. "This proves nothing," I argued. "Greg has no benefit if the Arts Society get the farm."

"If they're prepared to sell it, he does. He'll get a huge commission. From what I've learned, Dun Roamin' is one of the few remaining properties that he needs, and Blake's been offered a huge bonus if he gets all of the properties. Do you think the arts society would sell it?"

Damn skippy I did.

"It doesn't matter anyway," Ethan continued. "I'm not trying to cut you out completely. I'm just trying to get my share. I'll be more than happy to sell it to you if you want it." He rocked back on his heels and beamed. "Karma's a bitch, Tilly."

"Only if you are, Ethan. Only if you are." With that I spun on my heel and hightailed it out of there.

I sucked in some much-needed oxygen and tried to calm myself. I was unable to stand still as my body tensed and the muscles in my neck quivered. My pulse raced.

Would Ethan really get Dun Roamin' from me? How did he know about Greg and Blake and I hadn't had a clue? Had I missed the clues because I didn't want to see them?

Despite wanting to confront Dad, I hadn't been able to stay at the party. Instead, I said my goodbye to Mum, and told her I'd visit her soon. I then drove on autopilot back to Littlebrook, my mind preoccupied by Ethan and Tony and what would happen if I lost this battle.

A battle, I might add, I had no idea how to fight.

It was only as I was nearing the turn off to town that my phone dinged from the depths of my bag, diverting my simmering temper. I was planning to ignore it but it dinged again. And then again.

Constant dinging rattled my nerves. Someone really needed me in a hurry to be messaging this often, so I pulled the car to the side of the road and found my phone.

There in bold capital letters, shining brightly on the screen were three texts.

I TOLD YOU TO GO BACK TO WHERE YOU BELONGED.

YOU'LL GET WHAT YOU DESERVE.

DON'T SAY YOU WEREN'T WARNED.

My stomach took a dive south as my palpitations kicked up a

notch. Who knew my number? I hadn't given it to that many people since being in town.

Pushing the car back into gear, I slammed the accelerator down on my little Fiat and rammed her to her limits, heading straight for the police station. I was tired of this. I was tired of feeling anxious and worried and scared, not just for myself but for Noah and Wally and Randall. I needed to find who was behind this and make them stop. Surely Doyle would be able to trace the messages and find out who sent them? This way the whole scare tactic thing might just be over tonight.

If it was only the messages and graffiti to deal with, I probably could have laughed it off as the prank Doyle originally believed it to be. But the gunshot and the bullets told me this person wasn't messing around.

I needed this mystery solved, not just to get my life on track, but also to get Noah out of my bed. He was insisting on staying until the culprit was caught. Noah was hard to resist, even though there seemed to be no temptation coming from his end. Nope, all the longing was coming entirely from me. Yep, he needed to be safely back on his own side of the farm and out of reach of my dream filled fingers.

The lights on the police station were burning brightly as I pulled up outside, so I beeped the car locked and headed to the door. "Hello!" I called to the empty room.

Doyle was nowhere to be seen, so I sat myself down on the hard-plastic chair that was pushed against the wall. The sound of the ticking clock competed with the hum of the air conditioner and a chill danced over my skin. A twinge in my belly reminded me I hadn't been to the toilet for a long time.

The station was only small, but there were two doors and I sure hoped one of them was the toilet. My heels clicked against the linoleum as I pushed the first door back and saw what looked like a store room. A small window on the far wall allowed the moonlight to shine on row after row of metal shelving which held multiple cardboard boxes, scattered belongings that looked to be lost and found, and a multitude of odds and ends.

Something on the other side of the room sparkled, catching my attention. Ignoring my screaming bladder, I dashed across the room on my tiptoes. When I saw what the sparkling object was, I gasped. It was a long gold chain with a tiny key dangling on the end of it.

Matilda's key was cold against my hot palm. How had it come to be here? Had Doyle forgotten to give it to my dad? I seriously doubted it, because he would have mentioned it before now, and I distinctly remembered asking him if he'd seen it not that long ago. So why was it here? Had he just forgotten about it?

I closed my eyes and thought over the events leading to Matilda's death and about everything I'd been told. From all the photos I'd seen of Matilda, the common factor in every one was the necklace holding the key—from the marriage of my great grand-father to the last photo Noah took of her at Christmas.

Footsteps echoed on the back stairs, getting closer as they made their way up. I had to get my thoughts together to fit these new puzzle pieces.

Making a fast decision, I grabbed the necklace, hung it over my neck, and tucked it into my dress. If Doyle noticed it missing, maybe he'd just think he'd misplaced it.

I attempted to wipe the guilty look off my face and quietly closed the door, hoping to look as if I was about to use the ladies.

"Tilly! What are you doing?" His eyes darted between me and the store room door.

"Hi Doyle. I was looking for you, but then I needed the ladies, so I just hopped up wondering if it's in there." My speech was rushed and I knew I had to slow it down before I looked suspicious.

A deep crease appeared between his brows as he assessed me. "The bathrooms are out the back. That room is for approved personnel only." He nodded at the door.

"Silly me." I awkwardly stepped from one foot to the other, unsure where to move.

Doyle's frown deepened.

"Is there something I can do for you?"

"Ummm...yes!" My nerves were rattling, making clear thinking difficult. "I've ah, had a few messages I was worried about."

"You'd better show me," he said, a grim twist to his mouth.

He stepped further into the room as I fumbled to get my phone.

"I don't know who sent them," I explained, handing it to him. "But I was hoping you could do the CSI thing and trace it."

I fell silent as Doyle scrolled through the messages. "I'm not sure what I can find out, but I'll follow it up."

"Do you need to keep my phone?"

"No."

"But you'll need it surely?"

"Right now, I'm heading out to an accident on the highway. I'll call you tomorrow and we'll follow this up then. In the meantime, just be cautious."

Bugger. I was hoping to have this solved in the next five minutes. But as the key burned warm against my skin, the need to distance myself was almost overwhelming.

"Great! Then I'll give you a call in the morning," I trilled, my nerves making me sound over excited.

I didn't wait for him to show me out, instead I took a deep breath, and got out of there as fast as I could.

My plan was to go home and search for any locks the key might belong to. Plus, I wanted to ask Noah for his advice about Doyle.

Guilt and fear that I'd stolen from a police station weighed heavy on my chest and I felt the squeeze of panic with every breath. As soon as I'd found the lock which this key opened, I was going to make a trip back to town with the excuse that I thought I'd lost my bracelet and would Doyle mind me having a look around for it. I'd then find a way to get back into the storeroom while Doyle was distracted searching for my bracelet and no one would be any the wiser. Then I could innocently ask him once again if he'd seen the key at all. The thought that technically the key was mine did cross my mind, but that was a conversation I'd have when needed.

But first I needed to find what secrets it could unlock.

Pulling up outside the farmhouse, I felt my blood pressure return to normal and I smiled. I think that had a lot to do with Clifford bounding toward my car, using my headlights to guide his way. I got out and gave him a pat, wondering why I'd never owned a dog before, because one thing I knew for certain was that I had never had a boyfriend this happy to see me every time I came home.

"Hey gorgeous. Did you miss me?" I asked, roughing up his fur.

He didn't respond, but I took his wagging tail for a yes.

Once inside I started flipping light switches on as I made my way down the hallway, only stopping once I reached my destination.

I took a moment in Matilda's room, just standing at the end of her bed and looking around me. I knew that one day I would have to do something with her belongings, but it still felt too soon.

"Matilda, can you please give me some idea as to what this key is for? I know it's important. I just don't know why," I called, pulling the chain from beneath the collar of my dress. Not that long ago I would have been freaked by the idea of talking to a ghost, but now I needed her.

The coolness in the room had now gone and was replaced with the warm evening air, but it was still, the silence only broken by the sound of the cicadas as they played their night time song.

Clifford joined me as I started my search at Matilda's dressing table. When that came up with nothing, I moved to the wardrobe, scurrying through box after box, searching for a lock which belonged to the key. From the size of the key, it wouldn't be a large lock and my first thoughts were it might have belonged to a jewelry box. But I found nothing. No diaries, no jewelry boxes and no hidden locks.

I sighed as perspiration dripped down my neck and I pushed the window open. The full moon was now high in the sky bathing the landscape in its soft glow and I enjoyed the rush of cool air as I watched the trees sway.

The workers hut came into my view. That was another job I needed to do. One day soon, I'd have to clean all of Matilda's things out of the hut. Things she had loved enough to not throw away. How would I decide what to do with it all?

Hang on a minute. Matilda had loved that stuff enough to have kept it. Could whatever the key belonged to be in there? Surely if the key was valuable enough for her to have kept it on a chain, then whatever it opened should have been valuable enough to have kept too. And hiding whatever the special thing was in the worker's hut would have been a perfect way for Matilda to keep it away from prying eyes of anyone who may have been looking.

My skin prickled with excitement as I ran to the kitchen, found a torch and made my way into the moonlight.

The workers hut looked creepy from the outside, and I quickly made a pact with myself that if the lights didn't work then I would get up early and start my search when the sun was shining.

The three front steps groaned as I put my weight on them, and the building swayed just a little.

Taking a deep breath, I stopped at the door and pushed it open, my torch illuminating a path to the light switch. I flipped it and the dim overhead bulb lit the room, showing me the mountains of furniture, boxes and suitcases Matilda had stacked neatly in rows around the edge of the room. Spiders had spun their webs, decorating the scene and giving it a Halloween feel. The stench of dead rodents and possum poop clogged my sinuses, and a cast-off snake skin hung from the exposed rafters.

I shivered and seriously considered scampering back to the main house. But the mystery of what the key belonged to niggled me forward, so I pushed the door open to allow the breeze to dilute the smell, and tackled the task ahead of me.

If you ever want to know someone, like really know them, go through their stored possessions.

In the last hour I'd learned more about Matilda than I had in the entire time I'd lived here. I now knew she was a bit of a hoarder. A neat hoarder, but one just the same. I found a stack of newspapers dated from the end of the second world war up to just prior to her death. I flicked through a couple of them and discovered that in 1943 Lester Montgomery was the mayor. In 1944 he was a big wig in the local grain growers' industry, and the front page of the Littlebrook News showed a photo of him with his wife and kids standing outside the Littlebrook railway station on the day it opened.

Matilda certainly seemed to have an obsession with him, and it made me curious as to why. From the photo I could tell he was reasonably good looking, an air of confidence surrounding him, but other than that there was nothing remarkable about his looks. He definitely wasn't in Noah's league that was for sure.

Pushing the papers to one side I sliced open the tape holding a box closed (I'd earlier found some cutlery which had come in very handy).

Inside were more newspapers, only this time they were used to wrap a china tea set. The teapot was in perfect condition, the painted purple wisteria wound its way toward its spout, giving it a whimsical look. I put it to one side and hurriedly searched the rest of the box's contents finding the rest of the tea set to match it.

I wondered why Matilda had kept such a treasure out here, and decided this was something I wanted in the house. Carefully repacking it, I moved the box outside to the bottom of the steps, ready to take home when I left.

Outside, a soft glow of light came from the McKenzie's home. I took a few deep breaths of fresh air and watched for a few moments wondering what Noah was doing at this present moment. His bedroom light was out, but his Ute was in the carport, so I figured he might be in the lounge watching TV. I made a mental note to call him when I got back to the house to tell him I was home, then I turned to head back in to the abyss to find what this key belonged to.

As I turned, a movement near Goatie's paddock caught my attention and I thought I saw someone moving. Nerves jingling, I squinted toward the fence. Goatie was quiet and the movement had stopped.

"Noah, is that you?" I called, my voice echoing in the still night.

The cicadas stopped chirping and silence surrounded me. When no one returned my call, I shook myself, chastising my imagination, and headed back into the hut.

The stacks of newspapers and piles of discarded paperwork everywhere I looked were a bit overwhelming but I pressed on, moving bundles of wrapped paperwork marked tax returns dated from 1988 to 1999. Underneath them, another layer of treasure revealed itself, and this time my heart danced to a different beat. For there, sitting in amongst the cardboard boxes and stacked dining room chairs, was a small carved chest.

With a lock.

Excitement pounded through my veins as I frantically pulled the detritus away, clawing my way toward the box. I wasn't a fan of spiders, but I ignored the cobwebs and lifted my prize toward me.

The chest wasn't overly large but it was reasonably heavy, so I cleared a spot in front of it and sat on the dirty timber floor. The chain was warm in my hand as I pulled it from my neck, smoothing the dust from the carved camphor wood as I did so. Sliding the key into place, I heard the satisfying click as the lock turned.

I was almost scared as I lifted the lid, but this was the moment I was about to learn what it was Matilda held dearest. I was about to find out what she loved.

22

I sat looking at the papers around me, stunned. I now understood why this chest was hidden and why Matilda had kept the key protected her entire adult life.

Letter after letter sat opened on my lap. The words Lester Archibald Montgomery had written to Matilda were forever ingrained in my heart.

He'd loved her with all he had, only he belonged to someone else. He had a family, a wife, a child, and a respectable stake in the community.

But he loved her, about that I had no doubt. His words could not be denied. And she loved him too. I only had one half of their conversations in my hand, but from his words it was easy to see Matilda loved him back even though he could never be hers.

Only the papers which had me in a spin were the ones I held in my hand. I studied them, double checking I hadn't mistaken what I was reading, but the birth certificate did not lie.

John Milton Lockhart

Male

Born January 22nd 1944

Westport General Hospital, Westport

Mother: Matilda Mary Lockhart

Mother's Age: Twenty years

Father: Unknown

It didn't take a genius to figure out who the father really was.

Along with the birth certificate were adoption papers which stated the child's new parents were Milton and Emily Lockhart— Matilda's brother and his wife, my great grandparents.

The pieces fell into place and I understood why Matilda had an affinity for me. I was her great granddaughter, the first female to have been born into the Lockhart family since Matilda herself.

I leaned back against one of the cardboard boxes, with Clifford curled up on my lap, and I considered the implications to what I'd just read.

Did Ethan know about this? If he did, surely he would have wanted to stop me from learning the truth? After all, with this knowledge he had no chance of ever getting a share in Dun Roamin'. His grandfather was John's brother, the true child of Milton and Emily. Matilda was only his aunt not a direct ancestor.

Clifford's ears pricked as a clunk sounded in the distance. Clifford jumped off my legs, but I was too absorbed rereading the last of Lester's letters to Matilda to bother with him.

In the letter, Lester told Matilda that even though it broke his heart, they could no longer be together. He had to make a choice, and keeping his family together had to be his duty.

Tears pricked my eyes as I thought about how Matilda would have felt, carrying his child, but forbidden to ever tell. I thought of my great grandparents and how they took the child, keeping the Lockhart name and giving it a loving home. Because that I did know. I'd sat on grandpa John's lap and listened as he recounted the stories of his childhood, of the love his parents had for him and of the bond he had with his younger brother, Malcolm.

Lost in memories of my own childhood I startled as Clifford growled, and started to scratch at the door.

"What's wrong buddy?"

His hackles were raised as he stared at the gap under the now closed door.

Geez, how long had it been closed? I'd been so lost in thought I hadn't even heard the wind blow it shut.

Clifford frantically scratched at the chipped, cracked paint, his growling increasing to an aggressive bark.

"It's okay mate. Calm down."

The breeze blew under the door, pulling the distinct smell of smoke with it.

This couldn't be good.

I hurried forwards, turning the handle and yanking it to open, but it wasn't budging. I tugged harder. Still nothing.

The smoke now billowing in under the door, coupled with the terrifying sound of crackling flames spiked my anxiety. The orange glow contrasted against the night sky quickly filled the window.

I pulled Clifford to the middle of the room and looked around me for a way out. The flames were now destroying the old splintered timber of the window. I screamed as the glass shattered. The smoke thickened, and breathing became difficult. Memories flicked of the day Wally and I had set fire to the sorghum, and how quickly it had spread. This hut was old, dry and a haven for fire and I knew I didn't have a lot of time before it would be consumed.

I frantically pulled at boxes to get to the back window.

The fire increased intensity and was now roaring. Choking, I desperately gasped for air as black spots danced in front of my eyes. I knew I had to get down low and go, go, go, but there was nowhere *to* go. Instead I dropped to my knees, pulled Clifford close and held his collar tight.

With a loud buzz, the light bulb died, plunging me into a darkness only lightened by the glowing flames.

Clifford howled, tugging against the hold I had on his collar. The collar broke and he ran toward the window, disappearing into the blaze.

I tried to call his name but choked. The smoke stung my eyes as the flames licked the ceiling. The heat was unbearable, and I covered my face as timber splintered and part of the roof collapsed nearby.

I couldn't open my eyes anymore and I was losing my battle with breathing. Was it Clifford tugging on my sleeve and barking at me or was I dreaming it? I was getting very sleepy. So sleepy.

"Clifford!" Noah shouted. "Clifford come here!"

Noah's voice was real. I was sure of that.

I rolled onto my knees as Clifford helped pull me up.

I opened my eyes against the sting to see a dark figure looming above me silhouetted against the fire.

A second later, he had draped a soaked blanket over me and lifted me into his arms.

"Hold on Tilly," he yelled.

I didn't need to be told twice. I closed my eyes, buried my nose into his neck and held back the tears.

His body was tense, his heartbeat fast, but he felt strong as we stepped through the heat and the cool night air replaced the thick smoke filling my lungs.

Noah had saved me once again.

———

I didn't want to let go, but as he dropped to his knees and carefully laid me on the grass, I had no option.

Noah's hands patted my clothing as I sat up and coughed, the disgusting taste of smoke filling my mouth.

227

"Roll over," he commanded. "Your clothes are on fire and I can't put it out."

I squealed as he pushed me backward and then rolled me over, the dewy grass extinguishing the small flames.

Once he was done, he pulled me in to his arms and didn't let go until I coughed so hard, I thought I may have broken a rib.

"How did you know I was in there?" I asked when he finally let go.

"I didn't. I went in to save Clifford." He sat heavily on the grass alongside me. "God, I was terrified when I saw you lying there."

"You, you went into a burning house to save a dog?" I asked between gasps and coughs.

"Of course, I did."

"That's amazing." I smiled before giving into the wheezing fit.

"You'd do the same," he said, his hands rubbing my back fast while I shivered. "Are you hurt?" His voice trembled.

"No. I don't think so." I looked around us. "Where's Clifford?"

"I got him," I heard Wally say as he and Randall ambled up from behind us with Clifford in tow. "That dog saved your life."

"What do you mean?" I coughed again.

"We were sitting out the back of the house and didn't know anything about the fire until Clifford came barreling through our flyscreen. Threw himself at it like a mad dog," Wally said. "I knew something was seriously wrong."

"He was frantic to get me to follow him," Noah added, "He smelled of smoke, so I let him lead the way. Then I saw the old hut being consumed with flames and Clifford ran straight into it."

Wally let go of Clifford who bounded toward me.

I put my arms around him, buried my nose into his blackened fur and gave in to the tears which were spilling. "We need to call the vet. Get him to check that Clifford is okay." I sniffed, noticing his singed whiskers.

"He's on his way," Randall said. "I called him right after I called the rural fire brigade."

"Noah!"

We all turned to see Doyle hurrying toward us.

"Doyle, you got here quick." Noah stood to shake his hand.

"I was on my way back to Littlebrook when I heard the call about the fire come over the radio. Is everyone okay?" Doyle asked.

"Pretty much. Tilly was caught in the hut. I'm going to take her to the hospital in Westport in a tick just to get her checked out after the amount of smoke she's inhaled, but otherwise everyone is okay."

"That old hut has been a fire waiting to happen," Doyle mused, his face illuminated by the fire.

The sounds of sirens echoed over the crackling flames and I gave a sigh of relief. The hut was nowhere near any other buildings and Noah kept the grass around here mowed, so the fire posed no more of a threat, but the memory of being inside it would live in my mind for a very long time.

"Have you finished your shift for the night?" I asked Doyle when I noticed he was no longer in uniform.

"Yeah. It's been a long day, so I called it a night." He watched the remains of the fire. "I reckon the last of that building is going to collapse any second."

"It looks like Monty has all the fire out now." I replied, looking at Noah who was talking to Monty.

Wally and Randall had taken Clifford into their house to try to get him to drink while they waited for the vet, but Doyle wanted me to stay with him to give a statement, explaining how the fire had started before I was taken to be checked out at the hospital.

To be honest, I had no idea how the fire started, but apparently, he needed me to recount tonight's events anyway.

"Come and sit in my car while we chat," Doyle said, leading me by the arm. Only when we reached Goatie's paddock, did I start to question just how far we needed to be from everyone else.

"Where exactly did you park it?" I tripped on a bucket that had been left lying around. "Ouch," I cursed, stumbling and another coughing fit took hold of me.

"Get up," growled Doyle, his pleasant tone suddenly replaced by aggression. He pulled me up roughly by the sleeve.

"Hey! Careful!"

"Quiet! Come with me. We need to get away from here." His menacing tone caused fear to dance across my skin and I dug my heels into the dirt.

"No! What's going on?" I demanded.

Doyle stood square, his shoulders pulled back and instantly I recognized his silhouette. He was the shooter. The one who had destroyed my front tire.

"You were supposed to die in there." He covered my mouth with his large calloused hand and lifted me off my feet with an arm around my waist.

I kicked out and squirmed but Doyle was strong, holding me tight and dragging me along as he broke out into a jog, only stopping when we reached his car parked behind one of the sheds.

He released his hold on my mouth, as he opened the car door and tried to push me inside.

"Noah!" I screamed. "Help!"

I lifted my legs and braced my feet against the car, resisting him. He gave an exasperated sigh as he grabbed my hair and dragged me backward. My butt hit the dirt hard.

"Shut up and get in," he growled, pulling me forwards by the hair. "Or else."

"Ah!" I cried, grabbing my scalp. "Let me go!"

"Oh, for Christ sake," he snapped, whipping my head backward. "I said shut up, and I meant it." Tightening his grip, he fumbled around his belt.

I used the time to get some control before the air filled with the clicking sound of electricity and a searing pain hit my neck. My muscles felt like they were on fire and I dropped to the ground unable to move.

Dazed, I felt Doyle lift me off my feet and throw me into the back of the car.

23

The pain in my head pounded as I fought against the metal prongs of Doyle's Taser. Every time I even considered moving on the backseat, the clicking sound competed with his laughter and the searing pain started once again.

I needed to keep still, to try to get my thoughts together, and to find a way out.

I had no idea where we were going. The car rocked violently as he took corners at high speed. I heard Doyle's whispered comments into his phone, but I had no idea who he was talking to.

It felt like an eternity but finally the car stopped.

I held my breath as I waited, the night air now cold against my skin as it blasted in the open door. My fog filled brain couldn't understand what Doyle grunted at me but his hand on the Taser stopped me from resisting.

I stumbled from the car, and he half dragged me toward the building cloaked in darkness, the full moon temporarily hidden behind a brewing storm.

As a door swung open, light poured toward me, causing me to groan in pain.

"Seriously?" I heard a familiar female voice question. "This is the best plan you could come up with?"

"What, you could do better?" Doyle spat, throwing me through the open front door into the building in front of him.

I squinted against the searing pain of the light, desperately trying to put the pieces together.

"I don't like this Doyle." Eliza's pretty face danced in front of me, her brows squeezed in concentration.

"I had to think fast, and this was the best I could come up with."

"Well, why do I need to be here?" she spat.

"Because you're as much a part of this as I am," he growled.

"Where are we?" I asked.

"Somewhere safe. Well, safe for us anyway," Eliza replied, as Doyle tilted his head back with amusement.

"What the hell is going on?" I cried.

Doyle gave Eliza a knowing smile, before he took her place in front of me. "Tilly, I tried to do this the easy way, but you're nothing if not stubborn." His finger was firmly on the button connecting me with his Taser.

"What are you talking about?" I asked, scanning for the exits.

Would Noah be looking for me? Had anyone seen us leave? I had no answers, but I knew one thing from watching crime shows, I needed to keep these guys talking in order to give myself more time.

"I tried to get you to leave the farm, but you wouldn't," Doyle said. "So, I had to try to scare you off, to get you to go back to Westport. But did you go? No. You see, this is all your own fault." His tone was low and even.

"So, all of the sabotaging was you?" I squinted.

"Of course." He smirked.

"But..." Pain shot behind my eyes and I winced. "You're a police officer. You're sworn to protect."

I thought what was genuine regret flashed in his eyes but he quickly blinked and a cold, calculating look came over him.

"Why?" I whispered.

Eliza once again stepped into my line of vision. "Doyle tells me you found something tonight. Something which could destroy everything for us."

"We're this close to the old man, Lester, dying," Doyle snarled, using his fingers to show just how close they were. "We're his only living relatives. We get his entire estate. Just the two of us."

"So, you're related?" I asked, confused.

"Our parents were siblings. Our great grandfather Lester has outlived everyone except us. When he dies, if ever he bloody dies, we get his entire estate."

"But what has it got to do with me?"

Eliza sighed. "We know who you are. That your grandfather was the illegitimate child of the old man and Matilda."

Geez, I'd only figured that out tonight.

"We needed to prevent you from ever finding out. That way you have no claim to what is ours."

"And if you'd gone home and given Dun Roamin' to the arts society, no one would ever have known," finished Doyle. "It's your own fault Tilly. You should have gone when you first got here."

"How did you know about Matilda?" I asked, returning his stare.

"We found the old man's letters when we cleared out his crap," added Eliza. "Every single one Matilda had written to him."

"But she never told him about the baby," I argued.

"Yes, she did." Eliza nodded. "When he wrote to her asking her why she was leaving Littlebrook, she confessed everything."

"The important thing was you didn't know," Doyle said. "But then I saw you at the station tonight when you found the key."

"You knew what the key was for?"

"No. But I knew Matilda carried it her entire life. It didn't take a genius to figure out why."

"Why didn't you try to find the chest yourself?" I asked.

"We did," Eliza said. "We searched that house high and low and couldn't find anything it would have belonged to."

"Then you showed up. It was only a matter of time before you cleared everything out and found the evidence."

"Guess I'm a better detective than you are then, aren't I?" I glared at him.

That comment earned me a back hand across the face.

"Stop, Doyle! That's taking it too far," Eliza commented, walking toward me.

"Too far? What did you think was going to happen when I brought her here?" He yelled at her.

Eliza paled but held her stare.

"You told me to get the job done no matter what it took," Doyle continued. "You said if she was dead then the property automatically went to Marshall. The farm would be sold, Matilda's possessions would be destroyed and we'd be in the clear."

My stomach clenched at his words. "So that's what this is really about? Money?" I asked, winding him up to keep talking.

I'd already scanned for exits and had found one behind Eliza. I still had no idea how I was going to get him to release his hold on the Taser and escape, but I was doing my best to think rationally.

"Of course, it's about money! Do you have any idea how much the old man is worth? Millions! Tens of millions!" Doyle shouted.

"I'll give you something though, Tilly," said Eliza. "I never thought you would do it. I didn't think you'd even last a week. The day I met you at Monty's I thought we had this in the bag."

"Glad I disappointed you then," I retaliated.

Doyle moved close and once again smacked me across the face.

I thought I was going to throw up.

"Cut it out!" snapped Eliza.

"What does it matter?" he laughed. "We're killing her tonight anyway."

Eliza's eyes widened. "I just had a thought. What if Tilly's will cuts in first. If she dies as owner of the farm then everything will go to her benefactor. Doesn't it work like that?"

Doyle slammed his palm against the wall. "I don't bloody well know! All I know is that she needs to go! We've gone too far!"

"Noah's going to know I'm gone," I sniffed, giving it everything I had not to cry. "He'll know you took me."

"No he won't," Doyle sneered. "I've got a back-up plan. Billy Perkins has been sniffing around you and we all know he has a history of hitting women. I'm going to make it look like he took you." He gave me a satisfied grin. "Come on, don't look at me like that. If the bloody dog hadn't saved you, you would've died in that hut already, like I planned."

Nausea rumbled and I vomited.

"I don't like this," Eliza whispered. "I just want the money. I can't go through with killing her."

"What else do you suggest?" asked Doyle.

Eliza ran her hands through her long hair and rubbed them all over her face.

Doyle said in a low voice, "Go outside and wait. You don't have to watch it then."

Eliza blinked hard and nodded. Then she left the room without even a backward glance.

Any thoughts she would help me out of this disappeared with her retreating back.

"Where are we?" I asked.

"The old bakery. I thought if Billy Perkins was going to kill you, then I at least needed to get all my ducks in a row. What better place than in his mother's bakery. Maybe she even got in on the action. She hates you after all." Doyle sure was putting a lot of thought into this plan.

"Won't the residents of Littlebrook hear me screaming?" I asked, sounding much braver than I felt.

Nausea was swirling, my heart was pounding, and my blood pressure somewhere around the stroke zone.

Doyle moved in close, kneeling in front of me. "Nope. They're all on the bus trip to Ackwood for that stupid play. Except Billy. He's home, but I know for a fact he's out cold after inhaling a nice little packet of the good stuff I sold him. When he wakes up next to your dead body, he's not going to remember a thing. And as I'll be the first investigating officer, I'll make sure all evidence points directly to him."

I tried to gulp but all my saliva had dried up.

Doyle laughed, the evil sound echoed off the walls of the old bakery. "Ah, this is going to be so much fun. And the residents of Littlebrook are going to love it. The publicity may even bring some new life into the town."

The door was too far for me to reach, so I once again scanned the room. I knew the inside of bakeries well, I knew it would hold many things I could use as a weapon.

"Well if you're going to make it look like a woman bashing," I said. "Shouldn't I at least be standing? You don't want the evidence to look like I didn't even fight back."

Doyle glared at me before moving ominously close. "Fine," he spat, grabbing my hair and pulling me to my feet.

I screamed against the pain, but eyed the knife block sitting on the stainless-steel bench as he laughed manically.

He swung his hand backward, ready to backhand me, but I was faster.

Ducking under his arm, I knocked the Taser from his hand, and lunged for the knife.

I'd never had to fight for my life before. As I kicked into fight mode, I screamed against the pain as I pulled the Taser prongs from my neck and held the knife like I intended to use it. I had no idea if I actually could use it but I was prepared to find out.

Doyle laughed again. "Oh man, this is going to be a lot more fun than I thought. Ah, what a night. You know how I'm going to celebrate? I'm going back to Dun Roamin' and I'm going to kill that bloody dog Clifford."

Any rational thoughts I had in my head disappeared right out the proverbial window. I dropped the knife, instead grabbing the cast iron skillet. Doyle lunged toward me. When he was close enough, I swung the skillet for his head, my aim perfect as the clang sounded and iron and skull collided.

He staggered for a moment before swiping at the blood which now trickled down his temple. Licking his fingers, he turned to me, murder in his eyes.

My heartbeat pounded in my ears.

He launched himself off his feet and through the air, lunging toward me but I side stepped him, and he landed with a bang on the draining board.

Out of the corner of my eye, I spotted a bag of flour which I grabbed and swung at him as he turned to face me once more. A smog of flour filled the air between us. He coughed and cursed.

I bolted in the direction of the door on the other side of the room. But Doyle was faster than me. Grabbing my arm, he spun me around, hitting me hard across the face. I stumbled and fell, and he grabbed me from behind, this time using his fist to punch me in the back. Pain seared as I crashed into the oven.

I scurried across the floor toward the door. Doyle was on me, kicking me in the legs and hitting out with his hands. I curled into a ball, unable to defend myself from his strength, when the vision of Clifford filled my mind.

Doyle was going home to find him.

I couldn't let Clifford down. He needed my help and I had to do whatever it took. I couldn't let myself die.

Doyle lifted his leg to stomp down on me again, but I reached for anything I could grab onto, finding a meat tenderizer. I rolled onto my knees and swung the mallet, connecting deep in his groin.

His shorts did nothing to absorb the impact, and the pain registered in his eyes before he fell to the ground. Encouraged, I threw everything I could get my hands on at him. The stainless-steel pots, the rolling pin, the muffin trays. Everything clanged as Doyle used his arms to shield himself. I wasn't giving up. Rounding on the mix master, I pulled the lead from the power socket and lifted it above my head. Doyle attempted to stand, taking his eyes off me for a split second. That was all I needed. With all the force I could muster I brought that mix master down hard across his arm, the impact making a sickening crack. He staggered and tripped on the rolling pin, falling against the stainless-steel table.

Adrenaline pumped through my veins as I jumped on his back, anger at what he had done fueling my every move. I hit him hard, my fists pounding his flesh, rage blinding me. I was screaming obscenities at him for all the terrible things he had done, when hands grabbed me under the arm pits and pulled me up. I kept kicking out and screaming, thinking Eliza had come back to help, but Noah's deep voice echoed through my panic.

The Littlebrook police suddenly grew in employees. Sergeant Christopher Jenkins from the neighboring town of Ackwood had rushed to the area, ready to take Doyle into custody and to track Eliza down. I guessed Littlebrook hadn't seen this much action in a long time. The flashing red and blue lights of the police car reflected off the bus which had pulled up in the main street of Littlebrook, returning everyone from the play. The majority of the town's residents stood watching the scene in front of them.

Noah held me tight against him as Doctor Drew checked my wounds.

"We have a couple of ambulances on their way," the doctor said, dabbing at a cut on my cheek. "One for you and one for Doyle."

It appeared I hadn't killed him. He was going to have a hell of a headache and would be walking with a limp, but I was okay with that. Even in self-defense I didn't want to kill him.

Noah looked down at me.

"How did you find me?" I asked.

"When I realized you were gone, I saw Doyle was missing too. Monty said he saw him walking with you toward your house. Only neither of you were there. I had no idea why he would have taken you *anywhere*, and I started to wonder how he got to the hut fire so quickly. Unless he was actually at the end of our driveway at the time of Gramp's call, it was pretty coincidental that he was there when he was. So I put a call out on the radio asking if anyone had seen him or his vehicle and Jacob Brown said he'd seen the car outside the bakery. I got here as quickly as I could." Noah's eyes clouded. "I'm sorry I didn't get to you faster. Not that you needed my help of course. You seemed to be giving Doyle the beating of his life."

"Yeah well, he shouldn't have threatened my dog."

Noah grinned as his fingers reached out and tucked a few stray hairs behind my ear and I shivered at his touch.

"Sorry, did I hurt you?" he asked, pulling his fingers away quickly.

"No. No you didn't. I just..." Now didn't feel like the appropriate time to tell him how his touch made me feel. "Is everything in the hut gone?" I asked, already knowing the answer.

Noah nodded. "Saves you the worry of cleaning it out."

Sadness that all of Lester's letters to Matilda were gone, enveloped me. I wasn't worried about the birth certificate or the adoption papers which were replaceable, but I was sad for the part of Matilda's life that had gone with the burned letters.

"Hey, tell me, what were you doing in there anyway?" Noah asked.

Boy, did I have a story for him.

24

$\mathcal{I}$'d heard the car in the driveway long before I heard the faint knock on the door. My body ached, but I ignored it and shuffled toward the door. On the new steps that Noah had built was the outline of a man in a suit who was nervously flipping his briefcase from one hand to the other.

"Hello." I pushed the screen door open, forcing a smile. The serious face of Gregory Blackburn looked back at me.

"Tilly. I heard what happened. I'm so sorry."

"You've got nothing to be sorry about. You didn't do anything." I gave him a weak smile and stepped aside for him to enter.

"But I'm sorry you got hurt. You could have lost your life."

That thought had been dogging my nightmares.

"How are you holding up? Are you okay?" he asked, the crease line on his brow deepening.

"I will be." I smiled to alleviate his concern. "Would you like a coffee?" I asked him as I led the way to the kitchen, attempting to lighten the mood.

"That would be great. It's a fair drive from Westport."

"What brings you here today?" I asked, moving to fill the kettle as Greg put his briefcase on the table and sat himself down.

"I'm here on business."

"Oh?" My stomach flipped and nerves started to jingle. I had this fear he would one day turn up and tell me this was all a big mistake.

"When you asked me who Matilda's executor was, it made me start to think. I wondered if there was anything Bronwyn Brown hadn't been able to do in regards to the will. So, I paid her a visit."

"It's really nice of you to go out of your way like that."

"Nah, she's a lovely lady, so it wasn't a hardship." He smiled and opened his briefcase. Retrieving an envelope, he placed it on the table.

I frowned as I moved toward him.

"Her daughter had completed everything which needed to be completed, but she had forgotten to forward you this."

He slid the envelope toward me and I immediately recognized Matilda's loopy handwriting. My stomach fluttered as I read my name.

"Thank you," I said, my thumb sliding over the dry surface of the paper as I detected the faint scent of Chanel number 5.

Greg's intense stare seemed to be checking if I was okay, so I pushed the unexpected sting of tears aside, pulled my shoulders back and smiled.

"I'll open that later. It's waited this long so another hour won't hurt."

Greg nodded solemnly and questions I had for him niggled my conscience.

"Greg, it's come to my attention that you might have a conflict of interest in all of this."

His right eyebrow cocked. "Are you referring to my relationship with Blake?"

I nodded.

He sighed. "I spoke to Matilda about it when I took over from

243

my grandfather. I explained everything to her and recommended another solicitor. But she was adamant that she wanted to stay with me. She'd known my grandfather since he passed the Bar. She trusted him and felt that if he was happy for me to take the reins then so was she. I promise you Tilly that as much as Blake's work is important to me, I never once influenced Matilda's decisions. Besides, I wouldn't have stood a chance even if I had. Matilda was a force to be reckoned with."

I smiled. That was one way to describe her.

I waved him goodbye. I felt the warm breeze as it swirled gently, silently opening the door to Matilda's room before embracing me in a hug. The heady scent of a floral bouquet filled my senses and a feeling of calm overwhelmed me. I smiled and went to the kitchen, where I made myself a cup of tea in Matilda's fine china cup and then sat at the table, ready to spend some time in her thoughts.

Clifford sat across my feet as I slid my finger under the seal and revealed the subtle pink writing paper, her words laid out in front of me.

Dearest Tilly

My wish for you is that you will love Dun Roamin' as much as I did. That you will love the animals, find peace within them that you haven't yet found within yourself. The land gets under your skin and into your blood. It was my home and I hope it will be yours. But you need time, and it is my hope that within the twelve months I have given you, you will find what you have been searching for.

I've watched you from a distance over the years. Your father Paul allowed me to be a small part of your life for a while.

The day he knocked on my door and announced he was my grandson was a true blessing. He told me he was expecting a child - a girl, and over the following months we became friends.

You are the first female Lockhart since myself and I knew even before you were born that you were going to be special.

I was touched when Paul suggested you take my name.

Don't be mad at him, Tilly. Paul wanted me to be a part of the family that I never had. Only I refused. You see, the truth about my child could still hurt the one man I loved with all my heart, the one I sacrificed it all for.

Of course, I never forgave myself for not leaving Dun Roamin' to raise my child alone, but really the choice wasn't mine. My brother never loved the farm. He never loved the land. He felt trapped here, whereas I felt free. Father couldn't lose both of us and I couldn't lose Dun Roamin' as well as the man whose child I was carrying.

With Paul's help I got to watch you grow though. I got to be a part of your life, even if you didn't know it. I know that as you are reading this, I have gone, but the truth can still hurt many.

With this, I ask for your forgiveness and for your silence. Family is everything, and it needs to be protected. Even when that family isn't your own. Archie never knew the truth. He had his own family to protect and my secrets could have destroyed it all.

This was no one's fault but mine. I made my own destiny and I made peace with my choices.

I've done my best over the years to keep Dun Roamin' going, through the droughts and the floods. I love it. It's part of who I am. Which is why I have given it to you. You're a lot like me.

I'm sure you feel like you don't belong to the family at times – I felt the same. I was always the odd one out and I'm sure father wished that Milton had stayed and I had been the one to leave, but like I said the farm was in my blood in the same way it wasn't in Milton's.

I know you'll do what's right, Tilly. I know that in time you too will love Dun Roamin'. The sounds of the wind whipping across the plain, the smell of the dust and the feel of the hot dry air against your skin. It becomes a part of you that you can't leave.

I know you have what it takes to see it to the next generation. Believe in yourself like I believe in you.

You're a Lockhart and you're special.

With all the love in my heart

Your great grandmother,

Matilda xo

I stood in the hallway of my childhood home, momentarily closing my eyes. Unease swirled inside me as I considered the awkward conversation I was about to have with my dad, and I hated the feeling.

My fingers curled around Matilda's letter tucked into my pocket, giving me the strength to move forward. I hated fighting with my dad. He was a formidable opponent, but the letter had given me an understanding of the relationship he had with Matilda, and I always believed that if you understood others, you had a much better chance at a resolution. I still needed to hear him explain why he withheld her from us, to settle the unease I felt.

Taking a deep breath, I made my way toward his home office.

My childhood home wasn't stately. It was in a suburban housing estate with an average size yard, but it was on the right side of town, and was perfectly maintained. Mum's job was an interior designer and her home showed it. The minimal clutter, white walls and perfectly placed throw cushions created a scene that was magazine worthy, yet it lacked the feeling of home.

My friends had always been envious because we'd had a

swimming pool, yet I was always envious of the relaxed, cozy atmosphere their homes had given. Still, I wasn't complaining. I'd had a good childhood.

Dad was finishing a phone call as I popped my head around the door and gave him a smile.

He waved that he would be a second, and gave his full attention to his caller.

Dad was fifty last birthday, but didn't look a day over forty. He had sandy blonde hair which he kept cut close, big blue eyes (which he used to his advantage at every chance he needed to) and kept his body at amateur athlete performance levels. He also had an air of authority which was good when you ran business training sessions. When up against a difficult businessman, Dad would pull himself up to his full height of six foot four and bat his puppy dog eyes. The poor man didn't stand a chance. They were either scared or charmed. Either way Dad got the upper hand.

He ended his call and turned a full smile toward me. I moved toward him, giving him a hello kiss on the cheek.

"Tilly!" He stood and pulled me in close, and held me tight. "How are you feeling?"

"I'm fine," I mumbled, enjoying the security only a dad can give. "I told you at the hospital that I'm okay."

He grabbed my shoulders and held me at arm's length, his eyes rapidly assessing my condition.

"Are you really okay?"

"Yeah, I'm fine. Just a few bruises and they're healing pretty fast. And I'm going to see the psychologist like you recommended."

"Good."

He once again pulled me close and I had to swallow hard to dispel the emotion the hug caused. We weren't a family to show our feelings of love, and habit had me hiding how I really felt to him. If the speed of his heartbeat was any indication, he was doing the same thing I was.

"Now, what are you doing here?" He hurriedly released his hold, and sat back at his desk. He only faced me once the emotion had retreated.

"Oh, I was in the area and thought I'd pop in." It wasn't a complete lie. This was just the first important stop I had to make today. Later I was visiting Bronwyn to collect Matilda's ashes, but I pushed that thought down and smiled at Dad.

"At this time of day?" It was seven thirty in the morning and it was true I'd had an early start, but I hadn't been able to sleep much so why waste time tossing and turning, when I could be hitting my problems head on?

"Can't a girl pop in to see her parents once in a while? And anyway, I missed you at Aunt Christine's birthday party. I haven't heard how your holiday was." I forced myself to sit in the armchair opposite him. Too many emotions caused my body to be antsy and it wanted movement.

"Oh, don't remind me. Peru wasn't the kindest to me." He laughed a hollow laugh, his eyes wide, scanning me from head to toe.

"But you had a good time?"

He nodded. "Yeah, we did. Still can't believe we won it though."

We were making idle chit chat, but we both knew why I was really here.

No point putting it off any longer.

I pulled Matilda's letter from my pocket and handed it to him. He paused before accepting it.

"What's this?"

"Read it."

He gave an almost unperceivable gulp as his fingers opened the envelope. As he read the letter, I studied him, knowing exactly what words he was up to by his micro expressions. Once he'd finished, he carefully folded the paper up and handed it back to me.

The sound of the clock ticking loudly competed with the beating of my heart, as I confronted him.

"Why did you lie to me about her?"

"I'm sorry, Tilly." His eyes downturned, looking at his hands.

That threw me. Dad never apologized for anything.

"I didn't tell anyone the truth about her. Not even your mother."

"But why? I know that Matilda told you not to, but we're family."

His sigh was long and loud as he sank backward into his chair. For the first time I noticed the dark rings under his eyes and saw how tired he really was.

My heart squeezed.

"I wanted to. But you didn't know Matilda. She was kind and compassionate, but she was also strong willed."

I gave him the silence to get lost in the memory for a moment, before saying, "Yeah, I'm getting to know that about her."

"You're a lot like her in that way. You never did want to listen when I told you what you should and shouldn't be doing. You always wanted to learn the hard way."

"Dad, let's not get into my failings, okay?"

He gave me an assessing look. "You've never failed, Tilly."

"Really? That's not what you and Mum said when my shop closed."

"I never said you failed. I said you had poor management skills, and you do. But when you learn something in life, it's not a failure."

My muscles tensed as the desire to pace the room was almost overwhelming, but I took a deep breath and got the conversation back onto the track where I needed it.

"You haven't explained why you lied about Matilda."

He took a long breath before speaking. "I visited her and told her about all of us, asking her to be a part of our lives. But she was stubborn. She told me that she would leave you the farm in her will one day, but if I told anyone of our relationship, she would make sure that everything went to the Arts Society. You would have had nothing."

"This isn't about money!" I yelled. "Why is everything about money with you?"

"Because whether you like it or not Tilly, a fact of life is that you need it." He stood, towering over me. "You need money to put food on the table, to enjoy it. It gives you a security and stops you worrying about life. It's a fact you could never get a grip on."

"But I'm doing fine!" I yelled, matching his pose.

His look was skeptical.

"Okay, I've had a few mishaps and things haven't always turned out the way they should have, but I've given it a go. And despite what you think, I do know the importance of money."

"No, you don't. Not fully."

"Anyway, some things are more important than money," I argued. "I wouldn't have cared about the inheritance. I would have preferred to know my great grandmother. We could have had a relationship."

"You did know her."

I scoffed.

"You did! I told you stories about her all the time. She paid for your education, the pool in the backyard, even that school excursion you went on to the snow. You even have some of her things."

"What? You paid for all those things."

He ran his hands through his hair, his skin pale. "No. She gave me the money for it. All of it. She wanted to do it and it made her happy. I make an alright living Tilly, but I could never afford those kinds of things."

I suddenly felt wrong footed.

"I didn't need a pool or snow holidays, Dad. I would have preferred to know Matilda."

He swallowed hard. "You needed an education, and she gave you the chance to have the best Westport could offer."

I shook my head wanting this new information to fall into place so that I could truly understand it. "But...Mum would have known about it. And she swears she didn't know about Matilda."

"She didn't. I told her the money came from a good business deal. She had no reason to doubt me."

Shock pushed me to sit in the nearest chair as I digested what I'd just been told.

"Do you remember the stories I used to tell you about the elderly woman at work? Do you remember me telling you about Tilda?"

"Of course, I do. She would send me little things of hers, like that really ugly doll, and those red sparkly shoes I used to tap together like Dorothy. I still have them all." Dad had often made us laugh with anecdotes of what Tilda got up to. *Oh wait!* "You said she was the cleaner!"

His shoulder slumped as he put his head into his hands.

"I'm sorry Tilly, I wanted to tell you and your mother the truth, but this was her offer. She could give you the security that I was afraid I couldn't give you. I couldn't take the risk."

"But you're her rightful heir. If she'd have left the farm to the Arts Society you could have contested it," I pushed.

Dad shook his head. "This way was so much cleaner. So much safer. It's the way she wanted it."

Dad looked so defeated that I could no longer argue. And what was the point? Matilda was gone. I couldn't bring her back. All I could do now was to move forward in the way she wanted and honor her memory the way she deserved.

25

*I*t had taken me a week to get everything together. To organize the tables, bake the cupcakes and send the invitations. But I'd done it. Sure, I hadn't slept much in the last week, but with everything that had happened recently, sleep wasn't really on my radar anyway. I'm pleased to say I used the time well.

The day dawned bright and sunny, the spring air filled with hope and joy. Nature had brought her finest and I couldn't thank her enough.

Noah helped clear the field and set up the tables. I carried the hundred raspberry truffle cupcakes, all decorated with fresh peonies I had scoured Westport florists for (thank goodness Wally and Randall had a cold room I used to store them all in). Placing them on the tables I'd covered with white table cloths and vases of daisies accentuated with cotton stalks blooming with tufts of white fluffy balls, I smiled.

The urns were boiling and the tea and coffee was ready to be served in china cups. Matilda hadn't owned enough for everyone so I had put a note on the invite saying BYO china. Since the incident at the bakery the townsfolk had softened toward me. Even

252

Callie, who I knew would never call me a friend, no longer glared at me, and word of the street was that she was grateful that I won the battle against Doyle. I did point out to Wally who had recounted that tale, that she was only grateful because her son would now not be facing bogus murder charges, but I'd take the gesture in the vein that it was meant.

I had dressed in my prettiest pink dress, my now tanned legs highlighting my white Jimmy Choo's. They weren't the most appropriate choice of footwear but I felt like I needed to dress my best today.

I covered my healing cuts and bruises as best I could, adding an extra layer of lipstick to distract everyone's attention, and I'd then topped the ensemble off with the new Akubra cowboy hat Wally had given me, smoothed my hair behind my ears and spritzed myself with some of Matilda's Chanel number 5. It felt like the right thing to do.

I thought of the thirty or so people who were soon to arrive and took a deep breath surveying that everything was just as it should be.

"How are you feeling, Tilly?" Father Brian asked.

I shielded my eyes against the morning sun as it reflected off the dam and smiled up at him.

"Happy," I replied. "This is what Matilda deserved."

"I think so too," he agreed as we both turned to look at the pink china pot decorated with tiny roses, which held my great grandmother's ashes.

Clifford sat on the bench alongside Matilda's remains, almost as if he knew she was among us. Which quite possibly he did.

This was the place I had chosen for her to finally rest. Wally had helped me dig a garden bed and plant a magnolia tree right next to the bench where Lester had painted the dam with vitality and life. It was the place I was soon to spread her ashes. The place I believed she felt the happiest.

A lump formed in my throat as I thought of the woman and

the life she had lived, and now that the dust had settled and I realized where I truly belonged, I could be content.

I gave Father Brian a smile and I sat next to Clifford, adjusting his new collar.

"It's just you and me now buddy," I said. "I hope you're okay with that."

Thankfully Clifford had no long-lasting effects from running into a fire and after the bath I'd given him, he looked almost as good as new. He answered me by swiping a long tongue up my cheek. Not long ago this would have freaked me out, but now I laughed and kissed the top of his head, giving him a gentle squeeze.

"Are you ready?" a deep voice asked. Noah gazed down on me, his gorgeous eyes large and full of concern.

I gulped as I looked at the man standing in front of me. Today he'd worn a dark blue suit, his white shirt sharp and tied off with a silk tie. His hair had been cut and his whiskers trimmed, giving him the sexy five o'clock shadow thing. My heart stuttered as the corner of his full lips tilted into a small smile.

"As ready as I'll ever be," I replied. Once this ceremony was over, I had a whole speech I wanted to give him.

We'd had our roadblocks and fear had stopped me on more than one occasion confessing to how I felt, but Matilda had taught me to love while you can, and love freely. She had missed a life with her soul mate and it wasn't something I wanted to repeat. Today, when everyone had gone home, I was going to tell Noah my true feelings.

My stomach cramped with the thought of how horribly things could go wrong, but it wasn't going to stop me. If he didn't feel the same, then he could retreat to his side of the property and I would stay on mine, and I would pray that when he finally did find the love of his life, I would be blind by then and wouldn't have to see those gorgeous eyes look at someone else the way I wanted them to look at me.

I stood as the first car pulled up, straightened my dress and pulled back my shoulders. "Let's get this day started."

"I'd like to say a few words before we lay Matilda to rest," I whispered to Father Brian. The majority of Littlebrook residents had shown up to pay their respects to a woman they'd shared their lives with for so long, and I was more than nervous to address them. But never the less, I needed to say what I had to say.

"Of course." Father Brian stepped aside.

"Ahum," I cleared my throat. "Um, thank you all for coming here today," I said, pulling a sheet of paper from my bra strap and fumbling to unfold it.

My hands shook so badly I nearly ripped it in half, but Noah carefully took it from me and spread it out, only handing it back once it was straight.

"Thank you," I whispered, accepting the page. "The day I found out I'd inherited part of Dun Roamin' was a day that I knew my life had changed." I looked at my mum and dad as they stood at the front of the crowd, Dad's smile encouraging me to keep going.

"The day will forever be brandished in my mind," I continued. "How naïve I was thinking that I could move from being a city girl to being a country girl, and to be honest, I never believed I could do it. But Matilda knew better. Like so much in her life, she was strong, passionate, considerate, and above all compassionate. She loved with her entire heart and never stopped loving even after her death." Lester sat nearby in his wheelchair, and I gave his wrinkled face a smile as his cloudy eyes wept for the woman he had once loved. After I'd confronted Dad, I'd paid Lester a visit, allowing him to read Matilda's words. I'd wanted to meet my great grandfather and allow him to meet me. My heart ached for him and the family he had lost, and I hoped to get to know him a little better.

"She saw hope and joy," I continued, "and worth in things that other people couldn't see. She believed in life and treasuring it and protecting it, no matter how small or insignificant others thought it was." Clifford laid his head on the timber slats of the bench seat and I heard his small whimper. "I never knew her, and that is my tragedy, but I love her and thank her for her faith in me, for showing me a life where I belonged and where I fitted in. I cherish what she has taught me, and I thank her for the sacrifices she made."

I collected Matilda's hat from the table and signaled to Father Brian that it was time to set her free.

My tears welled as he blessed the urn, before handing it to me.

With shaking hands, I opened the lid and stepped up to the garden bed, Clifford moving to stand alongside me. As I knelt down and sprinkled the ash across the ground, covering it with a handful of Dun Roamin' soil, Clifford licked at my tears then moved to complete three concentric circles over her and laid across the earth.

The sunsets on Dun Roamin' were the most spectacular I'd ever seen, and tonight was no exception, as the red and pink hues were thrown haphazardly across the scattered clouds.

Everyone had gone home, leaving Noah and I to finish the clean-up, but now as the dust settled on the day, we stood shoulder to shoulder, almost touching, admiring the view.

"Do you think Matilda had anything to do with this?" he asked, smiling toward the sky.

I laughed. "From what I've learned about her, I would say she is sitting up there bossing the Gods around."

Noah laughed, nudging my arm. "So, what happens to your cousin Ethan now? Will he proceed to contest the will?"

"I think so, but I don't like his chances of winning. Lester said he was willing to legally change my grandfather's birth certificate saying that he's the father. That will prove my status in her family and we'll see what the courts have to say I guess."

"But then Ethan will learn that Lester is really your great grandfather."

"Yeah. Lester loved Matilda for protecting him for all those years, but he believes that it's time for the truth to be set free."

Noah placed his arm around my shoulders and pulled me in close, before his arms encircled me completely. The scent of his aftershave mixed with his deodorant and for a moment, my head spun and my breath caught in my throat at the sensation of his touch.

"Do you think she's really gone?" he whispered.

I nodded as tears prickled. "I stopped in her room earlier and it's different." I tried to explain, allowing my head to fall back against his shoulder. "It feels lonely in there now."

His heartbeat fast against my back and as he lowered his head, his breathing was strong against my ear. "You're not alone Tilly. You've got the McKenzies now."

I smiled as he hugged me tight against his chest, knowing that he was right. My family loved me, but here was where I was meant to be.

"I'm glad Matilda brought you here," Noah whispered.

I looked up at him. The sunset shone in the softness of his eyes as he looked down at me through his long lashes and as our eyes connected, a jolt of electricity went through me, and a longing pang started next to my heart. "Me too."

It was now or never. I had to tell him how I felt.

"Noah..." I started. But before I could continue, he lowered his head and his lips found mine, in a perfect delicate kiss which tugged on my heartstrings.

I moaned, enjoying his taste as our connection deepened as our tongues collided. Moving my arms around his neck and entwining my fingers in his hair, his hands found my waist, pulling me hard against him.

Our lips parted and a gentle breath escaped him, and at that moment I knew I didn't need to tell him a thing. He understood exactly what I felt for him. And if I wasn't mistaken, he felt the same way about me.

"So," he said, his voice husky, as a mischievous grin formed. "I was wondering. Have you had any more dreams lately?"

Oh boy! Had I what.

COMING SOON
Be a part of my reader team for updates on release dates, pre orders and cover reveals. And keep scrolling if you'd like a free book!

Beth's Cozy Companions

DANGEROUS DEEDS - CHAPTER 1

*I*t's probably important that I start this story by telling you who I am. My name is Lizzie Fuller and I'm the tallest female member of my family, measuring in at 5' 2". I'm average weight with a small waist and hips. Unfortunately, I was at the front of the queue when God handed out breasts. I got my brown eyes and long, dark, curly hair from my mum's side of the family. I also have dimples. I don't know who I inherited those from. Grandma Mabel was a bit of a wild card, so we don't really know what's hidden in the family gene pool. As far as intelligence goes, I'm not stupid but I'm not a genius either. Today I'm debating that.

I'm standing here trying to turn the sticky lock preventing me from opening my new front door. Well, new is a stretch of the imagination, but it's new to me, so I guess it's okay for me to say that. About a month ago, I had a premature mid-life crisis and realized that at the age of thirty-one, I didn't own anything of significance. Sure, I own my car and a collection of high-end fragrances, but if I was to take an unscheduled trip to the Pearly Gates, I had nothing that stated this was who I was. True to form, I rushed out and bought a house. No time like the present, hey?

Now, I'm wondering if I should have had an affair like every other sane member of society having a mid-life crisis. It would have been much easier…and cheaper.

"Hurry *up*. It's freezing out here," complained my sister Molly. Molly had come along today to help me move, but I was about to ask her what her definition of 'help' was. So far, I'd yet to see it.

"It's stuck," I grumbled, rattling the door in the hope that it would miraculously unlock itself.

"Use your shoulder," she suggested. "Give it a good shove."

The timber door looked pretty solid from where I was standing. "You're welcome to give it a go."

"Sure, but you're wearing jeans, whereas I'm in a skirt. Jeans are much more appropriate for the job." I'm not sure what occasion Molly had come dressed for today. It definitely wasn't moving house. Her skintight jumper, mini skirt and high heeled boots looked amazing, but that was all they were good for.

Looking at the door again, I reached out and picked at the peeling paint, considering my options. I'd never rammed a door before, but maybe Molly was right—it just needed some encouragement. And the condition of the house was pretty decrepit so maybe the white ants might have weakened the frame for me.

"Stand back," I warned Molly before I changed my mind. Taking a couple of steps backward, I then ran at the door. My aim was perfect, my shoulder hitting the door above the lock. I'll admit to not being the strongest person on the planet, but I gave it my best shot. Unfortunately, the door was stronger than I was and it held firm, causing me to bounce off it, landing on my butt on the timber boards of the porch.

Molly stared down at me, her hands on her hips looking thoughtful. "Maybe you should have just climbed the drainpipe and gone in through the open window up there," she said, nodding in the direction of an upstairs window.

"You couldn't have mentioned that before I threw myself at the door?" I snapped.

"I know you don't like heights."

I sighed and accepted her outstretched hand, getting back onto my feet and rubbing my shoulder as I moved.

Negotiating the couple of front steps, I stood on what was left of the front lawn, squinting up at the window Molly was referring to.

She was right. The timber casement window was ajar.

"Why don't you climb it?" I asked. "You were good at scaling drainpipes when you were a teenager."

Her smile beamed at the memory, before she looked down at her skirt and boots.

"What exactly did you come dressed for today?" I asked.

"Lizzie, it's important to always look your best." I sighed. "Come on, I'll tell you how to do it," she encouraged.

I knew it wasn't a good idea. I knew it. But I did it anyway.

"Take your shoes off," she suggested, "You get a better grip with your toes that way. Then you just grab the drainpipe and start to climb."

The window wasn't that high, and it was directly next to the drainpipe, so if I didn't look down, surely I could do this.

Doing as Molly instructed, I kicked off my sneakers and started my ascent. The plumbing creaked and groaned, but before I knew it, I was nearly at the top.

Once the window was within reach, I stretched to grab it. The bolts holding the drainpipe to the wall didn't seem too happy with the extra strain put on them, and with an almighty snap they gave way, allowing the drainpipe to fall away from the building.

I screamed and held on to the rusted metal pipe with all my might.

Molly yelled, but I didn't hear a word of what she said. The only noise that my brain was receiving was the loud groan of the metal, the sound of rust flittering past my ears, and my blood pounding through my veins.

I said a quick prayer that this would all end well, as the pipe gave its final groan and succumbed to my weight, plummeting to the ground with a mighty crash.

The descent had been much faster than the ascent, and as the air gushed from my lungs, I saw Molly's anxious face peer over me.

"Are you alive?" she cried. "Oh, please tell me that you're alive!"

I blinked.

As relief washed over her, she succumbed to an uncontrollable fit of giggles. By the time I had managed to roll over, push the rusty drainpipe off me, and sit up, she was on the grass next to me holding her sides as tears of laughter dripped off her chin.

"That was so not funny!" I cried.

"Oh yes it was. You should have seen your face."

Bloody sisters.

As I was considering if I'd actually broken any bones, a man walking his dog down the street, looked over the tiny fence toward us.

He gave me a small smile. "Afternoon ladies. Is everything okay?"

Brushing the rust and grass off my top, I smiled at him and explained that I had just purchased the house and couldn't get in.

"Oh, well I'm Edward. I live at the end of the street."

"Pleased to meet you."

"You should just go in the back door," he suggested. "It's never locked."

"Pardon?" I asked, as the heat raced up my neck.

"The lock doesn't work on the back door and the previous owner never bothered with it. Everyone in the street knew that if they needed to get in to her, that was the way to do it."

"Oh. Okay. Well...thanks then. I'll try that." Just why I hadn't thought to do that before listening to Molly's hare-brained ideas was beyond me.

Walking through the knee length grass toward the rear of the house, I struggled to remember what the hell possessed me to buy the very first property I'd seen. The house was a tiny, detached two-bedroomed Victorian. Probably the best way to describe it is a dilapidated cross between a gingerbread house and the house of horrors. It's a money pit. I know that. But my rival buyers wanted to knock it down, and I couldn't let that happen. All I saw was the memories the house would hold, and knew that now was the time to protect it. It needed to be restored to its former glory. But why I thought I had the skills necessary to do such a thing is beyond me.

"Why didn't you buy one of those new apartments they've just finished overlooking the river?" complained Molly, looking around the overgrown yard.

To be honest, I was now wondering the same thing myself.

Pushing my hands deep into my pockets for warmth, we walked to the back porch. The morning had started with the sun shining and not a cloud in the sky, but as the day had rolled on, the clouds had moved in and the wind had picked up. Typical Westport weather. I'd lived in Westport most of my life, only moving to the city ten years ago for work. But I'd had enough of working in the city, so I'd made a deal with my boss and would now be working from home.

I looked up at the old house and groaned. I really should have bought something with a usable office.

Reaching the rear timber deck, we negotiated the few steps. My first attempt to push the door open was unsuccessful, but with the use of my hip and a bit of force, we finally made it inside. Finding the light switch, I flicked it on and waited until the dim 60-watt bulb illuminated the room. I looked around and bit my lip. The excitement I'd felt when I awoke this morning was fading by the second. I surveyed the room, biting down on my disappointment. Molly followed me in. As she stomped her feet to warm herself up, I watched the dust rise and nearly consume her.

"Bloody *hell*," she coughed, waving her hand in front of her.

The smell of a stale, damp room hit me. I looked around at the dirty old kitchen cabinets and scarred timber flooring, and felt a lump form in the back of my throat.

"Leave that door open, will you Molly, and for goodness' sake *stand still.*"

Once the dust had settled, we silently walked through the house. I don't think either of us could find the right words to say. It was only as we were walking back down the stairs from the attic that Molly finally broke the silence.

"Who the hell thought this wallpaper was a good idea?"

It's funny, but I don't remember seeing the wallpaper the day I bought the house. To be honest, I don't remember the house looking this bad at all. That day, all I could think about was how it would look revamped.

The house had a simple floor plan. There was a main hallway with the staircase off the front door. To the right of the stairs was the lounge room and to the left was the kitchen. It's the same on the second floor, only to the right was my bedroom and to the left was the bathroom. The second set of stairs led to the attic, which was home to a second bedroom. The amount of work needed before this house was even livable made me feel queasy. The butterflies in my stomach were going crazy, telling me to run, but what the hell did they know? This was going to be fun, right?

"It's going to be great. A bit of a cleanup and you won't recognize it," I said, not daring to look Molly in the eye.

"A bulldozer would be better, but if you're insistent on

265

sprucing it up then you'll need a hot handyman to help you." Her petite nose wrinkled as she glanced around her. "What is that smell?"

"Rodents, I think." I blinked against the sting of tears. I hated rats. I mean, *really* hated them. Like phobia-hated them.

"Don't worry," said Molly. Sensing I was about to cry, she placed a hand on my shoulder. "The cat should help with that."

"What cat?" I looked at her, surprised. "I don't have a cat."

"Well, maybe he came with the house. He was sitting on the window seat in the lounge when we walked in and looked quite comfortable, if I may say so. Didn't you see it?"

"No. But there are a lot of things about this house I don't remember seeing," I said, feeling a weight on my chest. "How could I be this stupid, Molly?"

Molly pulled me into a big sister hug. "You can come and stay with me if you like."

"Thanks, but no. I got myself into this so I have to see it through," I said sniffing. I took a minute to enjoy the warm, safe feeling of Molly's hug before I stepped back and pulled myself together. Feeling sorry for myself was not going to improve this situation. "Now, where was this cat?"

I followed Molly to the lounge, and there, sitting on the window seat, was a particularly large, fluffy ginger cat. Damn, she was right.

"But I don't want to own a cat," I whined, thinking I have trouble looking after myself. I should never be allowed to own any animal. You see, I did fish-sit for my mum once and—between you and I—the results were disastrous.

"I don't think you have much choice."

Okay, the cat did look quite at home sitting there, leg in the air, licking his privates. It stopped mid-lick, tongue sticking to its fur and gave us the once over. Deciding we were of no interest, it resumed what it was doing.

"Do you think it wants food and then it'll disappear again?" I *was* hoping it had the wrong house.

"It's worth a try."

"There's enough bloody rodents around here it could have a smorgasbord." Maybe a cat wouldn't be a bad idea. This last thought was actually encouraging. I mean, a cat isn't like a dog, is it? You can forget to feed a cat and it will find food itself, won't it?

"I think you should go and get it some real cat food. It looks far too lazy to actually catch anything."

Bugger.

We spent the rest of the afternoon cleaning. Not that you could really tell where we'd been. The solicitor who'd handled the sale of the house told me it was empty for about six months, and prior to that an elderly lady had lived there. I guess that explains the three inches of dust on every surface.

Molly helped a little in the end, but not without complaints. By the time my dad arrived with the truck full of my belongings, we had dusted and vacuumed every inch downstairs. Now all I had to do was clean the bedroom and bathroom before I could go to bed tonight.

"Why don't you sleep at my place until you get this place straightened?" offered Molly.

"Thanks, but I'll see how I go. It's going to take forever to renovate this place, so I'll have to get used to it at some point."

"Yeah well, the offer stands. Even if it's midnight, just get in your car and head over."

I smiled. On the surface, Molly may look shallow and self-obsessed but it was all an act. On the inside she was a big softy.

After Molly and Dad left, I improvised a lock on the back door by pushing a chair under the handle, and made a quick trip to the local grocery store, which meant I could now feed not only myself, but also my squatter. I had a feeling Cat belonged with the house and that even after feeding him the best Kitty Kat food money could buy, he was not going anywhere. I'd also purchased every mouse and rattrap the store had in stock because my faith in Cat was pretty low. There was no way I wanted any of those little rodents crawling over me in my sleep.

Feeling tired and irritable I drove back to my new home. I was exhausted, everything I owned was in boxes and there was no way I was unpacking them until I knew all furry creatures had moved on. Most of the house was still filthy, I was responsible for a cat, and now the sun was setting, I was starting to feel Molly was right. I was pretty creeped out.

As I drove to the house, it looked dark, scary and lonely. Carefully driving around the black sedan parked opposite my driveway, I parked my car and contemplated spending the night in it. I could lock the doors and not have to face going inside the house until morning when it was bright and sunny again. But no, I had to stop being stupid and get inside. There was nothing in there that could hurt me. I had personally checked every cupboard for dead bodies and scary creatures earlier in the day. Checking again would probably put my mind at ease, but there was no freaking way I was going to check in the dark.

Entering the house, I turned on every light in every room, all except the attic which—as that particular light switch was at the top of the stairs—was way too creepy for me to even think about.

I stood outside my bedroom door and looked toward the darkened staircase, terrified. I probably should have ventured up there and turned it on. Peace of mind is a powerful thing. Oh well, I'll just lock the door, jump into bed and pull the covers over my head. That would work just as well.

Chapter Two

I'd been dreaming. Someone was standing over me, watching me while I slept. It wasn't a reassuring-angel-watching-you kind of dream. It was a scary, some-lunatic-wants-to-kill-you kind of dream.

I woke with a start.

The hair on my arms and back of my neck stood on end as I sat up and had a good look around. Everything was the way I'd left it. Everything except the bedroom door. It was wide open, swinging on its hinge.

Fear ran through me, ending its journey in my stomach, where it swirled around, mixed with anxiety, and left me feeling sick. I looked out onto the darkness beyond the hallway, knowing I'd left every light in the house burning. So why was it dark?

Thankfully my bedroom light was still on, so I reached for my phone and pulled back the covers before allowing my toes to curl into the dirty carpet as I stood. Grabbing my handbag, I quickly searched for a weapon.

I came up with a can of deodorant.

Oh well, it's the best I was going to get right now. I shook the can, and walked toward the door, my heart pounding against my chest. What I really wanted to do was run. Run through the door, down the stairs, out to my car, and drive as far from here as I could get. But I guess I should grow a set and deal with whatever opened that door. The closer I crept, the harder my heart pounded.

With the dream still lingering, I peeked into the hallway. The staircase leading up to the attic looked darker than ever, and not for the first time I wished I'd turned the light on up there before going to bed.

Standing still, I held my breath and strained to listen for any unfamiliar noise. Unfortunately—as this was my first night in this old house—every noise was unfamiliar.

I couldn't see anything or anyone that shouldn't be there, so I relaxed a little bit. Not too much though. I still needed to walk down the stairs to check the kitchen and lounge. Shit, I hated this.

Hearing the wind rattling the old windows, I wondered again why I hadn't bought a brand-new house.

The stairs creaked under my weight, alerting any intruder I was on my way. I also forgot one of the treads was loose and nearly sped up my descent as it slipped when I trod on it. Grabbing the railing I regained my balance, but not before a small scream escaped my lips. Well, I guess I could cross *Spy* off my ideal career list.

"Hello! Is anybody there?" I yelled, giving up on the creeping bit. I'm not really sure what I expected to get back. I didn't exactly think any intruder would jump out yelling, "surprise!", but I'd never been in this situation before, so who knew?

Waiting for what felt like an eternity, the only response I got was the sound of the wind. Reaching the bottom stair, I paused. I didn't know which way to turn. Should I check the kitchen or the lounge first? I decided on the kitchen as it contained the only other exit. I could see the lock on the front door was firmly in place, so that was comforting, at least.

Pushing myself as close to the wall as possible, I slowly peered around the corner. The light, thankfully, was blazing. Well, blazing was a bit of an over-statement, but it did give me enough light to see the room was empty and the back door was closed.

I let out a shaky breath when I saw it was locked. Now all I had to do was check all the windows in all the other rooms and I could go to bed and back to sleep. Maybe. Oh, who was I kidding? Sleep was something I figured would evade me.

Taking a deep shuddery breath, I entered the lounge. Thankfully, the only thing I found there was Cat snoring loudly on the couch. He didn't seem upset by anything so maybe my door was only open because the house was old. Timber moved, didn't it?

Picking up Cat, I walked into the hall and checked the switch for the upstairs light. No matter how many times I flicked it, it didn't work. I guess the bulb had blown.

My knees shook as I continued my rounds of the house feeling the loneliness creep in, threatening to smother me. Earlier in the day I thought it was because the house was unfamiliar, but now I feel like the house was watching me, letting me feel its sadness. I hugged Cat closer to me as a lump sat in my throat and I made my way back to bed, once again shutting and locking the door behind me.

Continue reading Dangerous Deeds for FREE from all major ebook retailers!

Find Your Copy Here

An irresistible series full of romance, mystery, laughter, and just a bit of danger...

Where every closed door hides a deadly secret...

They say love is blind. Of course, they weren't discussing dilapidated houses, but I'm sticking to this storyline rather than the one where I suspect I'm losing my marbles.

I knew that purchasing a fixer-upper, I would be diving head-first into the abyss of demolition, dust storms, and a bottomless pit of expenses. What I didn't foresee was the unexpected discovery of an engagement ring and a treasure trove of forbidden love letters hidden beneath the attic floorboards. Not to mention the cat with an undying love for naps, and a handyman who looks like he just walked off a magazine cover. Oh, and a stalker? He definitely wasn't on my vision board.

As the house slowly returns to its former glory, those letters persist in haunting my dreams. Who could be the mysterious author, and why was their love forbidden? And who's putting in so much effort to keep me from learning the truth?

Working alongside Riley, the hunky handyman is delightfully distracting, but I'm determined to solve this heartstring-tugging puzzle.

Only can I restore the house to its former splendor and unveil the mystery before my relentless stalker catches up with me? Or will I lose everything, including life?

'Dangerous Deeds' introduces you to The Westport Mysteries, a hilarious romantic mystery series that will keep you glued to your seat. If you're a fan of quirky families, thrilling and engaging reads, and a dose of sweet romance served with a twist of danger, this is your ticket to an unforgettable adventure you won't want to miss!

I'm offering a free e-book to everyone who signs up to my mailing list. I promise not to spam you and only send out a handful of newsletters a year!

www.bethprentice.com

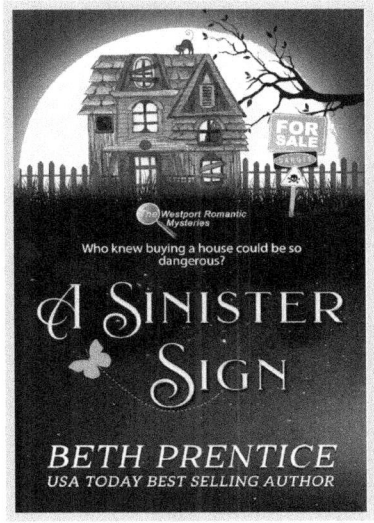

Who knew buying a house could be so dangerous?

I recently had the great idea that moving back home to Westport and being close to my family again would be good for my soul. But now that I'm back and sharing my space with Grandma, it's clear I need my own home. ASAP. I adore my family, but cohabitation isn't on my bucket list, especially now that Grandma's claimed my childhood bedroom. But lo and behold, I've stumbled upon a house that's either my dream come true or a full-blown nightmare. It's all about perspective.

The lonely run-down old Victorian in need of major renovations has tugged on my heartstrings, and before I can stop myself, I've fallen head over heels in love with it. Unfortunately, I'm not the only one who wants it, and the other bidders aren't playing nice.

Deadly accidents, missing real estate agents and a chilling stranger, are all sinister signs that this is not the house for me. Only I'm determined to rescue this fixer upper or die trying. Now all I need to do is to win the auction and stay alive.

If only it was that easy...

A Sinister Sign is the prequel to the light-hearted, romantic mystery trilogy. If you like crazy families, cozy reads, and a sweet romance, all tied together with a ribbon of danger, then you'll love The Westport Mysteries.

ABOUT THE AUTHOR

I'm Beth and I write funny, romantic mysteries (aka cozy mysteries), paranormal cozy mysteries, and the odd rom com because two of my favorite things are romance and mystery.

I'm the proud but often flustered owner of two dogs, two very noisy Indian Ringnecks, a Parrotlet named Axel, five chickens, and a duck named Dorothy. Oh, and I can't forget the Guinea Pig Herbie. I spend most of my days wishing for a quiet life but secretly loving the chaos!

When I'm not writing you can find me lost in a good book, passively watching documentaries (my hubby loves them and seems to have gained full control of the remote) and scrolling Instagram dreaming of holidays I don't have time to take, and perfect hair.

https://bethprenticenovels.com

www.ingramcontent.com/pod-product-compliance
Lightning Source LLC
Chambersburg PA
CBHW072351110726
47909CB00003B/669